I0735791

untangled vines

MICHELLE OUCHAREK-DEO

Untangled Vines

Michelle Oucharek-Deo

Wine, Love, and Friendship

Book Three

All rights reserved. Published by Live and Grow Press.

This book is a work of fiction. Any references to real people, real places or real events are used fictionally. Other names, characters, places and events are products of the author's imagination, and any resemblance to actual events or places or persons, living or dead is entirely coincidental.

Copyright © 2023 Michelle Oucharek-Deo

No part of this publication may be reproduced, stored in a retrieval system, or transmitted in any form or by any means, electronic, mechanical, photocopying, recording, or otherwise without written permission of the publisher. For information regarding permission, contact liveandgrowpress@gmail.com

Oucharek-Deo, Michelle B. 1969-

Oucharek-Deo, Michelle, author
Untangled Vines / Michelle Oucharek-Deo.

ISBN 978-1-988348-11-7 (paperback)
ISBN 978-1-988348-10-0 (html)
ISBN 978-1-988348-12-4 (hardcover)

Book Cover Design by Best Page Forward

This series is dedicated to my husband and son.
The two most amazing men in my life who walked
with me through this journey; poking, prodding, and
loving me every step of the way.

Character Index:

The Wells Family, Friends, and Others

Maya Wells – Traveled to Portugal as one of Netuno's contest winners after canceling her wedding.

Judith Wells – Maya's mom. Recovering from a clinical depression which plagued her most of her adult life.

Phillip Wells – Maya's father. Lawyer and former vineyard owner. Dedicated husband and father.

Jordan Wells – Maya's sister. Grumpy young woman. Resentful towards Maya and generally unpleasant.

Beth – Maya's best friend. Gradeschool teacher. Level-headed and patient but in search of something more.

Steven – Maya's ex-fiancé. Engineer. Jilted the night before his wedding with Maya.

Lazaro Family, Friends, and Others

Cristiano Lazaro – Flight attendant. Musician who loves to surf. Difficult family history. Fell in love with Maya.

Avo – Cristiano's grandmother. Raised him after his parents died. The maker of special bread.

Rosa and Michel Lazaro – Cristiano's adoptive parents who died in a plane crash in Egypt. History professors.

Pierre – Old friend and colleague of Rosa and Michel. Lives in Paris. Works at the Louvre.

Mrs. Dutra – An old friend of Cristiano's adoptive parents. Gatekeeper of Cristiano's apartment in Lisbon.

Jack – Old surfer from Texas who lives on the beach in Portugal. Friends with both Cristiano and Marcos.

Marcos and Euphemia – Cristiano's biological parents who live with their other two children in Porto.

Jacinta – Cristiano's sixteen-year-old biological sister.

Zef – Cristiano's eighteen-year-old biological brother.

Luca Palito – Cristiano's old school friend and police officer with Portuguese International Crimes.

Netuno Family, Friends, and Others

Josie – Sixty-five-year-old powerhouse. Divorced three times.

Dalley – Journalist. Complicated character and past.

Ravn – Finish freelance journalist. Reunited with Dalley after a ten-year absence.

Petra – High-powered ad executive. Works too hard.

Sachi – Quiet; engineer. Wants to be a chef. New temporary owner of Netuno after the attempted takeover.

Maggie – Widow and mother of twin sons CJ and Tim. Returned to Netuno weeks after CJ's death.

Tim – Eighteen-year-old son of Maggie. Travelled with Maggie to Netuno after his twin brother's death.

Puro – Manager of Netuno Wineries. Helped Cristiano and Avo after Cristiano's adoptive parents died.

Carmo – Works at Netuno; daughter of Puro. Engaged to Bento.

Reinaldo and Mateus – Brothers who owned Netuno before the takeover attempt. Reinaldo is Bento's father.

Bento – Engaged to Carmo. Hard worker. Will oversee Netuno one day.

Branca – Bento's mother and Reinaldo's disgruntled wife.

Francesco – Limo driver and friend to all at Netuno.

Jade– Beautiful; viper; toxic. Desperate for her father's approval. Daughter of Axel Axeline.

Axel Axeline – Ruthless businessman; father of Jade Axeline.

Richard – An inner-circle employee of Axel Axeline.

Dakar – Rogue leader of the Ptolemites who is after an Egyptian relic and willing to do anything to get it.

Saafa – Sixteen-year-old orphan who lives in Morocco on Dakar's compound against her will.

Prologue

Dalley

Netuno: The Morning of Maya's Kidnapping

Being a good friend is more difficult than it looks.

The drive from Lisbon to Netuno was deafeningly quiet. I insisted on driving and Ravn happily agreed, as he had been up most of the night trying to track down Maya and Cristiano but with few results. I could only hope the two of them were holed up somewhere breaking their most important relationship rule. My laugh broke the silence.

"What are you snickering about, Dalley?" Ravn asked, waking from a doze which left a little drool on his chin. *So cute*, I thought as he ran his sleeve across his face.

"Snickering? I wasn't snickering, I was giggling."

"There are a lot of things that you do, Dalley Price, but giggling is not one of them."

I huffed at him, knowing he was right. I would never be a giggler. "I was thinking about Maya and Cristiano and that maybe they're off breaking their one *rule*."

"You mean the one about no sex before marriage?"

"Yes, exactly."

"Well, if that is the only reason the two of them dropped off the edge of the world then I guess I could forgive them but …"

"Don't go there, Ravn. I just managed to stop thinking about the Ptolemites for two seconds, and now their back in my head. Nice going."

"I only meant …"

"I know what you meant, that maybe they're here in Portugal searching for the relic. Who knew an ancient hair fork worn by Cleopatra and rumored as the weapon she used to kill herself could cause so much trouble?"

Silence filled the car again as the familiar terrain of Netuno's luscious rolling vines came into view.

"It's stunning!" Ravn said.

"Thank you, Captain Obvious."

"Dalley, you need to settle down."

"Don't tell me to settle down!"

Ravn touched my hand. "I know you're stressed, but you can't talk to me like that."

I knew he was right, but I couldn't admit it just then. "Ravn, please allow me the distraction of reviewing my apology with me. I have to get this right, or they'll never believe a thing I have to say about Maya or anything else. I only hope the case of wine arrived last night and softened them up enough to listen. Maybe you should tell them about Maya and Cristiano. I don't think they'll believe me."

"Dalley, take my hand." I reluctantly agreed. "Yes, you made some bad choices, and yes, people got hurt, but you had nothing to do with Maya running off to find Cristiano or the Axelines' attempt to take over Netuno. In fact, if it hadn't been for you and your black file of information, Jade's father, Axel, and Bento's mother, Branca, would have succeeded in taking over of the family business and Carmo and Bento would not be getting married at the vineyard today. They should be thanking you for saving the winery."

A smile popped up on my lips.

"A little much?" he asked.

"Yes, maybe a little, but I get the point." Ravn managed to reduce my nerves from boil to simmer, giving me a chance to breathe.

When we arrived at Netuno, the wedding preparations for Carmo and Bento were in full swing. They had transformed the olive grove into a sea of tulle and ribbons and it looked exquisite. After parking, my anxiety began to grow again. "I can't go inside."

"Dalley, enough of this. Get out of the car and talk to them."

"You can't tell me what to do."

"Why are you fighting with me?"

"Just leave me alone."

"That's not going to happen, but I will sit with you until you stop being so nasty."

Although I resisted, he sat with me in silence until the anxiety passed and I found the courage to face my friends, if I dared call them that.

⁓

My knees shook as we walked toward the inn, but Ravn was there, holding my arm and giving me the strength to move forward.

Josie saw me first and stopped talking mid-sentence. All eyes followed her glare, as a quiet Josie only meant one thing: something was wrong.

Everyone stood frozen except Puro, who jumped in trying to break the instant tension that filled the veranda.

"Dalley! The case of wine you sent from France arrived yesterday— what a beautiful selection. Gervais confiscated three bottles as soon as it arrived. Looks like someone knows their French wines. I had no idea."

"Oh, Dalley has many talents she doesn't always share when people are getting to know her," Ravn added.

"And you are …?" Puro asked.

"Hello, Dagmar Ravn. I'm Dalley's boyfriend."

"Boyfriend?" The ladies on the veranda asked in unison.

I looked at Ravn, "What?"

"It's true," he whispered putting his arm around my waist.

Although I appreciated his support, it was time to be accountable for my actions and a case of wine could not take the place of the words I needed to say.

I took a step forward. "I'm sorry. I'm truly sorry." All eyes were on me as several more people stepped out of the inn, including Maggie.

"Maggie!" I uncharacteristically wanted to run to her. My heart ached for what she had gone through and for my part in making things worse. No mother should ever have to bury her child. CJ was only eighteen. I was familiar with all different kinds of loss but that's one I would thankfully never have to face.

Maggie pulled me back with her soft voice and smile. "Dalley, what are you sorry for?"

Ravn squeezed my arm. Maggie created an opportunity for me to get the apology right.

"In my career as a journalist I've come to accept there are varying degrees of truth depending on who's telling it. I can only explain my version of the situation and hope you believe and forgive me for my part of the mess I caused."

Ravn let go. "I'm here if you need me, but you're doing great," he breathed into my ear.

I smiled and continued. "When I was young, I created alternate versions of the truth to get through my days, and then one day I met someone who offered me a chance to be something more. I ran away from it, from him." I looked over at Ravn and then back at my friends.

"When I became a journalist, I was already jaded," Josie and Petra stifled a laugh. "Just a slip." I rolled my eyes. "I was stepping away from … I don't know, the right thing? Being a good person? I really had no frame of reference." My apology was going off track and I could feel the heat rising in my cheeks.

"Keep going, Dalley, we're listening," Maggie encouraged.

"Maybe a glass or two of wine?"

"No," Maggie and Ravn said in agreement.

"Okay, so no alcohol." I took another breath. "When I found out I was a winner in the contest, I was genuinely excited. I thought coming on the trip and writing cool stories about myself would be easy, earn me some new readers, and get me back in my editor's good graces. Write some articles, drink wine, have fun, and go home. That was the plan. But things don't always go as planned and if I were to do it over again, I would have abandoned the research I did before I left."

"Research?" Petra asked.

"Full disclosure?" I looked at Maggie.

"Yes, everything," she said in a stern, motherly tone.

"The night Maya punched me and everything fell apart, I left you a black file on Jade Axeline. That was not the only one I created." I searched in my bag and pulled out the other files, casting them onto the dirt. "I wrote backgrounders on all of you before I got on the plane."

"Are you serious?" Petra asked, flushed with anger.

"Yes, I'm sorry. It seemed like a good idea at the time. It all started before I met you. Before we went through everything we did. Before we became … friends. I took special interest in Maya after she canceled her wedding to Steven and even flew to Peachland and followed her around for about a week. She doesn't know that part yet, but when I see her …" I paused. "I promise I'll tell her that too. As far as the blog, things got out of hand, I didn't know what to do. I've never had close friends. I didn't want to lose you all."

"Well, I can assure you stealing Maya's journal and publishing stories about the rest of us is not the way to keep friends." Petra stated.

I wanted to push back, to be sarcastic but I stopped myself. "Yes, of course you're right, Petra. I *want* to be a better friend. That's one of the reasons I'm here."

"Please don't tell me I'm the purple one. I hate purple," Josie squawked, breaking the pressure.

"Since when?" I laughed. "No, you weren't purple. I left that one for Maya." My heart rate slowed, and I was ready for the next question.

"Dalley, why did you start writing the blog?" Maggie asked.

"When I began, it was supposed to be about me and my adventures here. Then Maya met Cristiano in Vancouver and their story seemed to outshine anything I could have written about. Like you said, Petra, their relationship was movie worthy."

"But her journal, Dalley. How could you have taken her personal entries and twisted them around the way you did?" Petra asked.

"My first blog wasn't from her journal. I just wrote about how they met and embellished the story a bit. Then there was an accident in the bathroom."

"An accident?" Josie laughed.

"Oh, you remember that night when we were all drinking green wine and Maya got really drunk? Well, later that night she was writing I assume in the bathtub, and her journal got wet. The next day I found it on the bathroom floor and decided to blow dry the pages. I knew how crazy she would be if anything happened to it. While I was drying it page by page I noticed my name pop up a couple of times. My curiosity got the better of me and I read the entries. I was blown away by her free style of writing and as I read, I couldn't stop just at the mention of my name. I could feel her falling in love with Cristiano and her desire to let go of all the fear and self-doubt she had about herself. I didn't plan to use her writing, it just kind of happened.

"I was selfish. At first, I made excuses and justified my choice and for a time, I liked the attention I was receiving online. Then all the stuff happened with Maggie and I started feeling guilty. I began to drink—a lot—and things got worse. You remember when we were working on our project, Petra? I tried to stop writing but my editor wouldn't let me. Then out of the blue, Jade happened. I thought we had gotten rid of her when she flew back to Montreal, but she obviously had an axe to grind with all of us. Especially Maya and Cristiano. She hijacked the blog with her images and tags. Just to be clear. We were not working together, and I had nothing to do with the Axelines trying to take over Netuno. When I finally stopped using Maya's journal for content, it was too late. Then came the yelling and the punch, and the rest you know. Saying sorry can't make up for breaking your trust, but I have been trying to set things right with Maya. I … I … There's something else I need to tell you, but I'm not sure you'll believe me."

"Believe you about what?" Josie asked.

"I said I want to be a better friend. And this is me being better. I think something has happened to Maya."

"What do you mean 'happened'?" Puro asked.

"When we left Paris, Maya and Cristiano were on their way to Porto to meet his parents, Euphemia and Marcos. About a day ago I got a strange feeling, like something was wrong or going to happen. I texted Maya repeatedly; she never got back to me. After everything we went through in Cairo, I …"

A woman stepped forward, with a gentle but firm smile. "Dalley, hello, I'm Judith. Maya's mom. We spoke on the phone before you and Maya left for Egypt. Thank you for helping her find Cristiano but I'm sure they're fine. I spoke with her before she left Paris and she was clear Cristiano needed to meet his family before she came back to Netuno. They should've arrived yesterday in Porto. I'm sure they're just enjoying some family time and don't want to be interrupted."

I looked over at Ravn, then back at Judith.

"Dalley, what's the matter?" Judith took in a quick breath and held it.

"Judith, I think we should all go inside." Ravn said.

✍

"Let's go into the dining room. The wedding guests will be arriving soon and there is no need to cause a fuss out here in the lobby." Puro offered.

Surrounded by wedding decorations and fancy napkins, Ravn waited until everyone was seated.

"As you know, Dalley and I went to Egypt to help Maya find Cristiano and we ran into some problems."

An older gentleman slammed his hand down on the table. Although casually dressed, his face was anything but relaxed. He had hard crease lines in his forehead and a grim look that outdid everyone else's in the room.

"What do you know about my Maya?" Phillip grumbled.

"Phillip, don't be so rude." Judith scolded him.

"I'm not being rude; I just want to know where my daughter is. Has anyone called his parents in Porto?"

I looked at Ravn, realizing I had missed a step.

"No, we haven't. As Dalley said, she texted Maya and left messages, but we haven't heard back from them. I was able to track them down to a hotel in Spain, but after that, nothing. I chatted with someone at the hotel but he spoke little English, and my Spanish is rusty."

Josie jumped in, "Why is that so out of the ordinary? Maybe after their ordeal, they needed some time alone."

"Or maybe Maya needed a break from you Dalley," Petra said.

Petra's words stung, but I deserved them. "I might have agreed before, but Pierre La Nou, Cristiano's friend from Paris, couldn't get in touch with them either."

"Well," Judith broke in, "let's call Beth then. Maya's best friend from back home. If anyone knows where she is, it would be her."

Judith pulled out her phone and made the call. "It's ringing."

"Beth? I'm sorry to wake you." Judith smiled and listened to Maya's friend. "We don't know. That's why we're calling you?" Judith looked around realizing there was a room full of people anxiously wanting to be part of the conversation.

"Beth, could I put you on speakerphone?"

"Hi everyone? What's going on? I can only imagine this has something to do with the wedding?"

"The wedding?" Judith asked with confusion. "Carmo and Bento's wedding?"

"No," Beth said hesitantly then went silent.

"Beth, are you still there?"

"Yes, I'm here. But Maya is going to kill me."

Maya's dad walked over to the phone, looking increasingly uncomfortable. "Beth, what is going on?"

"Well, I guess congratulations are in order." She laughed nervously. "Maya and Cristiano got married two days ago in Spain. They had a small ceremony at a nunnery. A local priest performed the service."

"They what?" Phillip's anger could be felt around the room.

"Yes," Beth said slowly.

"Those sly devils," I let slip.

"Dalley, shut up," Ravn interjected.

There was a strange split of emotion in the room. Several people were clapping with excitement, yet Maya's parents looked heartbroken.

"Well, I might have something to say about that," Phillip barked into the phone. "Beth, if she calls you, please have her contact me immediately. I'll try her right now."

Phillip walked out of the dining room as Puro rushed over to Judith. "They love each other. Cristiano is a good man."

"Thank you, Puro. I better go find Phillip."

A trail of on lookers followed Judith and I out into the lobby where Phillip was on his computer.

"Judith, it's right here all in black and white. There's no way the marriage is legal. She couldn't marry him in Spain without having to do months of paperwork beforehand. It doesn't matter that they were married by a priest, it doesn't count."

"Doesn't count? Phillip …"

He was ignoring his wife. "It's going to be okay. We can get her out of this," Phillip continued.

"Phillip? I'm sorry to interrupt, and I know this is none of my business. But Cristiano and Maya love each other very much. You don't know what they have been through," I said, trying to reason with him.

"You're right Miss Price. It isn't your business. You have already done quite enough. Anyway, Maya is still healing from her breakup—"

"No, Phillip, she's not." I had to set him straight. "What she has with Cristiano is the real thing. He asked her to marry him when they were in Egypt, and she did not hesitate even when we were being shot at—"

"Dalley!" Ravn stepped in and yelled, trying to stop me but it was too late.

"What? Who was shot at? What happened in Egypt?" Judith asked. The color drained from her face.

Ravn and I froze.

Phillip looked at Ravn and me, daring us to continue. "I don't know what's going on here, or what happened in Egypt, but as soon as those two surface, she's coming home with us."

"Phillip, let's take a breath. We don't want to do anything rash," Judith jumped in, seeing things were getting out of hand.

"You mean like leaving a series of crazy messages on the phone for our daughter?" Phillip asked.

"Yes, just like that."

"Too late. Judith, I have been mother and father to Maya since she was a baby, I appreciate you trying, but you have to let me handle this." Judith looked like she had been sucker punched but somehow pulled herself together and stood with grace and dignity even though Phillip's words had struck hard.

Puro came out of the dining room with the young wedding clad couple at his side. Carmo and Bento looked relieved. "I just got a text from Cristiano. He said they are safe and on their way to Porto to see his parents."

I grabbed Ravn's hand. "They're safe, did you hear that? I'm sorry everyone. I guess all that worry was for nothing. I don't know what got into me." I sighed.

Phillip was still pacing with his phone in his hand, fingers on the screen.

When Maya finally picked up, she barely had a second to say hello before Phillip launched into the 'you are not married' speech with the 'you are coming home with us' finisher. Maya started strong, yelling through the phone so we could all hear it, then Phillip kept on and she went silent. What happened next, though, reawakened my worst fears.

Phillip started yelling Maya's name again and again, but it was the look on his face that sent shock waves of fear through the room. Judith ran towards Phillip as the phone slipped from his hand and landed on the floor.

"What happened? What's the matter with Maya? Phillip, what's going on?" Judith yelled, shaking her husband.

"I heard a pop, a scream, and a crash. There's been some sort of accident."

"What do you mean? What are you talking about?" Judith swayed, but before I even needed to ask, Ravn grabbed her. It had only been several weeks since Netuno's lobby was home to the news that Maggie's son was dying and the thought that something tragic could have happened to Maya and Cristiano sent shockwaves through my body.

Further chaos erupted as everyone yelled at Phillip for more information.

During the commotion, Carmo removed the veil from her hair and picked up the phone. "Cristiano? Maya? Are you there? Shhh, I hear something. Everyone stop talking! Please let us know you're okay. Say something."

Carmo looked at me and Ravn, then turned on the speakerphone. We heard a cry of pain, and silence.

❧

A man holding an armful of bouquets bound joyfully into the lobby. "Carmo, why are you out here in your wedding dress?" His tone changed. "What's the matter?"

"Luca, there's been an accident. Cristiano and Maya are in trouble. They were on their way to Porto to meet Cristiano's biological parents when something terrible happened. I heard her scream." Carmo's wedding day had just taken a terrible turn.

Luca dropped the flowers and grabbed his phone.

"When did it happen? What do we know?" Luca demanded.

He was dialling before Carmo could fully explain. "Inspector Luca Palito," he barked into the phone. I have an emergency. There's been an accident outside of Porto." "Give me Maya's number," he yelled to the shell-shocked crowd. "They'll be able to locate her if there is still a signal, if not we'll have to wait until someone calls it in."

Phillip ran over to Luca. "I think I heard a gun shot. He better not have hurt my daughter."

"Who? Cristiano? You must be mistaken sir. Cristiano is not a criminal." Luca said.

"Criminal or not, he got my Maya involved in something dangerous. Just ask Dalley and Ravn. I don't know everything about Egypt, but I know they escaped from the country which usually means someone is chasing you."

"How dare you imply Cristiano hurt Maya. He loves her. And she is his wife now." Puro defended Cristiano.

"Wife? This is lunacy I …"

"Judith, I think it is best if you take Phillip to your room. We'll let you know when we hear something," Maggie suggested.

"Oh, I'm not going anywhere," Phillip said.

"Phillip. Join me outside while we wait for the call," Judith insisted.

After Luca called emergency services he contacted his police department in Porto.

Carmo and Bento changed out of their wedding clothes and Puro sent all the guests home. Everyone waited for Luca's phone to ring.

❧

"Emergency services found Cristiano. He will be transported to the hospital as soon as they can cut him out of the car."

"But he's alive." Puro grabbed Maggie's hand and squeezed until her fingers turned white.

"Yes, for now." Luca answered.

"And Maya?" Judith asked in a whisper. "How is my Maya?"

"Judith, they're not sure, they can't find her."

1

Where is Maya?

Cristiano

"Look in the ditch! She must be somewhere."

"I'm telling you; we've searched up and down the road. She's gone!"

"She didn't just walk away; there's too much blood in the passenger seat."

"Well, if she didn't walk away and she wasn't thrown out of the car, where is she?"

It sounded like I was underwater. I couldn't speak, I couldn't move, something was pressing into my chest.

"We need the hydraulic ram; the steering wheel has him pinned. Get the c-collar on him and the back board ready."

"What about the girl?"

"The police are on their way. It's out of our hands. Our only job now is to keep this guy alive. He's coming to; keep him still."

"Where is she?"

"You need to stop talking, sir."

"Where did she go?" I sputtered.

"My team is taking care of that now."

The next thing I heard was the song of sick twisted metal being torn away from my body.

"He's asking about his wife. Poor guy. Inspector Palito said they were just married."

"Focus on what you're doing. Ready! On my three!"

Judith (Netuno)

I was numb. Phillip was enraged and Puro was beside himself with worry.

When Carmo called Avo and told her about the accident there was no negotiating with her, she was coming with us to Porto, ill health or not.

While on the way to the airport, Avo asked if Euphemia and Marcos had been contacted. Luca offered to take care of it but I felt a motherly obligation to make the call.

"Ola," Euphemia answered.

"Hello, this is …"

"Maya, Is that you? Where are you and Cristiano? We were expecting you yesterday."

"No, this is not Maya. This is her mother, Judith."

"Judith? It's nice to meet you. Forgive me for my rudeness, but why are you calling? Where are the children?" I heard the crack in her voice as her instinct kicked in. "Has something happened?"

"Yes. There is no easy way for me to say this but, there has been an accident. Cristiano should be at the Santo Antonio hospital in Porto by now. He is unconscious, but still alive."

"Oh, thank God. And Maya? How is Maya?" Euphemia asked.

"We don't know." I paused; not sure I could say the words out loud. "She's missing, Euphemia. Maya is missing."

"What? That can't be. There must be some mistake?"

"No, there's no mistake." I spoke quietly at first, but my anxiety began to rise and dissolve the calm demeanor holding our conversation together. "We'll be there in less than three hours."

❧

Marcos met us in the hospital lobby wearing a grim smile.

"And you are?" Marcos asked extending his hand to Puro.

"I'm Puro, manager of Netuno Wineries. I have known Cristiano since he was a boy."

"And I'm Luca, Inspector Luca Palito, an old friend of Cristiano's from high school who happened to be in the right place at the right time."

Marcos extended his greeting to Phillip, but the gesture was not accepted leaving me embarrassed and worried about my husband. I had only seen Phillip like that one other time when he found out Maya was being bullied because of me and my depression. He was furious and threatening to sue the schoolboard if something was not done to stop it. I'm not sure what happened in the end, as Phillip shielded me from most unpleasant situations.

Marcos ignored Phillip's snub. "I took the liberty of booking rooms for everyone at the hotel down the street. Cristiano is still unconscious and unable to communicate. It might be best if you settle into the hotel for a couple of hours."

"That is not a liberty I choose to accept," Phillip responded.

Marcos became rigid.

Puro interjected, "Marcos, I think what Phillip is trying to say is we would like to stay at least for a little while, just in case he wakes. Besides, I don't think you're going to stop Avo. She's already on the elevator."

Marcos turned and Avo waved to him as the door slid shut.

"If you will excuse me, I'm going to the police station to see if there is any news about Maya," Luca said.

"Can we please head upstairs now?" I asked.

Marcos sighed and we followed him to Cristiano's private room. When we arrived, Euphemia was hugging Avo while Zef and Jacinta, Cristiano's brother and sister, were standing nearby. The first few hours were like walking through a murky fog. Cristiano was in bad shape and Phillip's angry comments were not helping the situation. I finally convinced him to head over to the hotel and give Avo, Puro, and his family some time with Cristiano.

The next morning when we arrived at the hospital, Cristiano began to stir but the scene that followed was not one of hope or joy. Before I could stop him, Phillip was yelling like a mad man and when Cristiano finally came to and was not able to tell us where Maya was, Phillip knocked him unconscious with one blow to the face.

Fatherly fists began to fly, igniting the room into further chaos. I stood frozen as Marcos hit Phillip, defending his son who lay in his hospital bed.

Maya was missing; our children were in trouble and our husbands were throwing punches like disgruntled teenagers. Ironically, it was Zef, Cristiano's eighteen-year-old brother, who jumped in before Marcos landed a second blow and broke my Phillip's jaw.

Words and tears sprayed around the room like noxious gas, burning our skin and our hearts as fear became the chemical weapon of the day,

embedding itself into my tastebuds and ensuring that sleep would be fleeting until I knew my daughter was safe.

2

The Magic Bread Falls

Judith

BEFORE WE HAD A CHANCE to breathe, Jacinta's high pitch cry cast the room into temporary silence. We turned to answer her call but found ourselves frozen in disbelief. How could one family suffer so many tragedies? Avo fell to the ground clutching the loaf of bread she brought for Cristiano. Everyone shouted in horror but were unable to do anything as hospital security arrived, sweeping every male from the space.

The chaos peaked as Avo was whisked away to the ER, leaving Cristiano's room filled with quieting sobs and the beeps of his machine. Jacinta, his sixteen-year-old sister, picked up the loaf of bread and placed it on the table beside her brother's bed.

"Cristiano, you need to wake up. Please, I need you. Maya needs you." She sat down beside him, holding his hand and whispering into his ear so her mother and I could not hear what she was saying.

The reality of our worlds stood between Euphemia and me like an uncrossable chasm. My daughter was missing, and her son had just been knocked unconscious by my husband.

It was not until I saw her face soften that I could take a breath. She took Cristiano's other hand, then looked at her daughter.

"Jacinta, could you check with the nurses about Avo? And find out where they are keeping your father and brother." She looked at me and smiled. "Could you please also check on Mr. Wells and Puro? I'm so sorry Puro was caught up in all of this, and as one of my son's oldest friends he deserves better."

Euphemia gave Jacinta a hug and kissed her on her forehead. The action was so tender, so natural. A part of me was jealous, as that was the kind of relationship I had always longed for with my daughters.

With shaking hands, Jacinta nodded.

"Don't worry dear, everything is going to be okay. I need you to take care of those things for me and then bring us some coffee."

Jacinta stared at her mother with the kind of sadness you never want to see in your children's eyes.

"Your brother is going to recover and we will find Maya."

Jacinta left without a word.

"You are so good at that."

"So good at what?" Euphemia asked me with genuine curiosity.

"Mothering." I sounded ridiculous. "I'm sorry Euphemia. It has been a long couple of days." I paused. "Do you really believe we will figure things out? I want to believe you, but …"

"But it's true, Judith. Cristiano will find Maya. I know it. I don't know how, but I do."

My stomach turned thinking of Maya alone and possibly injured. "I can't believe any of this is really happening."

That's when a wave of nausea came at me. Euphemia grabbed a tray as I vomited up the pain and fear I had been holding in.

"Better?" She smiled ever so slightly as she handed me a glass of water.

"I'm not sure if better is the right word, but ... Euphemia, we need to talk."

"I agree."

⁘

During Jacinta's absence, we talked about our children and shared our heartbreaking tales of my postpartum depression and the adoption that was forced upon Euphemia as a teenager. Although from different worlds and circumstances, we were the same in so many ways. Two mothers who loved their children desperately but were unable to be there for them as they grew up; two mothers who wanted the chance to get to know their adult children and would do anything to keep them safe.

"It's strange how the world brings people together," I said simply as we held hands and confirmed our newly formed bond. "You are a wonderful mother, Judith. Never doubt that." With the shift of her brow, I saw the change of subject on her face.

"Judith, your daughter loves my son, and he loves her equally. Phillip is angry about the marriage, but we must focus."

I pulled my hand back and smiled uneasily. "I know what we need to focus on, Euphemia."

Moving over to the window, I stared out, wondering where my girl could be. My heart ached as I felt her pain wherever she was.

"Maya wrote me a letter only a week after she had arrived here in Portugal. She talked about Cristiano and how special he was to her. She was falling in love. In the letter she asked me to forgive her. Can you imagine that? It was me who should have been seeking forgiveness. I was never the mother she deserved. If anything happens to her ..."

"Judith, we did what we had to do to make sure our children were safe when they were little." She smiled. "But they are not little anymore.

We both have work to do to build their trust. Our only goal right now is to find Maya. But first we must get Avo and Cristiano up on their feet and get our husbands out of jail."

"Yes," I agreed, wiping a tear away that had slipped out during our conversation.

"Jail? So, what are you ladies planning, a prison break?" Luca asked as he wandered into the room.

"Luca! It's lovely to see you. Have you heard anything yet?"

"No, nothing about Maya, but there was some chatter on the police scanner mentioning some sort of scuffle at the hospital with a patient's family. I took a guess."

"Were they really arrested?" I asked with my anxiety knocking at the door.

"No, I arrived in time, flashed my badge and convinced security to cancel the call. Everyone is being kept downstairs in a holding room for now. How is Cristiano? Puro mentioned he woke up for a moment. I am going to need—"

Euphemia cleared her throat.

"Oh Euphemia, I'm so sorry, this is Inspector Luca ... my apologies Luca, I can not remember your last name."

Luca turned to Euphemia with his broad hand, held out to her, "Palito, Inspector Luca Palito, and you are?"

"I am the wife and mother of two of the men being held downstairs ... and Cristiano's ..." her voice broke off as she turned to her son.

"So, you're Cristiano's biological mother. I met your husband yesterday when we arrived from Netuno."

"Marcos did not mention you," was all she could manage at first, but she soon pulled herself back together and continued. "I'm sorry. I'm not myself. How do you know my son?"

Luca smiled. "Cristiano and I are old friends; we went to high school together." Luca pushed his hair back and pulled out a notepad. He waved the pad in the air. "Old school, but easier for me to find what I am looking for," he laughed a little, then shifted his demeanor.

"Can someone please describe to me what he said when he woke up. I am just starting to put the pieces together. I did a conference call with Dalley and Ravn back at Netuno and they filled me in on all the details of what happened in Egypt, but …"

"Who are Dalley and Ravn?" Euphemia interrupted.

Luca's face was filled with compassion. "Euphemia. I know there are a lot of moving parts and people right now in this situation. Dalley and Ravn are friends with Maya and Cristiano and helped them get out of Egypt."

"Luca, Dalley mentioned back at Netuno that someone was shooting at them when they were away. Is that true? I need to understand." I had to fight the rising panic breaking through my delicate veneer.

"Someone shot at Cristiano and Maya?" Euphemia blurted out in horror.

Luca moved in and touched my arm. It was the same move the doctors used to make before they told me bad news about my depression. I hated that touch.

"Ladies, I understand you are both worried about your children right now. But please let me do my job and ask the questions. All you need to do is answer what you know."

Euphemia stepped in, "The last thing he said while conscious was, 'It was no accident. They're here.' What does that mean? What was he talking about?"

I could tell Euphemia's poise was crumbling, much like my own.

"I need for both of you to stay calm," he said, reading the motherly panic rise in the room.

"We are." I growled with agitation. "As calm as two mothers can be in a situation like this. Luca, what is going on? *They're here?* Who was he talking about?" I asked as the pit in my stomach grew. "Do these people have my Maya?"

He walked over to Cristiano. "What have you gotten yourself into, old friend?" Then he turned to us. "The Ptolemites."

"Ptolemites?" Euphemia and I asked at the same time.

"Yes, simply, they are terrible people who think Cristiano and Maya have something they want and will stop at nothing to get it."

It didn't seem real. I wanted him to laugh, but that was the hysteria sparking. It had been years since I had an episode and I could not afford to end up in a psych ward in Portugal while my daughter needed me. I reached into my purse and pulled out a pill I had been keeping for emergencies only. Looking into Luca's eyes I placed the dissolving tablet under my tongue and waited for the calm.

"Yes, Judith. I'm going to be honest with you. It is more than likely the Ptolemites took Maya," he answered solemnly.

Euphemia chimed in, "Surely there has been a mistake. Cristiano works for the airlines."

"Euphemia, it's not about Cristiano, but something that's surfaced from his parents' past."

"Michel and Rosa? That's ridiculous. They were the kindest and most honest people I have ever met. Anyway, they died twenty years ago."

"I don't have all the answers, but I'll do my best to figure things out. If this is a kidnapping, we will know soon. We will need a place to stage our equipment just in case they try to call." He looked over at me. "They need Maya right now. In their eyes, keeping her alive is the only way they are going to get what they want."

My heart shook, and my legs crumbled. Luca grabbed my arm and led me over to the nearest chair before I collapsed.

There was an odd silence in the room, but Euphemia's unexpected ramble with her unconscious son broke it in two.

"Ptolemites?" Euphemia pulled at Cristiano's sheets, straightening them as she talked. "What do we need to do?" she asked him. "Once your father and brother are out of holding, we can set things up at our house. We don't live too far from here, but you know that, you were there just over a week ago." She looked at Luca. "I don't want to leave Cristiano here. He's coming home with me as soon as he can."

"Euphemia, are you alright?" I asked, almost whispering.

She had gone back to straightening Cristiano's bedsheets and fluffing up an extra pillow, but the open hand for fluffing, soon became a fist for punching. I moved to get up, but Luca shook his head. Casting the pillow across the room, Euphemia ran towards me, falling on her knees.

"Judith, this is all my fault," she cried. "I pleaded with Maya to find him. We put her on the plane to Paris ourselves. I put your daughter in danger. It was me," she said, breaking down into tears. "I'm so sorry."

Before I responded, there was a commotion in the hallway, followed by a familiar voice, "Oh, don't you dare touch me. I have been up for over twenty-four hours and I'm in no mood to be handled. Nothing is going to stop me from going into that room!"

By the time she finished yelling at the guard, we were all staring at the door and there she was, the one person Maya had depended on, since she was eight; hair tied up in a loose knot, backpack slung over her shoulder. The typically mild-mannered and methodical schoolteacher was nowhere to be seen as a newly fired-up Beth barged past security, looking fierce and ready for a fight.

3

Still Alive

Maya

THE HEAT WAS STAGGERING AND the air rank. I was still alive—at least, I hoped I was. Because if not, I surely had ended up in hell and somehow that didn't seem fair. It felt like a rucksack was covering my face and when I ventured to open my eyes, I couldn't. If there was ever a time to panic, that was it. My lips were the only exposed part of my face. I could taste the dust, but I didn't want to swallow, or I couldn't.

My breaths were shallow as I tried to calm myself and sort through a series of fragmented memories, but any shred of rational thought disappeared when I tried to move and found my hands strapped to the bed. I thrashed my legs, but bolts of pain shot through my body, rendering the action useless.

"Let me go!" I screamed again and again until my voice cracked, and my panicked silence filled the space. I lay still, trying to catch my breath, trying to keep the panic from consuming me. My heart beat so hard I wondered how much more it could take.

Is this how I'm going to die? I wondered. After everything I had been through, was that it? Then I heard it: the scuffle of feet, a click, and the sound of unfamiliar music. "Who's there? Please help me. Where am I? Where is Cristiano?"

I knew someone was in the room, but they wouldn't answer. I focused on my breath, trying to slow my heart down, trying to hear anything.

"Please, let me go," I said quietly at first. Nothing. "There are people looking for me right now," I said a little louder, finding my voice again. "Who do you think you are? You can't keep me here," I screamed with everything I had, twisting my wrists and moving my body in any direction I could. As I yelled, new pain points erupted in my body like mini volcanos spewing molten lava, but I had to push through it. "If you have done anything to Cristiano, I will tear you apart! Let me go!" I felt the whoosh of air leave my lungs before the throb in my gut; then came the laughter.

The music got louder and louder, tearing at my ears, invading my thoughts, erasing everything else. I just wanted it to stop. I shook my head side to side hoping it would somehow dull the bombardment of the sound. "Stop it, stop!" I croaked out, finally giving in.

"Are you done?" A caustic voice yelled into my ear.

With one last effort, I spat out my words, "It's too loud."

"Then stop yelling, you stupid girl, and say please," the voice hissed back at me.

She turned down the music enough that I could think again. "Could I *please* have some water? I am so thirsty."

"No. They said we're not supposed to give you anything," the woman scoffed.

"Maybe we should," another younger voice broke in. "We *are* supposed to be taking care of her."

"You need to shut up, too. Our only job is to keep her alive, not comfortable. You bandaged her up. That is more than she deserves. I am not doing anything for her." I heard her gather the saliva in her mouth, then felt the wad of spit land on my exposed lips. "Don't say I didn't give you anything to drink." She laughed again, then stepped away and pounded on the door. "Let me out of here. I have more important things to do." A bolt slid across the door and an icy shiver ran over my body; the door opened then slammed with a finality that made my stomach turn.

I knew I couldn't move, so what *could* I do? I could talk and smell and hear and with any luck, when they took the bandages off my eyes, I hoped I could see.

"Hello? Are you still there? The other one? My name is Maya …"

I heard a shuffle again. I needed her help.

I lay still for several more minutes. Then I felt an internal shift from fear to frustration. "Hello?" I tried yelling over the music. "Hello. Can you please wipe the spit off my face? And while you're at it, turn the music off. Honestly, it's giving me a headache," I said.

The music went off, and I heard a little giggle. There was silence. I could hear her footsteps scurrying across the floor; a cupboard opening and closing, and a twist of plastic. Next, I felt a cool cloth wiping my mouth and a straw being placed near my lips.

"Sip slowly. You have been unconscious for several days and are showing signs of dehydration."

"Thank you," I responded, not sure how much gratitude I should be showing. She differed from the other woman who had been in the room. Maybe it was a trick, but I sensed a kindness in her voice and had to trust that. I had to trust myself. "Tell me, how old are you?"

She hesitated, but finally answered, "Sixteen. I turn seventeen in a few months. Please, don't ask me anything else," I could hear the fear in her voice.

"Can I at least know your name? What should I call you? I don't want to get you into trouble, but can you at least tell me where I am? What am I doing here?"

The young lady paused and lowered her voice. "My name is Saafa. I can't tell you where we are. I'm sorry."

"Fine. Do you know what they want from me?" I asked, annoyance growing. "I don't have any money."

"They don't want money; they have *lots* of money," she answered flatly.

"Then what *do* they want? You must know." Irritation and fatigued continued to ooze out of my tone. "I don't even know who's holding me here."

"Yes, you do," she said emphatically. "Think about it."

"I can barely concentrate on swallowing. I need your help. What do you know?" I pleaded with exasperation.

She leaned down closer to my ear and whispered. "I heard them say they went through the suitcase *again* after the car crash, but it was not there."

"Again … the suitcase? Cristiano's parents' suitcase?" That night in Cairo at the storage facility. "Egypt?" My heart pounded again. *The relic?* I asked myself, then answered. "The Ptolemites."

"They took you so *he* would give it back," she said, speaking swiftly.

"The crash, the accident … Cristiano?" I said his name in terror. "Where is he? You want the relic? We don't have it. We never found it."

"Oh, I want nothing to do with the relic. I am not here by choice. I am not one of them," she said, sounding insulted.

"So, Cristiano is not here, but he's still alive."

She paused, clearly not sure if she should answer, but finally relented. "Yes, your husband is not dead. I heard he is at the hospital in Portugal, unconscious, but alive."

"So, we are not in Portugal?"

"I never said that."

"You didn't have to."

"Yes, like I said, your husband is still alive."

"My husband." I said the words carefully as my father's voice flashed loudly in my memory. Yelling at me, telling me Cristiano and I were not married, and the ceremony performed by the priest in Spain was nothing more than that: a ceremony.

I took a breath. "Like I said, we don't have it. We never found the relic."

"Shhh, don't say that." She placed her hand over my mouth and then turned the music back on and whispered directly into my ear again, "If he thinks you don't have it or know where to find it, he *will* kill you. Or worse …"

I shook my head, releasing her hand over my mouth. "Worse? What are you talking about? People don't just kill normal people like me. Anyway, what could be worse than him killing me?"

"There are many things worse than death in my world. Please stop talking."

"Okay, if I can't ask where I am, can you at least tell me what's wrong with me?" Why do you have my hands tied down? And the bandages on my face?

I could hear her hesitation, but after a few minutes, she relented.

"The ties were actually my idea. When you came in, you had injured your face and there was glass all around your eyes. I think I removed it all."

"You think?" I asked, feeling my stomach drop.

"Yes, and I was worried if you reached up in your sleep or something, you might disturb the wounds."

"Wounds?" I repeated, trying to process the information.

"Yes, now please be quiet. He's coming."

I could hear her breath quicken and feel the fear rise in the room as she waited for the door to open.

"Please, whatever you hear, don't say a word."

This young woman was possibly the only ally I had; if she disappeared, so likely would I.

"Thank you, Saafa," I slipped in. As the bolt slid across the door, she quickly whispered, "I gave you something to sleep. Don't fight it."

"No, Saafa, please."

"It's better for both of us. Trust me."

Saafa ran from me to the other side of the room. Just as the door opened, I felt a heaviness come over my body.

"What's the matter with her? I was told she was awake!"

The last thing I remember hearing was the crack of an open hand on a cheek and a body crumpling to the ground.

When I woke, my lips were dry and cracked and my body felt heavy. I momentarily forgot about the ties and bandages and when I tried to move, panic ricocheted around my frame. "Saafa?"

"Stop talking!" the voice snapped back. "No, Saafa is not here. The two of you have caused me nothing but trouble."

"Me and Saafa?" I asked, with a note of confusion.

"No, Cristiano!" He yelled at me. "You *are* as stupid as Naheim said. A part of me feels sorry for him; stupid and ugly, not what you want in a new wife."

I tried to turn my head away from his acrid words, to stop them from landing, but there was no getting away. I could feel them planting roots the moment they settled over my heart.

When I got to Portugal, I started over. I briefly believed I was beautiful, that I had something to offer the world, to Cristiano … but the man's words were already taking root.

The acid-toned voice continued, but I only caught a piece of what he said, "Ever since the two of you landed in Cairo, you have caused me nothing but trouble, but that will all be over soon. Just give me what I want, and we can all return to our lives." I could smell his lies and putrid breath as he hovered over me. Then, thinking the moment could not get any worse, I felt his rough, calloused finger scraping against my collarbone, my body pushed back into the cot, trying to avoid his touch.

"Stop touching me."

"Oh Maya, give me some credit. I don't need to tie my women down to get them to do what I want. Well, except maybe you," he laughed with an air of superiority.

"I'm not your woman, and I will give you nothing!"

"Really? Nothing? I don't know about that. Let's start with something simple. Why did Cristiano go to Cairo? Why did you follow him? Why did you collect the luggage? Why did you run from us?"

I could feel his fingers stroking my neck, scraping my skin, then felt the pressure.

"Come on Maya, just give me something and I'll let go a little."

I coughed, and my body ached.

"You were shooting at us! Of course we ran." The pressure increased.

"Oh, I think you can do better than that."

I coughed again. "I followed Cristiano to Cairo because he needed my help."

"Looking for the relic?" He pressed harder.

"No, we knew nothing about the relic." His fingers tightened around my neck. "At first. Stop! You're hurting me."

"*Of course* I am hurting you. That is the point."

"If you kill me, you will never get the relic."

The pressure lessened, and he removed his fingers.

"You're not as stupid as I first thought. Clearly this is going to take more time, but I didn't walk all the way down here for nothing. You may not want to *give* me anything but you do have one thing I want to take." I froze, preparing myself for what he was about to do.

I could feel his rough fingertips meandering along my neck until they stopped and lifted the chain that held my tear of bravery. *Be brave.* I told myself. He snapped the necklace from my body and a piece of me went with him—a piece I didn't know if I would ever get back.

I heard his heavy steps move farther away and the door opened. "This stone is going to make a lovely gift for another guest I have staying with me." The door slammed shut and the bolt slid into place, ensuring that even if I could move, I was not going anywhere. I stayed quiet for some time, trying to erase the feeling of his fingers on my skin.

"Hello? Saafa? Are you there? I need to go to the bathroom." I called, but no one came.

When I was young, I used to think I couldn't ask for help, that I was all alone. But being there, covered in my blood, sweat, and everything else, I redefined what being alone truly meant. As the room cooled, my emotions shifted from helplessness to anguish. Next came the sobs and with that, white-hot pain echoing around my ribcage and traveling up into my head. I screamed. No one knew where I was and there was nothing I could do. So, I stopped.

If I was going to get out alive, I had to find my own way. I had to think smart. Who were the two smartest, most kick-ass women I knew? Beth and Dalley. Beth, my best friend from back home who never cracks under pressure, and Dalley, my newest friend from Netuno who would do anything to survive. So, I started with channeling my inner Beth and using the square breathing technique she taught me before coming on the trip. I visualized my breath moving around a literal square, filling my lungs with fresh air, while pushing the pain and fear out of my thoughts. Breathe in and up, Out and Across, In and Down, Out and Across.

After some time, it worked, and I called on my inner Dalley who gave me a chance to assess the situation and start formulating a plan on how I was going to escape.

The room was cooler than before and I could feel a slight breeze; it was evening. I did not know how many nights I had been there, but at least I could start counting from that point on. Reaching around with my hand, I found a sharp edge on the cot. I scraped my palm, feeling the sting as the skin broke open, marking day one.

4

Where is She?

Euphemia

"Cristiano, wake up. I need you to open your eyes. We need your help."
I sighed; not sure what else I was supposed to be saying to him. Judith
suggested we not mention Avo's condition or that Maya was missing, but
I thought it might help to motivate him if he knew the truth, so I went
against Judith's recommendation. "Your old friend Luca is here. He wants
to help, but he needs you to wake up. I have some news my dear, and in
any other circumstance I might hold back, but if this can wake you up,
then … here it goes. Maya is missing, it appears the Ptolemites have taken
her. Her family are beside themselves. She needs you whole and healthy.
But that's not all." I hesitated. "Avo has had a stroke. She is in intensive care
and may not have long. Cristiano, I am fighting for you. I am so happy
you and Maya found each other and got married; not everyone feels that
way right now, but Judith and I are working on it. Your father and I know
a thing or two about parents trying to keep love apart, and I will not let

that happen." I paused. "I'm sorry, Cristiano. Listen to me going on and on. Wake up, my son. There are lots of people who need you."

I looked over to where Beth was sitting, her eyes closed, body folded into the hospital chair. Judith had finally convinced her to have a rest, but I wondered if she was asleep. When she had barreled through the door, and I found out who she was, I could not help but smile at meeting someone who would do *anything* to save her best friend.

"Cristiano, Maya's best friend Beth is here. She arrived earlier in the day, just after the ruckus with Phillip and your father. I think she wants you to wake up even more than I do if that is possible. She has been sitting in the corner for hours, refusing to go anywhere just in case you wake." I grabbed his hand and squeezed it again. That's when I felt it: a little pressure on my palm. "Jacinta, Beth, he's waking up."

Cristiano

Somewhere in the darkness, I heard her voice; she was talking to me, telling me to wake up. Did I hear her correctly? She said something about Maya and Avo. They're in trouble. I have to wake up ... I ... have ... to ... wake up.

My eyes flashed open and there were three women staring at me, holding their breath. I recognized Euphemia, but the others were strangers.

I was the first to speak. "Where is Maya?" I croaked out.

They all looked at each other, not sure how to answer.

"That's what we wanted to ask you." A young woman stared back at me.

"Jacinta, why don't you take Beth out of the room for a minute? I'll have a chat with your brother and call the two of you back when he is more alert."

"My sister?" I asked quietly to myself. Yes, I remember seeing her on the balcony the day before I ended up in Spain.

"No!" Beth yelled back at Euphemia. "I'm not going anywhere until he tells me what happened."

"Beth? Maya's Beth?" I asked.

"Yes, Maya's Beth," she responded defiantly.

"Beth, dear, Cristiano can't help us yet. Jacinta, please take her down to the cafeteria."

Beth left the room in a huff with my new sister close behind, leaving me all alone with my mother for the first time in my life. I stared at her, not believing it could be true. Then I felt her hand brush against my cheek, and I leaned into her palm. She cried.

"Please don't cry. I'm sorry."

"What are you sorry about, Cristiano? This isn't your fault, none of it." She grabbed the water jug, her hand shaking. "Are you thirsty?"

"No. My head is swimming in pain and memories. What day is it?"

"It's been four days since the accident. You have been in and out of consciousness since your arrival."

"I feel like I've been hit by a truck."

"Yes, well, it was something like that. The car was totalled."

I winced, then attempted to move.

"Your injuries are serious, son. You dislocated your shoulder, cracked several ribs, and received a concussion."

"Son …" I said, trying to find a place to put my new reality. "And my face?" I touched my jaw.

"Oh, yes, that would be from when Maya's father punched you."

"He hit me?"

She nodded with a grimace. "You woke and said a few words, Phillip lost his temper, then your father followed suit." She paused. "Sorry, I'm not sure how you want us to refer to ourselves. Well, anyway." She swallowed hard.

"Euphemia, please tell me. Where is Maya?"

"Maya is missing Cristiano."

"Then it wasn't just a nightmare. They have her, the Ptolemites have her." Beads of sweat emerged on my forehead as I tried to move but my body wouldn't comply.

Euphemia placed her hand over her heart. "Inspector Palito has been working hard to find her."

"Luca Palito?" I asked.

"Yes, it's a long story, I can explain later, but all you need to know right now is he's using all his resources within the international crimes department to find out as much as he can. He believes Maya is safe, for now; until they find what they are looking for. Do you know what that is?"

"Yes. I know exactly what they want," I said grinding my teeth together.

"Cristiano, I'm not sure how to tell you this, but something else has happened."

"What? To who?" I followed my mother's eyes until they landed on a loaf of bread with a piece torn off. Then I felt it. "She was here, I remember, the bread against my lips. Avo? Where is my Avo?" The blood rushed to my head and my face heated up.

"Maybe it is time to take a break. Have a sip of water."

"No! I don't want any water!" I screamed, knocking the cup from her hand and sending it crashing to the floor. "Euphemia, where is she?" My chest tightened.

My mother walked into the bathroom and came back with a towel, then bent down and started wiping up the floor.

"Please, just tell me where she is." I reached my hand out to her. "I need to know."

Euphemia fumbled with the words at first, but then took a breath. "Avo had a stroke. She's in the ICU right now." I didn't want to believe what I heard but by the look on her face, I knew it was true.

My heart was smashed. Once again, I had caused harm to the two women I loved most in the world. I hauled myself up in bed, embracing the pain. "Take me to Avo. Now."

I could see the worry in Euphemia's eyes. "Please, I need to see her."

She went into the hallway and grabbed a wheelchair. With great effort, she helped me into the chair. When we arrived at the ICU, the nurse stared at me. "Are you family?"

"Yes, I am. I need to see my Avo."

"Should you really be out of bed?" She asked.

"Yes," I stated.

The nurse smiled at me awkwardly. "She is resting now. You can only stay for a few minutes. I can take him from here," she said to Euphemia, motioning to the chair.

"No, thank you. My mom can take me in."

"But …" the nurse tried to interject.

"But nothing," Euphemia barked at her. "My son needs me."

I smiled when I heard the satisfaction in her voice of calling me her son.

Euphemia pushed me through the doors to Avo's bedside. Her eyes were closed, but I could see her chest rhythmically rising and falling as she breathed in the extra oxygen. Her skin looked grey, and I longed to see her pink cheeks and determined grin. "Avo? Are you awake? Please wake up. I'm so sorry."

Her eyes fluttered, and she opened her mouth, but could not speak. There was sound, but no words I could understand.

"No, don't try, not right now, anyway. We need to get you strong again, and then you can scold me and tell me what I am supposed to do. You're going to be okay. I'm so sorry Avo. This is all my fault, like usual." She blinked and shook her head ever so slightly, disagreeing with me. Her eyes tracked over to Euphemia and I saw a slight smile land on her lips.

A different nurse came over and let us know it was time to go. With pain, I lifted my arm and touched her hand. Her skin was almost translucent and for the first time in my life, I realized Avo was not invincible. "Mmmm … mmmm … maaa." She struggled to express the words stuck on her tongue.

"Mama?" I paused.

She shook her head.

"I think that's enough for now," the nurse interrupted her.

"Just one more minute, please." I thought for another second, and then my foggy brain gave me the answer. "Maya." She smiled, then I saw the question. She was asking about Maya; Avo would know if I was lying. "Maya is still missing, but I will find her, I promise." Her frame shook. She closed her eyes and drifted back into sleep.

"Mom, I need to talk to Luca."

By the time she wheeled me back, the adrenaline had burned off, leaving me only with my pain.

Jacinta was sitting in a chair with a book open on her lap. She leapt up to help me and tried to smile, but I could see the concern in her puffy eyes and her tear-stained cheeks. They helped me into bed, and she dragged the chair close to me.

My mom observed her.

"Cristiano, get some rest. Jacinta, can you stay with your brother? I'll go for a little walk and call Luca."

"Of course, mom, I'm not a child." Jacinta rolled her eyes at me; I could not help but smile back.

"*My* eye rolls used to get me into so much trouble with Avo," I said to my new sister. "Where is Beth?"

"Oh, I left her with Luca in the cafeteria. She's still mad."

"It's understandable. Beth and Maya have been best friends since they were eight years old."

"Wow," Jacinta said, hugging her book. "I have lots of friends, but I don't have a best friend, someone who would travel around the world to find me."

"You still have lots of time to meet that kind of best friend," I paused again, looking over at her book. "What are you reading?"

"Just some poetry. I like to read and write it."

"Really? That's so cool!"

"Most people don't think so. I'm odd that way."

"There is nothing odd about writing poetry. I've written a poem or two." Cristiano thought about the poems he wrote to Maya when he met her.

"Do you read it too?" she sounded excited.

"Just when I was in school."

"When Maya was at the house, she mentioned that—" she stopped mid-sentence.

"Maya what? What did she say?"

"When she was at our place, she told me about the letter and the poem you wrote her and I … I read them on the blog."

"Oh yes, the blog. That seems to be the biggest piece of news in Portugal right now."

"Oh, it will soon pass. None of my friends are reading it anymore. And once teenagers stop following something, it's pretty well done."

"Is that how it works?" I chuckled, holding my side.

I could see she was finally relaxing, but I was fading and needed to rest. "Jacinta, can you read something to me as I close my eyes?"

"Oh, how about some Keats?"

"John Keats?"

"Yes, he is an English poet."

"I know who John Keats is," I laughed, wishing Maya was there with me, helping me navigate my new relationship with my sister.

"What are you doing reading some old, stuffy English poet?"

"He's not stuffy; I love his words and the stories he tells."

"Then yes, read me some Keats." I closed my eyes, and she began.

"'To Autumn' by John Keats
Season of mists and mellow fruitfulness,
Close bosom-friend of the maturing sun;
Conspiring with him how to load and bless
With fruit the vines that round the thatch-eves run;
To bend with apples the moss'd cottage-trees,
And fill all fruit with ripeness to the core;
To swell the gourd, and plump the hazel shells
With a sweet kernel; to set budding more,
And still more, later flowers for the bees,
Until they think warm days will never cease,
For summer has o'er-brimm'd their clammy cells.
Who hath not seen thee oft amid thy store? …"

Her voice was shaky at first, but it didn't take long for her to fall into a rhythm of ancient words and beautiful storytelling. As she read, I fell deeper and deeper into my imagination and soon Jacinta's words and my images of Maya became tangled. I could see Maya sitting on the grass near

Avo's cottage, laughing, then getting up and running toward my tree. She was happy; we were happy.

⊷ 45 ⊶

5

Twisted Metal

Maya

I COULDN'T MOVE, BUT I could see him beside me; pinned between the seat and the steering wheel. Was he breathing? I couldn't remember. Think Maya, focus on his chest. Did you see it move? Yes, I saw it, which meant two things: before they took me, he was alive and I still had my sight at the time of the accident.

Cristiano's arm flung across my chest, trying to hold me in place when they hit us, but once the bullet shattered the windshield, there was nothing he could do. He lost control of the car and we crashed. I remember being on the phone with my dad. He was yelling at me, telling me I wasn't really married and I had to come home with him. He said not even the church would recognize the marriage; that I needed to walk away.

Awake and covered in my mess, the signs of yet another panic attack were bearing down on me, but I refused to believe getting married in Spain did not count. It did; every magical footstep on the labyrinth of stones, the silk ribbons floating over my back, my wedding dress which he so skillfully removed after saying I do and promising ourselves to one another.

It didn't matter what my dad, the government, or the church said; God was the only one who mattered. He was there when we said our vows. It was the only piece of truth I could hang on to at that moment.

I heard the soft shuffle of footsteps moving across the floor.

"Saafa, is that you?"

"Yes, Maya,"

"I needed you last night, but you didn't come."

"I know. The guards wouldn't let me in. They made me stand outside the door when you were yelling for help. I tried to convince them, but it was no use. They said it was my fault. So, I stopped talking and hoped they would let me see you in the morning."

Saafa began untying my hands. "Please do nothing."

"What could I do, Saafa? I am weak and injured. I'm sure I can barely sit up and I am a mess."

"I brought you some other clothes. How are you?"

I thought about it for a moment and then laughed as she tried to normalize an impossible situation. "I'm scared, but hungry."

Saafa giggled. "Well, I can't do anything about the scared part, but they decided I could feed you, so I brought you some food."

As Saafa unwound my arms, I could feel the pressure release; I was almost afraid to move.

"Here, let me help you sit up." Saafa carefully supported me from behind. Painstakingly, she helped me remove my soiled clothes and wiped me down with a damp cloth and then had me lean against the wall as she lay a blanket over the cot. "I'm sorry, but there is nothing else I can do. It will dry."

"At this point Saafa, a dirty cot is the least of my worries." I scratched at the stone wall with my tired fingers. "Saafa, when you were removing glass from around my eyes, how bad were they?"

She paused for a moment. "One good thing. There were bruises around your eyes which I imagined came from your sunglasses. I think they saved your sight."

"So, you think I can still see?"

"I think so, but … the rest of your face was very cut up. Some gashes were deep, and I had to put in a few stitches."

"You had to do the stitches yourself?"

"Yes, otherwise *they* were just going to leave them open, and I was worried about them getting infected."

"Oh!" was all I could say, feeling deflated.

Saafa's voice quivered slightly like a child's. "I tried my best; watched a few YouTube videos. I even used some superglue on a few of the smaller cuts. Those shouldn't scar very much, but there were a lot of them. I did my best," she said again, squeezing my hand.

"Can you help me? I need to sit down. Saafa, when do you think we can remove the eye bandages?"

"Soon."

"Today?" I asked with hope.

"We could try later, but let's get some food into you first."

"I don't think I'm hungry anymore."

"Maya, please eat something or at least have some water."

"Are you going to drug me again?" I asked, half joking.

I heard a huff of annoyance.

"I sedated you. Believe me, you were not ready for the interrogation he was planning."

"Interrogation? I know nothing. What is the matter with these people?"

"He believes he has the right to do *anything* to *anyone*."

"He?" I asked.

"Yes, the man you met. He's in charge of everything."

"And you? What do you believe, Saafa?"

"I can not afford to believe anything except that when I open my eyes, I am still alive. I'm just as much a prisoner here as you. The only difference being that when he gets the relic, he will probably let *you* go."

"You don't belong to anyone, Saafa. We are both going to find a way out. I promise."

"Please don't make promises you cannot keep."

She placed a glass of water close to my lips.

"Drink, Maya. Then rest. We will talk about taking off the eye bandages later today."

"Saafa, how old are you again?"

"I'll be seventeen in three months."

"You sound so sad when you say that."

"I am. Seventeen here is like a death sentence for me. I've been told Dakar has already picked me a husband and I'll have to marry when he takes me to Egypt."

"Dakar? Who's Dakar?"

"Oh no, please forget you heard that name, please, Maya."

I could hear the fear in her voice. He must be the person in charge; the bastard who stole my tear of bravery. I took a breath.

"Where is your family?"

"Dead."

"What right does he have to keep you? To make you marry anyone?"

"He may not have the right, but he has the power and the control. If I want to live, I need to do what he tells me. He can make me disappear Maya." She paused. "I have to go and let him know you are ready. Do you want anything to eat from the tray?"

"Maybe a piece of some bread?"

She placed something flat in my hand, another clue to where I was being held.

"I don't think I need to keep your hands tied down anymore. Please don't give *him* a reason to tie you up again."

After she left, I nibbled on the bread slowly, feeling each morsel slide through my system and land like a weight in my empty stomach. After five bites, I was exhausted. I tucked the rest of the flat bread under my pillow, knowing I had to try again later. Getting strong was the only solution to finding a way out for both of us.

I heard a set of heavy footsteps coming towards the door, and braced myself, knowing it was him, Dakar.

When he unbolted the door and walked in, I could smell his anger before he said a word.

"Don't even try to pretend you are sleeping. You and Cristiano have caused me a great deal of trouble and cost me money. I do have to thank you though. Until about a week ago, I still thought the hair fork was buried under twenty years of sand, so you can understand my people are keen to regain what is rightfully ours."

I considered how I was going to respond and kept in mind what Saafa said about not admitting to anything directly about the relic.

"Yes, that must have come as a shock and a relief."

"A relief?" I caught him off guard.

"Yes, discovering a piece of information once buried can often help us find the things we are looking for."

"What are you talking about?"

"Oh, sorry, it must be the pain. Am I not making any sense? It has been a stressful couple of days." I stayed as calm as I could, listening for his reaction.

Then he laughed. "Oh, my, you are a tricky one. Good for you. Just for that, I will give you another day to heal before we talk, but tomorrow we begin. In the meantime, I will have one of my people reach out to your Cristiano and see how he is doing. When I left him at the crash site, his injuries looked terrible. I would hate if anything else happened to him. People die in the hospital because of complications every day."

"Don't touch him, you bastard!" I flung my arms out in front of me, reaching for him. My nails landed on his forearm. I pressed down puncturing his skin and giving him a taste of his own medicine.

"You bitch!"

The next thing I knew, he had pinned my arms to my sides and shoved his knee into my chest. I could hardly breathe, but it was worth it. I wanted him to suffer.

"Oh, this is going to be fun." As I gasped for breath he spat into my mouth. His sour saliva triggered my gag reflux and I started to choke.

I heard a gasp.

"Well, Saafa don't just stand there and let her die, make yourself useful. It's in your best interest to keep her healthy."

It did not take long before a familiar set of hands gently rolled me over and kept me from choking on my bread and water.

"Well, there she is. Now that's better. I always like to pull the feral creature out from the women I meet. Until tomorrow then, Maya Wells." He laughed. I heard his boots slide across the floor, like he was taking his time; thinking about something else to say. "Maya, my new friend is going to love her necklace, such a pretty pendant. Saafa," he bellowed. "Clean up that mess and get her ready for tomorrow. I want to see the look in her eyes when she tries to trick me again."

6

Morocco

Jade

THE HEAT WAS UNBEARABLE, BUT at least I had a beautiful room, and the servants did everything for me without question. Beautiful and smart. If my father ever had any doubt about my abilities to take care of my business, I proved him wrong and exacted some special revenge on Maya at the same time. "Choke on that, Maya Wells!"

I could play with the big boys and my dad could no longer deny that. He would have to take me back, give me an office, and fire that bitch of a secretary.

As I sat and waited for my breakfast, I thought back to the hotel in Lisbon and revelled in how it all unfolded. After seeing Dalley at the hotel, I set it all in motion. I didn't have to wait long before receiving a call from a very interested Dakar. I told him where he could find Maya and Cristiano. The only glitch in my plan was Dakar wanted to meet me in person to 'thank me'. I agreed, as I did not want to take any chances of him backing out, but what I didn't expect was 'in person' meant a flight to Morocco on his private plane. I was told by his men that Dakar wanted to share his gratitude and hospitality. His plane was much nicer than the one my dad chartered for all his flights, so I didn't mind. It was good for once to be with people who treated me as I deserved.

When I arrived in Morocco, Dakar asked me a few more questions about Maya and Cristiano and I was happy to fill him in on the whole situation about the blog. I loved telling the story. He laughed about Maya's misfortune and commiserated with me about getting fired by my father. It was such a relief to talk to someone who understood my value.

While waiting for my food I wandered around the room noticing the decorative bars on the windows as well as double cylinder lock on my door to the hall. Flashes of my conversation with Richard, my dad's right-hand company man, landed in my thoughts and made me pause for a second. When I pressured him for an introduction to the Ptolemites he warned me how dangerous they were; obviously he had been misinformed. Dakar and his men had been perfect gentlemen since our first encounter. Besides, why would I turn down staying at a luxurious villa on the ocean in Morocco while I had him doing my dirty work? The least I could do was accept his hospitality. I checked the door and looked out into the hall. I saw a young girl carrying a breakfast tray hoping it was for me. I was starving.

When I stepped back into my room the young girl was right behind me. What I wasn't expecting to find was Dakar sitting at my table. I was surprised but ignored the fact that somehow he could get into my room whenever he wanted. Refusing to let him see his intrusion bothered me. It was time to go.

"I heard you have been keeping my staff on their toes, Miss Axeline."

"Oh Dakar, it's been several days. Please call me Jade. And yes, I've never had much time for pleasantries. I expect people to do their jobs and not get in my way."

"So lovely to see you this morning. May I join you for breakfast? I have something for you."

"Oh dear, what happened to your arm?" I saw he was wearing a bandage and blood was seeping through.

"There are lots of wild animals around here. You should be careful," he said, smiling widely, holding out a chain.

"I love presents."

"I had to get a new chain, as the original broke. I know you will love it."

"How do you know?"

"Oh, let's just say the spoils of war. Thought you would appreciate the irony."

"The spoils of war? Mine or yours?"

"I guess you could say a bit of both."

Before I asked another question, the diamond pendant swung down from the chain catching the light and sending speckled rainbows onto the wall. "I love diamonds but hate rainbows."

We laughed as he clipped the necklace around my neck. I knew exactly whose neck it had been torn from.

"She's not dead, is she? My father would be furious if you got me caught up in some murder story." I laughed light heartedly while pushing away the prickles forming under my skin. "That's not quite the revenge I was looking for," I chuckled.

"No, they're not dead. Not yet anyway. Mind you, the girl is injured and is going to wish she were dead once the bandages come off."

"Bandages? That's perfect. I love it," I said, holding the diamond up to check the clarity. "The pendant will go with everything I own. Dakar, thank you for your generosity, but I think I may need to head back to Montreal. It sounds like you have everything under control here and since you've found what you are looking for …"

The smile faded from his face. "We have found the who, now we need to locate the what."

"What are you talking about? What does this part of your plan have to do with me?" I asked warily, moving to the edge of my seat.

Dakar leaned forward and grabbed a few strands of my hair. "I'm not sure, but I'm not ready to let a pretty thing like you leave, yet." Dakar smiled.

"Look, I did you a favor, and you did one for me. We are even."

"Oh, no, Miss Axeline, Jade, your part in this has only just begun. But I am a generous man, as you can see." He pointed to the pendant. "I will give you a choice. You can choose to stay here as my guest, or you could share a room with your good friend Maya?"

The pendant became heavy around my neck. I reached to remove the necklace.

"Oh, that would be a bad idea. I brought that especially for you. You would not want to insult your host, would you?"

"Of course not, Dakar. I appreciate your hospitality and generosity." *Be smart Jade,* I thought to myself. "Whatever you need. If you'll excuse me, I think I've had enough breakfast and would like to go for a morning swim."

"Yes, you have my permission. There is appropriate swimwear in the closet. Be careful though, the sun is very hot here. I don't want you getting burnt."

After he left, I ran to my purse and searched for my phone and passport. They were gone. So was my favorite shade of lipstick. "Bastard."

As I lay in bed that night, I started thinking about Maya being all messed up. I know I should have felt bad for her, but I didn't. The only thing that mattered to me was creating an exit plan to get away from

Dakar. If I was going to figure it out, I would have to draw on my inner Axel and not give a shit about anyone but myself.

Axel

"Angie?? Can you please get me the most up-to-date credit card statement for my extra expense account?"

"Mr. Axeline, I put it on your—"

"Just bring me the damned piece of paper, with no extra commentary."

"Yes sir, right away, sir," she said with a hint of sarcasm which I did not care for.

Angie had only been working for me for a short time, but since we lost the Netuno deal, it had felt like she was getting too familiar, like she had forgotten who the boss was. I needed to sort that out or fire her. Maybe Richard was right, it was time to get a new secretary who knew how to do her job.

"Angie, call Richard and tell him I need to see him right now—in person, in the office," I added as an afterthought.

"I think Richard is taking the day off today. It's his anniversary."

"I don't care what day it is. Get him in here now!"

"What is so urgent Axel, that you could not wait until tomorrow? Bea is very pissed at you."

"Oh, I'll send her flowers. I need to ask you something. Where can I find one of those older secretaries? One that doesn't have a good ass."

Richard paused and stared at me. "What the hell are you talking about? What do you really want? Besides, I never thought you'd give up that ass."

"You may be wrong about that, but you are right about why I called you in here. There is something else I need you to investigate for me. Jade."

Richard flinched, like I had stuck him with a hot poker. "What? Are you afraid of me saying her name out loud?"

"No, don't be stupid. What's the matter?"

"When I fired her, I let her think I had forgotten to cut off one of my expense cards. I didn't. I have been monitoring her carefully. Richard, something is wrong. I have not seen one charge on the account for days. That is not my Jade. I checked her bank accounts too, and she has withdrawn no other funds." Richard raised his eyebrow.

"What? Yes, I have access to her accounts. It's my money. So what? The question right now is, what is she up to?"

I saw Richard's feet shift and his breath changed. I had been in the game far too long not to see the signs of when someone was getting ready to lie to me.

"Richard, before you open your mouth again, I want you to think carefully. If you tell me one lie, I will blow your life up. I will tell Bea you screwed my daughter on Valentine's Day last year and you had a trail of others before and after her."

Richard texted someone, then went over to my bar and poured himself a drink. "You're not going to like this."

He picked his phone up as if waiting for a response.

"Put your goddamn phone down!"

"Like I said, you will not like this, Axel."

"More than the fact you slept with my daughter?" I snickered, then paused just long enough. "Richard, I don't care about that. I'm sure she had her reasons. She's very smart, you know."

Richard sighed and shook his head as if disappointed in me.

"A few days ago, she called me. She was agitated, working on a deal. She said she had information that could be valuable to some people and needed my help to find them. I told her no at first, but she is her father's daughter."

"Good for her. Now that's what I like to hear. But? Richard, you're being very cagey. Why all the secrecy? Who did she want to contact?"

Richard looked over at me from the bar, picked up his phone, and took another drink. "The Ptolemites."

"Put that thing down," I roared.

"Axel?" he tried to interrupt.

"The Ptolemites? Are you out of your mind?" I could feel an unfamiliar sensation prick my heart when he said the name, but I pushed the feeling away and in two steps was standing in front of him.

"I told her they were dangerous, but she wouldn't listen."

"She wouldn't listen, or she blackmailed you?" I screamed.

Richard raised his drink to confirm my suspicion.

"How could she be so brilliant and stupid at the same time? Pour me a drink and tell me what happened."

"I called a guy who knows how to contact them and then gave him Jade's number. After that, I don't know. She never called me back."

He looked down at his phone again.

I swirled the whiskey in my glass, trying to think through the situation. "Check your phone already. You are driving me crazy with that thing." Richard sent another text, looking more nervous than before. "Richard, what exactly did she say to you?"

"She said she had information about some people they were looking for." I saw a light go on for Richard. "Axel, where is the latest credit card statement?"

"ANGIE!" I screamed.

"It's on your *desk,*" she said, punctuating the last word.

"Richard, she has to go."

He nodded. "Nice ass or not, I agree."

I ran back to my desk and shuffled through some papers. I had a strange feeling in my gut, but figured it had to be the whiskey. When I couldn't find the statement, my heart raced.

"Richard, I can't find it." He joined me at the desk and plucked the statement off the top of the pile.

"You're worried about her," he laughed a little. "So, the great Axel Axeline has a heart."

I took a moment to review his opinion and realized he was partially right. "Worried yes, heart no."

"Whatever you say, Axel."

I grabbed the paper out of his hand. "The last two charges were from a hotel in Lisbon and a car rental. Where was she going? She never drives herself anywhere. I don't like this. Unfortunately, I can only imagine it has something to do with Netuno and that Maya girl. Whatever you do, don't contact the Ptolemites yet. If she is with them, we will need to play our cards carefully. The last thing I need is her taking up with some political zealots just to spite me. Besides, it would be bad for business."

"Ah, and he's back." Richard rolled his eyes.

"Fatherly concern can only go so far," I said, finishing my whiskey and burying the useless new emotion.

Richard's eyes flashed to his phone again. His usually tanned and taught skin went grey and limp.

"What is it, Richard?"

"It's Jade. She never texted me back. She always texts me back, just to yell at me."

7

Shadows

Cristiano

WHEN I WOKE AGAIN, THE room was quiet and the only light I could see was coming from the hallway under the closed door. I thought I was alone, but I heard a grumble from the corner and saw a shadow move from the chair.

"Cristiano, at least Dakar didn't have to lie to her. You *are* still alive and so is she, but the question is for how long?"

My heart rate spiked, and I wanted to jump up and destroy him, eradicate the vile people who wanted to harm Maya, but I was broken and couldn't move. I had to play the moment as smart as possible. "The relic."

"Yes, the relic, that is all we want. Then you can have your little mummy back in your arms to do with whatever you want."

"Mommy?" I asked, not understanding what he was talking about.

"Mummy, covered in bandages," he said, laughing, like I was an idiot. "Yeah, she's in a bad way. The sooner you give us the relic, the sooner you'll get her back. At least, that is the deal right now. Dakar likes feisty women, and from what I hear, she put up quite a fight today."

"Don't you dare—"

"Oh, you are in no position to tell us what to do. Your grandmother is dying, your not-so-wife Maya is strapped to a bed far away from here, and you aren't even walking yet. It's simple: find the relic, save the girl."

"Not my wife?"

"Is that all you heard in that conversation? Oh Cristiano, you're in for quite the surprise, then. I have to go, but we'll be in touch."

Before I could say another word, a gentleman in a lab coat, with a chart in his hand, stepped out of the shadows. When he opened the door, the light from the hallway illuminated his face.

"Just remember, she is safe for now. My boss thinks you have it, but from the look on your face, you don't have a clue where it is. Find the relic, save the girl. It's as simple as that."

I pushed the emergency call button but it had been disconnected, so, I pulled myself up and struggled out of bed. My body was a mess, but at least I had my legs. I negotiated myself around the bed and made my way to the door. When I finally managed to open it, I saw Euphemia and Judith walking down the hall together. As soon as they saw me, they ran. It was a good thing too, as my strength was waning, and the corridor was spinning. The women scooped me up and dragged me back into the room.

"I can't, let me go. I must find her. They have her, he has her."

"Cristiano, what are you talking about?"

"One of them was here, just now. He was here. They have her for sure. Where is Luca?"

"He's back at the house; they are setting things up and waiting for a call."

"No need. They made a house call tonight."

"What do you mean?"

The two women helped me back into bed. My body screamed at me to lie down but my heart yelled louder: find the relic and bring Maya home.

"Cristiano, what did he say? Where is Maya?" Judith stepped closer to me, trying to be calm, but I could see the terror in her eyes. The terror a parent feels when they know their child is in danger. I saw it in Maggie's eyes when I flew back to Vancouver with her as she tried to reach CJ in time. And I saw it in Judith's eyes when she asked about Maya. I had a chance to make a difference. Like he said, find the relic, save the girl. That's all I had to do.

⁂

"Euphemia, can you write some notes? The medications are messing with my head, and I have to remember everything he said to me."

"Easier than that. I can record you and send it over to Luca. I have already texted him and he is on his way."

She pressed record and began asking me simple questions, helping me to remember as many details as I could. In silence, Judith paced back and forth as I spoke. When I got to the part about Maya being wrapped up like a mummy, she stifled a gasp, but my mother and I heard it.

"Judith, maybe you should step out while Cristiano finishes."

"No, I need to stay."

When I mentioned what he said about us not being married completely, I turned to Judith. "Is it true? I vaguely remember the phone call Maya had with Phillip in the car before the crash, and then he mentioned something about it again before he punched me."

Judith cringed when I mentioned the punch. "It's true, legally, you're not married. We understood from Beth that you were married by a priest while you were travelling through Spain."

"Yes, it was perfect. How naïve of me to think it could be that easy."

"Do you love my daughter?" she asked in all earnestness. "Do you believe you are married?"

I looked at my mother, then at Judith, "Yes, loving Maya is the easy part ... yes, I love her with all my heart and yes, when we took our vows, I promised to protect her and keep her safe until death do us part. I would give my life for her."

Judith took a deep breath. "Well, I'm glad to hear it then," she said, looking me in the eye. "I would, however, restrain from having this conversation with her father at this point. Mr. Wells and I have a different opinion on the subject. Let's just get her back and then we can work out the details."

"Thank you, Judith. I can see where Maya gets it from."

"What would that be?"

"Courage, determination."

"You think I'm courageous and determined?" she laughed a little, then paused.

Luca burst through the door, along with Beth at his side.

"Is everyone okay?" Luca asked.

Beth ran to Judith, arms stretched out like she was the parent. It was clear their history ran deep.

"Cristiano, now that Luca and Beth are here, I don't think I need to keep playing detective. Luca, I just sent you the notes about the intruder."

"Thank you Euphemia. My life would be a whole lot easier if I had one of you taking notes for me all the time."

Euphemia smiled but I could see the strain on her face.

"Why don't you and Judith take a break. I'm safe with these two protecting me."

Euphemia grabbed Judith's hand. "I'm not sure about you, but I could use a shower and some rest. Let's get you and Phillip moved out of the hotel and over to our place. We have a guest house you can stay in. What do you think?" Judith nodded her head. The strength Judith had been drawing on was starting to wane and I could see the fear and doubt creep across her face. Maya would never forgive me if anything happened to her mom while she was missing.

"Judith, please go with Euphemia. Luca and I will talk things over and come up with a plan on how to get Maya back."

"Judith, Cristiano is right. Maya would kill me if she didn't find you in shipshape when she gets back," Beth said. It's time to eat and get some rest."

Before leaving, Euphemia leaned down, kissed my forehead, and whispered in my ear, "I love you, son." I never knew I needed to hear those words so much in my life, but when she said them, it made me feel like I could do anything.

8

Old Friends

Cristiano

LUCA JUMPED IN ONCE ALL the motherly energy had left the room.

"Cristiano, you need to tell me everything that happened with the Ptolemites before tonight. Ravn and Dalley told me their version but I need to hear your side of the story to fill in some gaps."

I cast my eyes towards Beth; Luca understood immediately.

"Beth, can you get me a cup of coffee, please?"

Beth looked annoyed and was about to say something when she changed her mind and walked out of the room. I looked at Luca and he smiled. "We came to an arrangement. If she wants to help, she needs to let me do my police work without getting in the way. What can I say? Was I really going to turn down a beautiful woman who came halfway around the world to find her best friend? And who knows maybe she needs a place to stay."

"You haven't changed a bit since high school, except maybe the gun and badge thing." I laughed a little and held my chest to lessen the pain.

"On a scale of one to ten. How bad does it hurt?" Luca asked.

"Eight. You ever crack a rib?"

"I broke two on the job a couple of years ago when I was undercover. Couldn't work for weeks."

"I can't imagine a pain worse than this," I said on reflection.

"Cristiano, your pain isn't from the ribs."

I paused, "I know. It's the Ptolemites."

"Yes, the Ptolemites," he reiterated. "How did your parents get mixed up with them?"

"It all started with their friend Pierre La Nou. They worked together collecting artifacts from around the world for museums and private collectors. Pierre would identify what was needed, and during the summers my parents did the collecting, except for this one time, one relic."

"One relic?" Luca asked.

"Yes. Cleopatra's hair fork. It had been a piece rumored as the weapon she used to take her life so as not to be captured by her enemies. Pierre knew there was some risk involved and decided to go to Cairo himself. He was determined to find it but …"

"But things didn't work out as he planned? They rarely do." Luca interjected.

"He was run out of the country by the Ptolemites. Several years later he got a call that the hair fork was spotted in an antique shop in Cairo. My parents had always wanted to go to Egypt, so when they heard about the relic they jumped at the opportunity. Pierre convinced himself it had been long enough, that the risks were low … and so he never told them about the Ptolemites."

"Was the plane crash really an accident?" he asked matter-of-factly.

"I don't know. It doesn't matter anymore, does it?"

"Everything matters in an investigation. The more pieces to the puzzle, the easier it is to understand the picture coming together."

"The only thing that matters now is us finding Maya before anything else happens to her."

"Cristiano, there is no *us* right now, not until you are on your feet. But as I said the more detail you give me, the better. Do you have any idea where the relic could be? That seems to be the biggest ask from them at this point. The sooner we find it, the sooner we can try to make the exchange."

"Try?" I choked back.

"Sorry, Cristiano. I won't lie to you. Exchanges of this nature don't always go as planned. I need you to file that away somewhere in your mind."

"File what away?" Beth asked as she came back into the room.

"Like I told you before, Beth. We must stay very practical while approaching this situation," Luca said very slowly, like somehow that was going to keep her calm.

"Practical? This coming from the man who has the most impractical hair I have ever seen in my life."

"What does my hair have to do with this?"

"Nothing really," she said, rolling her eyes and crossing her arms.

"Did the two of you really meet only twenty-four hours ago? I'm sure Maya would appreciate the banter, but not right now."

They both looked at me and then at each other.

"Right then, what happened next?" Luca asked.

"I already went over all of this in the recording she sent you."

"Thank you. I still have some questions I need to ask. I'll listen to it later but for now I'm looking for any extra details you might have missed while talking with your mother."

While Luca took notes, Beth stood frozen, listening to the entire tale as I strained my brain to remember everything I could from the minute

Pierre and I started doing research in Paris about my parent's plane crash, to the wedding in Spain and the moment the Ptolemite left my room.

Beth was rubbing her arms as if she was cold, then I saw the shift.

"Luca, go back in your notes. Cristiano, you mentioned you talked to Avo the night before the wedding."

"Yes, I wanted to let her know …"

"You said she mentioned a package addressed to Pierre La Nou that arrived from Egypt after the plane crash. Where is the package now?"

"I assume it must be at Avo's cottage," I answered.

Luca grabbed Beth and swung her around.

"Hey, be careful, I don't want you throwing your back out," Beth scrunched up her face at Luca.

He ignored her comment and kissed her full on the lips. "You are brilliant Beth. I'm not sure how I missed that."

"Ahh, we all miss things sometimes." Beth was flustered but did her best to brush off Luca's kiss. "So, what are we waiting for? We need to get to Avo's cottage and find the package."

Luca smiled. "Okay inspector Beth, that's a good plan but maybe we should wait until morning. We can fly out first thing."

"You're really going to let me come with you?" she asked.

"Well, I think Maya needs your help and I get the feeling you wouldn't let me go on my own. Anyway, it's better I know where you are. The last thing I need is another Canadian beauty going missing in my country."

"Beauty? You think I'm beautiful? Oh, never mind," she said, before Luca had a chance to answer.

Before Beth and Luca could say another word, the loud slap of flip-flops hitting the floor echoed in my room.

"You're alive, you idiot; too bad. I thought I'd be able to start using your favorite surfboard."

"Stop where you are!" Luca stood between Jack and the bed, ready to draw his gun.

"Whoa, pretty boy," Jack said, stopping in his tracks. "Cristiano and I are friends."

Luca turned back to me, and I nodded. "I know, hard to believe, right? This is my best friend, Jack."

A smile broke across Jack's face. "Best friends? Well then, what can I do to help?"

Luca looked at me and then at Jack. "Can you stay here with him while I fly back to Netuno? If anyone comes by, call me. Don't leave him alone. I will have a policeman stationed at the door but I would feel better if there was someone with him at all times. Right now, though, I need to go back to my place, have a bite to eat, and get some rest." He looked over at Beth. "You coming?"

❧

Jack pulled a chair up beside my bed and sat quietly, then handed me my phone I had dropped that night in Setubal when I broke down his door and knocked him out.

"I charged it and everything," he said awkwardly.

"Thank you … Jack?" I didn't want anyone to see the terror I was feeling, but having Jack there reminded me again. Reminded me of everything Maya and I had been through to find our way back to each other. "What if something happens to her? What am I going to do?"

"Nothing is going to happen to her, brother."

"Brother?" I asked with a hitch in my voice.

"Best friends, brothers. I figure we are a good mixture of the two. But, hey. You got married without me. I thought I would at least get an invitation to the wedding."

I couldn't help but crack a smile. "Well, it appears you may still get your chance. Maya's mom confirmed tonight we are not legally married."

"You didn't have time to consummate?"

"Jack, stop being crude."

"What? It's a valid question."

"No, in that way we are very married," I sighed thinking about the red and blue buttons flying around the room as I tore my wedding shirt off her body, "but apparently, in our haste, we missed a few steps with Spanish law."

"Well, I heard the whole thing took place in front of a priest and a bunch of nuns. From my perspective, you're stuck together now like Texas French toast smothered in syrup," he laughed.

"What are you talking about?"

"Something my mother used to say." His smile faded away. "The only thing that matters is you find Maya and bring your bride back home in one piece." He paused again. "I still owe her a surfing lesson or two, and I'm not giving up until I see her riding that wave by herself."

I didn't realize it, but while he was talking, tears formed in my eyes. I had missed this Jack, the Jack from a long time ago. The Jack who had no secrets about me.

"That Luca guy seems like a good man."

I nodded my head in agreement, suddenly exhausted and fighting to stay awake.

"You look tired, old friend. Close your eyes. I'm not going anywhere."

"Just for a little while." I drifted away, thinking of the waves, seeing myself in the ocean paddling out to the next swell. Something caught my eye. Another surfer? No, it was Maya. She was sitting on a board, waving, bobbing up and down. I swam toward her, but no matter how hard I tried she kept moving farther away. Then I saw it, the nightmare of every surfer, the shadow in the water and the fin breaking the surface. I screamed her name again, but she couldn't hear me. She kept waving and waving—and then she was gone.

"Cristiano, wake up! Wake up!" I heard his voice. "You're having a nightmare."

"No, I'm not. She's in trouble, Jack; she needs me now. She needs me before they eat her alive."

9

Just a Ferret

Maya

I COULD FEEL THE WARMTH of the early morning sun shining on me when I woke. It almost seemed pleasant until I reached up and felt the bandages on my face. It was the day I would find out if I could see.

Next came the sliding of the bolt and the door opening. My body shrunk back into the cot as I remembered the putrid smell of his breath.

"No, it's okay, I can do it myself," I heard Saafa say as the door opened.

"Well, just as long as you have her ready for when he arrives. You have thirty minutes," the other woman barked at her.

The door closed again, and I heard her sigh.

"Well, are you ready?" she asked with hope.

"As ready as I can be. I think? I'm scared."

"Don't be afraid. I have been praying all night your eyes are well."

"Praying?"

"Yes. I pray to my God; do you pray to yours?"

I laughed a little. "Sometimes. Do you think our God is the same?"

I heard her take in a breath. Then she answered. "I think anyone who gives themselves the gift of prayer opens themselves up to a different life.

Your prayer or mine is neither better nor worse, just different. I have met good people who do not pray, and I have met many bad people who do. I can only hope I am in the third category, good people who like to pray."

"I think you missed one category."

"What would that be?"

"Bad people who don't believe in anything but their own interests."

She squeezed my hand. "Let's get the eye bandages off."

She had me sit up for a few minutes, then began. I heard the snip, and she unwound the gauze. She was slow and steady, and I could not imagine how a sixteen-year-old girl had gathered that much experience and wisdom. Truthfully, I wasn't sure I wanted to know.

As the bandages kept coming off, I felt a mixture of excitement and trepidation.

"Okay, we are getting closer. When I remove the next bandage, I want you to hold the gauze pads that are resting on your eyes. Don't take them off as there may be blood stuck to them. Your skin is so sensitive right now and I want to be extra careful."

I was seconds away from knowing and I could feel my stomach turn. I took a breath in and held the pads to my eyes. Next, I felt a warm wet cloth placed around the edges of the gauze.

"Okay, here it goes." She slowly peeled the bandages off. "Keep your eyes closed for a minute. It is going to be bright. It might be blurry to start too."

I waited until she touched my arm. "Maya, go ahead."

I opened one eye and then the other. At first, all I saw were shapes, and I panicked. "Maya, you need to breathe."

The light was so bright.

"Try to avoid squinting. Let's shield them instead."

I covered my eyes and then opened them again behind my palms. Looking down, I could see the bandages that were still on my nose. Slowly, I lifted my hands and the room and Saafa took shape.

"I can see, but it's blurry. You are so beautiful." Saafa covered her face and touched her hijab as if feeling embarrassed about something. "You are beautiful," I said again.

Our shared joy was temporary as we both heard the boots coming down the hallway. I touched my face again.

"Do you have any idea what the rest of my face is going to look like when these come off?"

Saafa could not or would not say a word when I asked her the question. But her facial expression told me more than I wanted to know. When the door opened, it almost felt like a relief not to have to think about it for a second; then I saw him. When I looked over at Saafa, I could see the fear rising in her cheeks and I realized worrying about the bandages was the least of my problems.

"Well, well, the ferret can see." In three steps, he was by my bed. "Look what you did to my arm." I had to decide again: fierce or vulnerable. Which would give me a greater chance at getting out of that place alive? I didn't know if Cristiano could ever find the relic, and I couldn't put all my faith into the possibility. I had to depend on myself. If there was one thing I learnt after Cristiano left, it was that I'm stronger than I thought. I went with fierce, and hoped I had enough strength to deal with whatever might come next.

"Pity, I thought I might have left more of a mark." I threw back at him.

He recalibrated, obviously not prepared for my response. "I rarely start this part of the interrogation this early, but for you, I'll make an exception."

He was swift and the open-handed blow was hard, but not hard enough to knock me out. My memory flashed to the night I punched Dalley and knocked her unconscious. I didn't know what I was doing, but he was very skilled and apparently had done this before. He didn't want to hurt me, not yet anyway. I was sure though, that would come later.

At first, I only felt the lingering sting, then I could feel the ooze and knew he had opened up at least one set of the gashes on my face.

"You drew first blood with the arm, Ferret, now we are even. Saafa, I'm going for something to eat. Don't you dare change the bandages. Everyone needs a good scar. It tells a better story. I'll be back in an hour."

He locked the door and I fell back on to the cot, holding my face. Saafa ran over to me. "What were you thinking? He could kill you."

"Yes, he could, but he won't; not yet anyway."

"Let's get you cleaned up as best as we can."

Saafa didn't dare touch the bandages on my face. The bleeding eventually stopped. As she finished wiping me down, I had to ask, "Saafa, I need to know. How damaged is my face? You said you removed all the glass and you did stitches."

She looked down at the ground. "Well, I didn't actually do stitches with a needle. I used tape to hold the big gashes back together and then crazy glue for the little ones, like I said before. The glue ones should be okay."

Saafa took a deep breath and looked at me. "I tried my best. I'm not sure what it's going to look like."

And there I was, holding on to a sixteen-year-old girl who was just as much a prisoner as I was, trying to stay alive and before I knew what I was saying, the words tumbled from my lips. "Saafa, when I get out of here, you are coming with me. This is no place for you."

She smiled but was not sure how to respond. "I'm not sure either of us is going to get out of here alive."

"Of course we are. Cristiano will find a way and if he can't, we will."

"You love your husband very much."

"Yes, I do." I said, asking myself whether I had a right to call Cristiano my husband.

"Rest now. He will be back soon, and you'll need all your wits about you."

～

My eyes flew open when I heard the bolt on the door. But I didn't move. Then the door opened.

"Wake up, Ferret, no time to sleep. I have brought some food for you."

It appeared my show of strength was the right move, even if it meant I would have a bigger scar to show for it.

"Could you please not call me Ferret?"

"Why? I like it. And I do whatever I like."

I had to adjust. "Then let's share a meal together. I once heard it is the best way to get to know someone."

"So, you want to get to know me, Ferret? I can arrange that."

"Thank you for the offer, I think? But I am a married woman," I said, forcing a smile.

"Technically, you're not."

My body reacted more than I would have liked, showing my vulnerability. "Well, I'm not so sure about that. We may not have a piece of paper to say we are married, but I'm pretty sure a blessing from God surpasses all other authorities."

He looked at me and laughed. "Maya, I am the authority. There is no one else."

I took a breath. "Category 4."

"What? What are you talking about?" He looked momentarily confused.

"Nothing, you're right. You're in charge and there's no changing that."

I smiled inside, but my little win was short lived as he had one more trick up his sleeve I wasn't ready for.

"Oh, a colleague gave Cristiano a visit last night. He looks in rough shape, Ferret, but his pretty face appears to be intact. I can't say the same for yours. I have one question for you. What good is a disfigured ferret to a man when he married a beautiful rabbit? I'm telling you now, you will never be a beautiful rabbit again, Ferret."

His words stung more than the slap, and as much as I didn't want to show it, my eyes must have betrayed me.

"Don't worry, Ferret, we won't tell him about the face. We'll let it be a surprise. Besides, I want my relic back, and who knows how motivated he would be if he knew the truth?"

My words escaped me, replaced by a sliver of doubt. *What if he was right? What if I was so hideous under these bandages Cristiano never wanted to hold my face, touch my chin, kiss my lips, ever again?*

"I can see you're not hungry, Ferret. Maybe you'll have more of an appetite tomorrow."

When he left, I lay down and cried. "Who am I kidding? I'm not fierce, I'm not fierce at all; I'm frightened."

Then Saafa spoke, "Maya? Why does one have to rule out the other? Rest now. I'll stay with you until you fall asleep."

10

Tick Tock

Dalley

I WAS DOING EVERYTHING I could to distract myself, from obsessing about Maya's kidnapping, Avo's stroke, and the mystery package at her cottage. Nothing was working, including writing my long overdue blog entry. What could I write that would not sound trite compared to everything that was happening? Not about the kidnapping obviously, but it needed to be something important. The last blog I wrote was my grand apology. It wasn't the most popular thing I ever posted but it was the most honest. Some readers seemed to appreciate my new style, while others wanted to burn me at the stake. And of course, the rest of them just wanted more salacious details about Maya and Cristiano.

As I sat in the lobby trying to figure out a headline, Ravn got a call from Luca letting us know they had just landed in Lisbon and were on their way to Netuno. Luca had called the night before letting us know about the package. As it was his only lead to finding the relic, he insisted we wait until he arrived to go to the cottage.

"What did he mean when he said 'they' landed? Who are they? If he thinks I'm just sitting around here while he and his little friends play detective, he is dead wrong." I drilled into Ravn.

"Dalley, you need to pull yourself together. If you keep acting like this, there's no way Luca will let you come along. Oh and the *they*, is Maya's best friend Beth. She arrived in Porto a couple of days ago and Luca invited her along."

"What? Is she a detective or something?"

"No, she teaches grade one," he said flatly.

"Oh, yes, now I remember Maya talking about her. Saint Beth, the best friend in the world. The Chocolate Chip Cookie."

"Chocolate Chip Cookie?" Ravn asked.

"Never mind. What is she going to do here, except get in the way?"

"Be nice, Dalley."

"Yes, I'll be nice. But I can't promise I'm going to like her or that she'll like me."

"Why? I like you," he laughed a little.

"*Why?* Maybe because I blew up her best friend's life and got her kidnapped."

"The kidnapping was not your fault, Dalley." He shook his head.

"And the blog?"

"Well, yes, that was your fault, but you're trying to make up for that."

"Yes, I am. But if *I* was her, I wouldn't want to forgive me."

"Dalley, you need to stop looking for absolution from everyone else and start figuring out if you are still that person. Ask yourself, would you do things differently now or make the same choices?"

Ravn's words froze me in my seat.

"I would never do anything like that again," I said, taking offence to his statement.

"Then that's what you tell Beth. When they arrive though, we will have little time for any kind of friendship tug o' war over Maya. I haven't known her for long, but she struck me as someone who might have space in her heart for two, maybe three, friends." He stopped for a second, while I digested what he was saying to me.

"You asked me what Luca needs from us. He needs us to be ready and waiting when he arrives. We need to go to Avo's cottage to find the package."

"Dalley, I know what you're thinking and no we can't go ahead of time.

Ravn and I went back and forth. In the end, he won out and so we waited. Thankfully, though, we didn't have to wait long. We could hear the police siren before we saw the vehicle coming down the road.

When the car stopped, Luca climbed out and so did the Chocolate Chip Cookie. She wasn't what I expected. Beth looked like a normal person and her hair was a mess. She wasn't wearing designer shoes and there was no size two in sight, but the thing I noticed most were her eyes because she was glaring at me intensely.

"Dalley, there is no time for me to tell you what I think of you, or … what you did. But I've been told you're coming with us to help. So, let's get on with this, then."

I saw Ravn and Luca smile at each other, I said nothing.

"Ravn, please join me in the front." Luca said, giving me no option than to sit beside the Chocolate Chip Cookie.

I stared at Ravn and climbed reluctantly into the backseat with Beth. Carmo and Bento ran out of the inn, waving an old skeleton key in the air.

"Luca, you are not breaking any windows to get into Avo's place."

"Oh, I'm better than that, Carmo, I know how to pick a lock now, but a key is even better," he laughed, obviously referring to something that happened when they were teenagers.

"Well, there is no way you are going to find Avo's cottage without a little help, so we're coming too." Luca shrugged his shoulders, smiled, and nodded his head in their direction.

The little thread of calm I was hanging onto snapped, "Well, if everyone is finished, do you think we can make our way over to Avo's or do you want to go for a cup of coffee so you can revisit your teenage delinquency?" My eyes locked with Luca's and then I saw it. We were running out of time, and he knew it.

We followed Carmo and Bento down the winding roads. I couldn't help but think of Maya during the contest, walking back and forth from Avo's, carrying her freshly baked bread to share with all of us. Avo taught her how to bake, how to live a new life, to leave behind her sadness and push past the memories. She chose strength over weakness. I could only hope wherever she was, Maya could hold on to that strength.

The drive only took minutes, but it helped me take a needed breath and reminded me why we were there.

The cottage was like something out of a fairy tale with its little fence and outdoor oven, but as we walked closer to the front door, there was no key needed, as it had been kicked in and the windows smashed.

Luca drew his gun. "Everyone, stay here."

When Luca finally emerged from the cottage, he was fuming.

"They trashed the place."

Ravn and I looked at each other. "Those Ptolemite bastards," Ravn growled.

"They must have done it last night." Luca shook his head.

"How did they know about the package?" Beth asked.

"I don't know, but I can guarantee they don't have it."

"How?" I asked.

"Because they left us a note."

TICK TOCK. NO PACKAGE HERE.
YOU BETTER FIND IT BEFORE WE DO!

Luca carefully folded the paper. "Where could she have put it?" He asked with frustration.

"What are we supposed to do now? If we don't find it soon, they're going to kill Maya. I just know it."

"Dalley, stop," Ravn said.

"Why? Because I'm the only one willing to tell the truth, willing to admit what the Ptolemites can do?"

Ravn looked at me, then over to Beth, her brave face crumbling and once again I had hurt someone else Maya cared about. I really was the worst friend in the world.

Carmo grabbed Beth, trying to comfort her and slow the sobs. Then her voice emerged through the tears.

"Dalley's right." She sniffed. "Luca, you need to call Cristiano, and ask him to go see Avo. She's the only one who knows where it is."

Cristiano

"The package is missing, and they tore our home apart. Luca is right, I need to see Avo." I managed to get myself out of bed and into the wheelchair, and when I peeked through the open door the police officer guarding my door was chatting up a nurse at the station desk. Quietly, I slipped past the preoccupied couple and with the help from another patient made my way down to the ICU.

"Mr. Lazaro, I hope you are feeling better." The older nurse ushered me in. "Avo will be happy to see you."

"Is she awake? Is she better?" I asked.

The nurse carefully avoided answering my question directly but when I looked into her eyes, I knew the answer.

"She's awake off and on. Very weak. Not eating. She's been trying to say a few words, but they're jumbled right now. That's common with this kind of stroke."

"The room is so dark. Can we get some natural light in here? My Avo does much better in the sunshine." The nurse smiled and pulled up the blind, casting a brilliant shaft of light across her bed. I sat quietly, eyes closed, holding Avo's hand. Her ragged breath hurt my heart and I ached to have one last conversation with her.

"Avo, you should have seen her on our wedding day. She was enchanting. It was perfect. The nuns made us get married in our bare feet. You would have loved it. Maya loved it. There was a labyrinth and the garden walls were made of stone, it was…"

Something changed in her breathing, it was as if it became easy again. I swallowed hard.

"Avo, what am I supposed to do without you? How could this be it? I just found my way back to you. Thank you for loving me when I didn't know how to love myself." I felt a slight pressure on my hand from her weak fingers, she heard me. "Avo, Avo? Don't go, not yet. Please, I need you. I love you. I promise I'll find Maya and bring her home."

I rested my head gently on her chest and listened as her heartbeat slowed. Looking up, I saw her eyes flutter and she uttered one last word to me, "love."

I'm not sure how long I sat holding her hand, but it was not until I heard my name that I stirred. "Cristiano," my mother said as she touched my shoulder. "Everyone is here to say goodbye."

Puro ran to Avo's bedside and kissed her forehead. "You were one of the unique souls put on this earth to make a difference, and you did it in your own quiet and stubborn way. Thank you, Avo, for every loaf of bread you ever baked."

Judith stepped over, "Thank you for loving my girl and for helping her find the Maya she has been searching for all these years."

Marcos, Jacinta, and Zef stood at the door, waiting respectfully. I motioned for them to come in.

Jacinta broke past our father and ran to my side. "Cristiano, I'm so sorry." She burst into tears.

"Jacinta, it's going to be okay. Avo lived a good and long life. I'm sorry you didn't have time to get to know her better, but I promise, I'll tell you everything you want to know about her."

"She was going to teach me to bake." She cried even harder.

"I'll teach you; I promise."

I made eye contact with my father. He smiled, then guided Jacinta out of the room.

I saw my brother standing awkwardly by the door, trying to find the right words. "Our sister has an enormous heart," he paused. "It was nice to have Avo in our lives, even if it was for just a couple of days. Cristiano I'm really sorry …"

Marcos stepped back into the room. "Zef, please go sit with your sister. Your brother and I have to discuss a few things."

"I want to be part of the conversation."

I looked over at him and felt my heart shift. It was odd. It was wonderful. I had a brother who wanted to be part of my life.

"Zef, give us a few minutes, please. Zef looked impatient but listened to Marcos. "Cristiano. Puro and I have already spoken with the hospital administration. We have arranged for them to send Avo home. Puro will take her as soon as they have her prepared. You can have a service as soon as you are well enough to travel."

"No, no service until Maya is back. I'll ask the priest here at the hospital to do last prayers, then Puro can have her cremated as soon as he gets back to Lisbon. No funeral until Maya is home."

"Cristiano, it—" My mother tried to reason with me.

"No, listen to me. I know what Avo would have wanted."

Euphemia and Marcos paused and looked at Puro, waiting for him to say something.

"Whatever you want, Cristiano." Puro said. "I will take care of her until you can come home."

I looked back at Avo. "Well, I guess it's time to get to work. The grief can wait." As I leaned in and kissed my Avo goodbye, I noticed a small smile on her lips. "On second thought, tonight we bake."

11

Cracking

Maya

I WAS FALLING, FALLING FAST, wind pushing around my body as I cut through the sky like a hot knife through butter. The whirring sound was so loud I could barely think and when I forced my eyes open the earth was fast approaching, offering to swallow me up and take the pain away. I blinked hard and everything stopped. I hung in the air hovering over a pit of moving dirt, afraid to breathe, afraid to move.

When I opened my eyes, Saafa was shaking me.

"Maya, wake up, you're having a nightmare."

"I ... I ..." my heart was pounding so hard, it felt like I had fallen a thousand feet. "Saafa, I need a pen and something to write on."

"Why?" she asked. "What do you need a pen and paper for?"

Taking a breath, I explained. "Saafa, have you never written down your deepest thoughts? Committed them to paper? Found a way to express feelings you never wanted anyone else to know?"

She shook her head. "No, there was no time or space in my life to engage in such an activity. Besides, I was not allowed to have secrets from my parents. And if they ever found it, they would have read it."

I winced at the idea of people reading your thoughts.

"I understand, Saafa. I recently went through something similar."

"Your parents read your journal?"

"Yes in a way, and the rest of the world too. But it wasn't their fault. A friend broke my trust and posted my journal entries online."

Saafa looked horrified.

"Since then she has apologized, but it still stings to think about it. Do you have access to the Internet here?"

"Some people do, but Dakar cut me off after he discovered I was doing course work online to continue my studies. Saafa paused. "Have you always kept a journal?"

"I started when I was in high school. I used it to write poetry and thoughts and dreams. It meant the world to me. Then I stopped until recently."

"Why? Why did you stop something that meant so much to you?"

I paused for a moment, knowing the answer but embarrassed to say it out loud, "Let's just say I started lying to myself and the words I was writing on the pages were no longer true."

"When did you start writing again?"

"When life gifted me the chance to be honest with myself again. What about the pen and paper?"

Saafa looked like she wanted to ask another question but changed her mind.

Jade

"Another night of this heat and I think it's going to kill me," I said. The young girl who brought me my breakfast just stared. "Do you see what it's doing to my hair? Where is Dakar? He said we would have breakfast together."

The girl looked at me like I had two heads. "What, you don't speak English?" She ran out of my room before I could yell at her, but came back with another girl, a teenager.

"Hello, I'm Saafa, Rabia said you needed some help."

"Thank goodness one of you knows how to speak English."

"Yes, I do."

She wasn't afraid of me.

"What can I do for you?" Saafa asked.

"I was supposed to have breakfast with Dakar this morning. Can you please let him know I don't appreciate being stood up?"

"Dakar is doing something else right now."

"Well, let him know I will not wait for him. Jade Axeline doesn't wait for anyone."

"Ms. Axeline, if Dakar told you he was having breakfast with you, then I would advise you to wait."

"Who are you to advise me about anything?"

The young woman took a step closer and stared at me. "Believe me when I tell you, it is much better if you just give him what he wants. Dakar *always* gets what he wants," she said.

A shiver ran over my skin. "Well, tell him I'm only going to wait for ten more minutes." I saw her shaking her head as she left the room. "I hate teenagers."

Maya

When Saafa returned with the pen and paper, she looked distracted, but I didn't have time to ask why.

"He's on his way. Make sure you hide that or we'll both be in trouble."

"Saafa, is everything all right?"

"There's a guest staying at the main house who is causing everyone trouble. She is rude and mean. Not the type of woman Dakar usually brings back to the house."

"I'm sorry, yes, I have met a few of those in my life. If you can, stand up to her. I don't want you to get in trouble but do your best." We heard the heavy boots hitting the concrete floor. "He's coming, quickly hide the—"

I slid the paper and pen under my pillow just as he walked in.

"Dakar," I said with vehemence.

He looked at me with surprise and turned to Saafa with hardened eyes. "I will deal with you later."

I had made a mistake, and now Saafa was going to suffer for it. I had to lie.

"Saafa didn't tell me. I heard the guard outside my door mention your name." I paused. "What does it mean?"

He laughed. "What? My name? Cat. My parents named me after the most revered animal in Egypt. I'm royalty, if you didn't know. Well, a descendant of royalty, Cleopatra VII."

"Dakar, Miss Axeline is waiting to eat breakfast with you in her room," Saafa interrupted.

I took a step towards him. "What? What did you say, who?"

"Oh, that's right!" Dakar laughed again. "Your little friend from Netuno is here enjoying my hospitality. I'm sorry you can't be up at the main house with her. I would imagine the two of you have a great deal to talk about."

"Why is she here? Did you take—"

"Oh," he laughed even harder. "Did I forget to tell you? Jade Axeline and I are partners now. Well sort of; that's what she thinks anyways. She's such a snake, isn't she? Almost as dangerous as an asp. Truth is, she's the one who contacted us. Quite the schemer, that one." He was looking at my face as I tried to put the pieces together. "She sold you out, Ferret. She told me what you did."

"What I did? She's crazy."

"Whatever happened is irrelevant to me. And yes, she may be crazy, but she still hates you and I can use that. I have always found hate to be such a useful emotion."

I grabbed on to the sides of the cot, not sure what to say or do.

"Dakar, what would you like me to tell Miss Axeline?" Saafa interjected, not missing a step.

"Tell her I'll be there soon, and she may have some tea while she waits."

I needed to calm down and play the moment out correctly.

"Jade? Well, that doesn't surprise me. She hated me from the first time she saw me."

"Oh, I would love to hear more about your rivalry, but I have more pressing matters to deal with regarding you. Let's make this easy. First, congratulations are in order. I see your sight is intact. You have beautiful eyes. That would have been such a shame to lose those too." Without warning, he cuffed me across the head. "Where is it, Maya?"

"Where is what?" My heart pounded as his open hand turned into a fist.

"Oh, that's good, but not good enough. I see the muscles around your eyes twitching. You're nervous. What do you have to be nervous about? Just tell me the truth and I'll let you go."

"What truth do you want, Dakar?"

He leaned in and I readied myself to be hit again.

He smiled. He was winning. "The truth that is going to help me find the relic. I need to find the hair fork, Maya." He grabbed my arm twisting the skin. "This business with you has become rather distasteful; I would prefer to be having breakfast with Miss Axeline than to see your mangled face. You're making me hurt you."

"I can't make you do anything; you're in charge remember?" I said, feeling a surge of confidence.

He let go and took a step back.

"Jade Axeline, really? She's your first choice for a breakfast companion? That's very sad, Dakar."

When he stepped even closer, I prepared myself for another smack or a punch, but it was worse. He started running his finger up and down my arm, gently at first, then he grabbed me and squeezed. "Your face may be a mess, but I do like a woman with a little more meat on her bones."

I tried to withdraw from his touch, feeling a darkness in his fingertips, but he wouldn't let go.

"Calm down, I was only teasing. What I really wanted to tell you was that we got a head start on helping you find it. Aren't you excited?"

I was confused.

"After learning about the package…"

"What package? What are you talking about?"

"Oh, you didn't know anything about it. He's keeping secrets from you already, how unlucky for you. Not a great way to start a marriage, even yours. Cristiano's parents sent a package back to Avo's cottage before their untimely accident."

As flash of hope filled my body, then came the flood of confusion. "What have you done?"

"You're asking the wrong question. You need to ask me what happened next. Well, let me tell you. I wish I could have been there. But alas, I am here babysitting you."

"Dakar?" My body shook.

"A few of my colleagues paid Avo's cottage a visit. Unfortunately for you and the cottage the package was nowhere to be found. Are you sure you don't know where it is?"

I got one solid strike in before he twisted my arm around my back, wrenching my shoulder until I thought it was going to pop.

"I'll kill you if you did anything to Avo."

"Avo?" He laughed. "I can assure you *I've* done nothing to harm her. She's up in Porto. Where's the package, Maya? It wasn't in the cottage."

"I don't know where it is!" He suddenly let go.

"Well then, we have a problem, don't we? You don't know, Cristiano doesn't know, and it's not at the cottage.

"Oh, I almost forgot. My condolences. Avo's dead. Sounds like all the stress was too much for her. Too bad. I heard so many nice things about her. I have a little goodbye video for you. Call it a gift." He pulled out his phone and pressed play.

There he was, there she was. She looked so fragile. Cristiano's head was on her chest. I reached for the phone.

"Oh, no. You just get to watch. Unfortunately, this is a silent movie."

"Cristiano?" I called out to him.

Avo's eyes fluttered open, and she fought to say a few words. Then she was gone.

My heart cracked in half. My body reeled and I could feel the sobs ready to erupt, but I was not willing to give him the satisfaction of seeing it.

"It appears you may need a few minutes. I'm off to breakfast."

12

Phone Calls

Dalley

"Shh, everyone, it's Puro," Carmo yelled as she picked up her phone and put it on speaker.

"What is it, Dad? Luca already talked to Cristiano. We just got back from the cottage."

"Carmo, please listen to me." Puro sounded on the brink of tears.

Carmo's face drained of all color and Bento ran to her side.

"Puro, what is it? Did something happen to Maya?" Bento asked.

Luca took a step closer to Beth.

"No … but there's no easy way to tell you this. After Cristiano got the call from Luca about the trashed cottage and the missing package, he went down to the ICU to see Avo, hoping to discover at least a clue to the where abouts of the package. He didn't get the chance to ask. Avo died about an hour ago."

Carmo sucked in a breath.

"Puro," Bento took the phone off speaker. He stood still for a few moments, listening. "We'll see you soon. Puro, just one more thing. I know this is terrible timing but the tempranillo grapes in the east field are ready for harvesting. I've spoken with Sachi and my father and uncle; we started picking today. Bento stood still for another long moment, listening intently. "Thank you. I'll let them know. Goodbye."

Everyone was staring at Bento waiting to hear more news.

"Let us know what?" Carmo asked between her slowing sobs.

"Puro is heading back to Netuno with Avo's body. Cristiano has insisted that a cremation be done in Lisbon as soon as possible. He's choosing to wait on the funeral until Maya is home. Puro also asked if we could put a crew together to fix up Avo's place. He wants it ready for Cristiano and Maya when they come home. One good piece of news: Cristiano is leaving the hospital today. They're heading over to Marcos and Euphemia's so he can continue to recover there.

"One other thing. I know many of you have heard the stories about Avo's magic bread or were lucky enough to have a loaf baked for you."

As Puro continued to talk, I thought back to that first day when Maya and I arrived in Lisbon and tried to make Seafood Stew. Our supper was a salty cod disaster, except for a loaf of bread given to Maya by a local vendor, who turned out to be Cristiano's grandmother, or Avo as everyone knew her, so when Bento told us that Cristiano and his family were going to bake bread in honor of Avo and asked if we would like to do the same, everyone agreed.

"What do you think Sachi, will Gervais let us in the kitchen to bake bread?"

"I think he'll be the first one with his hands in the dough."

❧

I hesitated at first on the group bread making, not sure if I was ready to be working in the kitchen with all of them again but Ravn insisted, saying having friends meant you did not have to do certain things alone.

With reluctance, I agreed to bake and help mourn the loss of a woman who touched so many hearts.

Avo's death strangely hit Ravn hard; he had only met her briefly after we heard the news about the accident, but it was clear it had unlocked a series of memories he wasn't ready to share with me yet.

As much as Luca wanted to stay for the bread making, he had to head back to Porto to continue the investigation. And although invited to stay at Netuno, Beth did not want to let Luca out of her sight. Ravn and I planned to go into Lisbon to do some research and get back to Luca as soon as possible, so after an unexpected afternoon of mixing dough with my friends, Ravn and I took off to Lisbon while the loaves were still rising. As we were driving away from the inn, I remembered the night Maya presented her loaves to us, wearing Avo's handkerchief. She looked so calm, self-confident, like she had found her way. I wondered where the handkerchief had gotten to.

"Can we turn back?" I asked Ravn.

"Only if it's an emergency."

"No emergency, but it is important. A friendship thing."

"Then, yes. We'll turn around."

"You're not going to ask me why?"

Ravn looked at me. "No, not unless you want to tell me. If it's important to you, then it is important to me."

Ravn did a four-point turn, and before I could say another word, we were heading back.

⚜

"Dalley, at least wait until I stop the car."

"I'll be right back," I yelled as I ran into the inn and up the stairs to our room. I still had the key. It did not take me long to find it, as Maya had folded it up carefully and placed it in the drawer beside her bed, making sure the most beautiful part of the embroidery was facing up. I tucked it carefully into my bag and ran.

❧

Ravn and I didn't quite know what we were looking for going into Lisbon, but when I got a call from the hotel that we had been staying at, it put us on the right track.

"Dalley, put it on speaker," Ravn insisted.

"Miss Price, please."

"Yes, this is her. What can I do for you?"

"Management wanted to see if you received your money from our other guest."

"What guest are you talking about? What money?" I was baffled by the question.

"The day you checked out; she came to the front desk. She said she was a friend of yours and had borrowed some money from you and wanted to return it."

"I have no friends in Lisbon, and I don't lend money to anyone. What are you talking about?"

Ravn poked me.

"I'm sorry to upset you Miss Price. She knew your name. She made it sound like you were old friends."

"Please go on. What did you tell her?" I asked in my fake nice voice. "What was her name?"

"I only told her you were going up to Netuno. She asked for me to book her a car. She was going to surprise you, but she never came to get the vehicle. A group of men met her in the café and then she left with them."

"Willingly?"

"Yes, she was smiling. They drove off in a limo. The men came back later without her, paid her bill, and picked up her luggage."

"Stop! Does this woman have a name?" My body twitched.

"The mean lady. She tried to be nice, but everyone knew she was mean, beautiful, but mean." I looked over at Ravn and he shook his head not believing it.

"Jade? Jade Axeline?" I asked.

"Yes, that's it. I'm sorry if I did something wrong."

Ravn jumped in. "No, you did nothing wrong. We'll be there in an hour. Do not let the staff who spoke with her leave. Goodbye."

I stared at Ravn in disbelief. "Jade Axeline was in Lisbon? At the same hotel as us?"

"Well, this adventure just got a lot more interesting."

"What mischief have you been up to, Miss Axeline?" Ravn asked himself as he continued to drive. "And who were the men you left with?"

Ravn's questions dangled in the air until we arrived at the hotel. Then it was time to get to work.

❧

"Ravn, I'll check with the front desk. You check with the staff on the floor."

"Ola, Dalley Price, you called me earlier." I held my hand up and gave the man at the front desk a forced, friendly wave.

"Oh, Miss Price, it is nice to see you again."

"Thank you. I'm trying to track down Ms. Axeline. You were right, she borrowed some money from me, a lot of money. I cannot believe she just ran off. Can you tell me more about her stay here?"

"Oh dear, I am so sorry about all of this. She was here for several days and complained about everything, but mostly about the food. On the day when you and Mr. Ravn checked out, she approached me, asking about you by name. The waiter later told me she had been acting strange and was hiding behind a planter while you were checking out. He thought she was trying to listen in to your conversation."

I stopped paying attention to the concierge and tried to remember what Ravn and I had been talking about. We were discussing Maya and Cristiano; not having heard from them, I mentioned Porto and we were worried about the Ptolemites coming up from Egypt. We needed to get to Netuno. Then I realized she heard everything. That cunning, manipulative bitch heard everything.

"But what did you do, Jade?"

Ravn was almost running when he arrived in the lobby after receiving my text.

"Ptolemites," we both said at the same time.

"Somehow, she has gotten mixed up with the Ptolemites. Dalley, we need to call Luca."

"Yes, you call Luca. I need to call someone who can get us different kinds of answers."

"You're calling Axel Axeline?" Ravn asked.

"No, Ravn, keep up. Didn't you listen to the stories Maya told about Sachi and her father? It was her family who saved Netuno and robbed the Axelines of gaining control over the vineyard. I'm calling Sachi."

"Are you sure? Axel might know something about Jade and why she is here."

∽

"Hi, Sachi, we need your help. Or more directly, we need your father's help.

I hung up to find Ravn stepping towards me, with his fingers over his lips, wanting me to be quiet.

"What do you want? And what do you know about my daughter?" I heard a man bark through the phone.

"Actually, Mr. Axeline, we were going to ask you the same question. I am with the Polícia de Segurança Pública." He shrugged his shoulders at me, hoping Axel would buy it.

"Did you find my daughter?"

"Can you confirm she was in Lisbon? And that she rented a car several days ago but never picked it up?"

"Yes, that's what I called you about. Has she shown up yet?"

"What was she doing in Lisbon, Mr. Axeline?" Ravn continued to pepper him with questions.

"I already had this conversation. Don't you guys talk to each other?"

"Different department, International Crimes."

"International Crimes?" he paused. "Well, I guess that makes sense."

"What do you mean?"

"I told the desk sergeant, or whatever you call yourselves, over there she had been in contact with some new international business associates and was trying to close a deal."

"What kind of deal?" Ravn asked, trying to be routine.

"Oh, I don't know the details, but I think it had something to do with brokering information."

"Interesting, yes. That would make sense."

"What, what makes sense?" I heard something shift in his voice. He almost sounded concerned.

Ravn threw out one more half-truth, "Hotel staff reported she left with four gentlemen who were speaking Arabic."

"So, what are you going to do about it?" he yelled at Ravn.

"Mr. Axeline, there is no need for that. From what we know, she went willingly, not like the woman the Ptolemites supposedly took by force a couple of days earlier. Your daughter appears to be running with a very dangerous crowd."

"I didn't mention who Jade was working with. Who are you? What did you say your name was?"

I looked at Ravn, worried we were done.

"Luca Palito. Inspector Luca Palito."

"Well, Inspector." He spat out. "I expect to hear from you as soon as you find my daughter."

"What if she doesn't want to be found?"

"Just find her. I don't really care what she wants … do your job or else."

Ravn hung up. "Hm. I had better call Luca and let him know what we found. And that I just impersonated him while talking with the great Axel Axeline."

Ravn and I sat in the hotel café with pen and paper in hand, going over the timelines and information we had discovered. As we filled in the gaps, it became clear Jade was the link to the Ptolemites.

"It was Jade. She heard us talking, took the information about Maya and Cristiano, and told the Ptolemites how to find them. She did this." I paused, trying to gather my thoughts. "I'm going to ruin her, destroy her life." My hands shook.

"Dalley. You're right, it sounds like all roads lead to Jade, but listen to me. Vengeance will send you in the wrong direction. I've been there before," he said, squeezing my hand and looking so deep into my eyes I could only imagine what had happened to him. "And I won't let that happen to you. I can't. Karma will take care of her eventually. You just have to be patient."

"Patient? You promise?"

"I promise you." I heard a plea of desperation in his voice; he wanted me to be safe, to be happy. No one had wanted anything good for me before, so I stopped and took a breath.

"Will I get to watch?" I smiled, knowing he was right, knowing I had to fight the urge to make this all about Jade.

"I can't promise *that,* but I can promise I'll do everything I can to help find Maya. Now I had better make that call to Luca and we need to catch a flight to Porto. We make a pretty good team, if I say so myself."

"Yes, you bring out the best in me."

Leaning across the table, he stroked my cheek. "I'm really proud of you."

"For what?" I blushed, unable to stop the physical response to his words.

"For making the right choice."

⤺

Maya

I held the pillow to my face and screamed.

"Jade. How could one person create so much chaos?" I said before that I hated her, but that's not true. The embodiment of hate is when one person is willing to destroy another to achieve their goal. I wanted to hate her but as I ran my fingers over the bandages, I knew I could never do this to anyone, even Jade. After I finished crying, I realized the tears had soaked through some of the bloody bandages and loosened them. It was time.

I found one end of the bandage and started unwinding the gauze one inch at a time. I tried not to think about what I might look like and rationalized it would not be that bad. When I was just about done, I heard the bolt slide from the door and I froze. Saafa walked in, closed the door quickly and ran over to me.

"What are you doing? They're not ready to come off."

"Ready or not, I have to see what is happening. Saafa, I need to know."

Saafa nodded her head and took over the unwinding. "Maya, can you tell me who this Jade woman is?"

I smiled at the teenager as she tried to make sense of how Jade was part of the craziness that ripped me away from my life.

"Jade is an unhappy woman who lets hate and pain rule her world. She thought by doing this to me—telling the Ptolemites how to find me—that it would solve her problems. But I can guarantee you, I am the least of her problems now that she has invited Dakar into her life."

Saafa paused, then gently pulled the last layer of bandage off my face. Her eyes told me more than I wanted to know as she stared at me.

"I'm sorry Maya. I tried my best. I'm sorry." The tears came fast as I saw the young woman turn briefly into a sad little girl. I held her tightly and wondered if it could really be that bad. Touching my skin, I could feel the multiple cuts and open wounds, some long, some deep. I needed to see it.

"Saafa, can you please get me a mirror?

"No—Maya, I don't want you to see it. Let me clean it up a bit."

"Saafa, I need to see it right now."

As much as I appreciated Saafa's attempt to change my mind I had to see my new reality. Saafa stepped out to find a mirror and while I waited, my imagination took me back to my first real date with Cristiano at the medieval festival; the lights, food, costumes and the intense connection we experienced. It was the first time I truly felt alive, not just because of Cristiano but something inside of me had started to change.

When Saafa returned she was tapping her pocket. "I have it."

Then we heard the boots and the bolt.

"Saafa, you need to yell at me for taking off my bandages. Now!"

"What have you done?" she tried to say with anger but failed.

"Louder! Meaner!" I whispered. "Call me stupid!"

Just as he walked in, Saafa began berating me. Screaming at me for removing the bandages. Yelling that only Dakar makes those decisions.

"Get out, Saafa!" Dakar stood on the other side of the room staring at me with shock and disgust. "What a waste. But then, I can't really say, can I. I didn't see what you looked like before, but now, well, it's hard to even look at you." He paused, holding up his phone and shaking it in my direction. "On another note, I thought your dear *husband* has suffered long enough. He needs to know you're alive. I think he needs a little motivation. So, this is how it's going to work. I'm going to call him and put it on speakerphone. When I'm ready, I'll let you say a few words. You will tell him you're safe, that you're being treated fairly, and that all he needs to do is find the relic and I'll let you go. It's that simple. He has one week."

My body was shaking with a mixture of fear and anticipation. Anticipation, in hearing his voice and fear, as Dakar had not said what he was going to do to me if Cristiano could not find the relic.

"What's the matter with him? Why isn't he answering?" Dakar asked.

The phone rang three times before I heard his voice. "Ola?" He answered in almost a whisper. It didn't sound like him.

"Cristiano," was all Dakar said in his brisk, angry voice.

"Who's there? What have you done with Maya? What have you done with my wife? I'll kill you; I'll kill you if—"

"Cristiano. Stop. Is it really a good idea to yell at me? Threaten to kill me? I have someone here who is dying to talk to you—well, almost dying," he laughed.

"Maya? Maya, my love, are you okay? We are doing everything we can to find you."

"Cristiano. I thought you were dead. You looked dead when they dragged me out of the car."

"No, my Maya, I am very much alive, and we'll be together again soon. I promise. Everyone's here at my parents, even Beth came."

"Beth is there?" I couldn't get distracted with emotion. "Cristiano, all you need to do is find the relic."

"Maya, you don't sound like yourself. The firefighters said there was blood all over the car." I could hear him teetering on the edge, and I knew I only had a few more seconds before Dakar would lose his patience.

"Listen. I'm alright. I am safe. We can't talk long. I was told to tell you they are treating me well, but you need to find the relic. Once you've done that, they will do an exchange."

"Maya, when you're back, we'll get married again, in the chapel, just like you wanted. I'll hold your beautiful face and we will start over."

Dakar laughed. My heart lurched at the thought of being near Cristiano. His touch on my skin, his lips on mine. Then I reached up to my face and froze.

"Dakar says we have one week!"

"Bitch!" Dakar took the phone and threw it across the room.

Cristiano

"Maya!" I shrieked, but it was too late.

"You stupid bitch, you said my name."

"Yes, I did, didn't I? It must have slipped out," she pushed back defiantly.

"You're going to pay for that!" Then I heard a smack and a punch, a crumple, and a groan. "Clean her up, Saafa, I'll be back after I finish my breakfast with my special guest. At least she appreciates my hospitality."

Then I heard Maya's voice; quiet but fierce, "Yeah, having breakfast with toxic waste is always a great idea."

I could hear the footsteps coming closer and felt the boot heel crushing the connection.

13

New Friends

Cristiano

I sat on the couch at my parents' home, police scanners and people everywhere. Judith was the first to run at me. "She's alive," I breathed out; feeling the blows she took to give me his name.

"Cristiano, we need to break down the call and pull out any sounds and information we can. They have given us seven days," Luca said with little emotion.

"A week is too long. He hit her. I don't think she has a week."

The room went silent. Luca ran his hands through his hair. "It's going to be a long day. Can everyone give me and Cristiano a chance to go through the recording? Try to get some fresh air, have something to eat. We will let you know if we find something."

Ravn and Dalley had just flown in from Lisbon and arrived at the house amped up with newly discovered information about Jade and a promise from Sachi that she would call her father.

"Ravn, can you join us, please?" Luca asked, avoiding the daggers Dalley was sending his way.

Luca guided everyone out of the office except for the three of us.

"Luca, it might be better to have Dalley in here too," Ravn offered.

"No, not right now. I need your experience with no emotional distractions. Simply, you might hear something we do not. I've learnt the hard way emotions can cloud what we see and hear in a situation like this."

"Fair enough. Dalley is not happy about being sidelined."

"Yes, I know. She and Beth can commiserate and think of ways to get back at me, but for now, my only job is to find Maya. And it's too damn noisy around here. I need to think."

I saw him rub his hand over his forehead and, for the first time, signs of fatigue broke through. "Luca, why don't you take a few minutes? Ravn and I will listen to the recording while you close your eyes. We promise we'll wake you if we find anything."

"Just as long as you don't go rogue, Ravn, and pretend to be me again."

"I promise Luca, no more playing inspector. I'll just go back to being an investigative journalist. Much safer," he laughed.

I traded places with Luca. He lay down on the couch and I shuffled over to a chair to join Ravn, who was setting up the recording and two sets of headphones.

❧

Dalley

They kicked me out of the office. I could understand everyone else. But me? Ravn was going to get an earful for not insisting I stay to help. So, there I was, standing in the living room, Beth staring at me with laser eyes.

"What? What did you want to say? Clearly, you have something on your mind."

"I do, but first, why are you mad at me? I've done nothing to you. You're the one who started this whole mess," she stated, folding her arms across her chest like I was a six-year-old from her class.

My initial reaction was to fight, to lash back like I had always done when someone was calling me out. So, I stopped. "You're right."

"Oh," she said, altering her posture. "Well, that's not quite true, is it? It wasn't all your fault." She breathed in deeply and sat down on the couch, looking out the handcrafted bay window at a view that went on forever.

"Tell me more about them, about Maya and Cristiano. She never had time to share their story, only that she had met a man and fallen in love. I was worried at first, thinking it might be a rebound thing, then when I reflected on it, she never really loved Steven. She had only been going through the motions, doing what she assumed everyone wanted her to do. I figured Cristiano was a fling, an infatuation."

I shook my head. "She loves him, Beth, and he cherishes her." I paused, almost not believing I was the one saying those words. "He asked her to marry him in the back seat of a taxi while we were being shot at and in the middle of all that chaos; she said yes. Her response was as natural as breathing." I smiled and rolled my eyes.

"Someone was trying to kill all of you? She missed telling me that part of the narrative when she called about the wedding," Beth said.

"You asked how they met." I offered, trying to distract her. "Let's see. *I* first met Maya in person on the airplane."

"In person?" Beth asked, picking up on the subtle disclosure.

"Yes." I could feel the prick of guilt creeping in.

"I discovered who the other contest winners were and did some research on everyone before I got on the flight." Beth's face wrinkled up like she had eaten something rotten. "I know, it was bad, and the worst thing is I flew to Peachland to see where Maya was from. She was the one person in the group I found unusual—well, more boring—but I kept thinking she was supposed to be interesting. I'm not sure. There was just something about her."

Beth laughed. "I know, right? She never saw it. So you were following her around?"

"Yes."

"Oh my God, that makes so much sense now."

"What are you talking about?"

"A few weeks before she left, she mentioned feeling like someone was following her. I just thought it was her anxiety. I told her parents and we all hoped she would hold it together long enough to get on the plane for the trip."

"No, Maya wasn't paranoid, she was listening to her instinct."

"Keep going, Dalley."

"Well, the day we left for Portugal, I almost missed my flight, but Cristiano saved the day by getting me on board. After I joined Maya on the plane, there was a bunch of drama about her losing her journal and pen, and then … *he* returned them."

"Cristiano? Seriously? You didn't write about that in the blog."

I feigned annoyance, but she was correct. I deserved the jab. "I know. She left them on a chair in the waiting room after the tea catastrophe—"

"Tea catastrophe?"

"Well, more like, she spilt a hot cup of tea, and he came running over to save her? Meet her? I'm not sure, but I think that was when it happened, when something shifted for each of them. I didn't see it. But from what she said and the way the two of them acted afterward, it didn't take a detective to figure out they were meant to be.

"Well, the rest of the story was the same. Every time I saw them together, it was intense. After the death of Maggie's son, which I'm sure you read about." I shook my head, still feeling ashamed for telling a story that was not mine to share. "Cristiano returned after escorting Maggie back to Vancouver and then whisked Maya away for the evening. It was a mixture of the most romantic and tragic moment I had ever seen. He ran through the doors at Netuno and kissed her like something had torn them apart and they found their way back to each other. I laughed it off, making jokes about them. But I was jealous.

"I could go on and on because that was their entire story. One dramatic moment after another; the night club, and the trip to Paris, and the bet—"

"The bet?"

"Yes, the bet. The other ladies and I ended up making a bet. The two of them kept stealing away together every chance they got, but Maya hinted they had not *been* together yet. So, one night, with a few extra bottles of wine, the rest of us made a bet about whether they had sealed the deal."

"Sealed the deal? I thought you wrote they did it on the airplane."

"No. I made that up." I laughed. "You can't believe everything you read."

"Oh, I wondered about that. It was out of character for her. But then so was cancelling her wedding and taking up with a Portuguese flight attendant. I'm not complaining, mind you. I knew there was another Maya in there, but I didn't know she had it in her to run off and find Cristiano after that debacle with Steven."

"Yeah, what was all that about?"

"Oh, Steven is a dolt. He loved her in his own way. I told him not to come, but he didn't listen to me. That's all irrelevant now. Back to the bet."

"The two of them *actually* waited and as much sexual tension as everyone saw between them, they were still holding out. I think they were waiting until they got married. She once talked to me about doing it the *right* way."

"Hm, that's very interesting. Thank you, Dalley. I remember in one of our calls, before she left to go look for him, I asked her if he was worth it. She was so mad at me. Then the next call I got from her was telling me she found him, and they were getting married. She was happy. The happiest I had ever heard her. You had all made it back safely from Egypt and she said she was ready to start her life, a life with Cristiano. I was ecstatic for her and asked her to take pictures, and that was it. That was the last time I spoke with her."

I could see the tears forming and I braced myself.

"Dalley, what am I going to do if something happens to her? She's my best …"

Supporting crying women was not my strong suit, and Maya was the only woman I ever attempted to help and ended up failing miserably. Moving towards her, I gently placed my hand on her shoulder. Jumping up, Beth unexpectedly threw her arms around me. So, I did what Maya would do, and hugged her back.

"Sorry, Dalley, you must think I am an emotional basket case," she said withdrawing suddenly. "I'm just tired and confused about a few things."

"Confused? What are you confused about?"

"Embarrassed would be more accurate."

"Come, sit down. You are talking to the queen of embarrassment. I just went through the largest humiliation of my life and had to apologize to almost everyone on the planet. I'm sure I can help you out with your situation."

Beth stepped away and started pacing.

"Well, I'm sure you noticed. I'm not like the rest of you."

"What does that mean?"

"You, Cristiano's family, Luca, everyone here is so beautiful. Even Maya underwent a transformation over the last few weeks, but she had something good to start with. I'm just a teacher from Peachland; plane Jane, and as you can see, not a size two."

"Beth, what are you talking about?"

"Oh, Dalley, don't be coy. I saw how you looked at me the first time you saw me. It rarely bothers me." She paused. "This is a stupid conversation. Maya is missing. I should not even be thinking about this."

"Yes, Maya is missing, but she's alive. And those boys kicked us out because there was nothing else we can do right now to help. So, if we can solve a different problem, then I am happy to do it. But I need to know what you're talking about."

"Luca."

"What about Luca? You like him?" I guessed.

"No, well, I don't know. But I think he likes me?"

"What do you mean?"

"See, you don't even think I'm attractive enough for him."

"Oh, be quiet, Beth, that's not what I meant. You need to know Maya is the first real female friend I've ever had in my life and I did a crappy job in the beginning. I don't have friendship skills, so forgive me if I don't say things in the right order. Beth, so what if you're not a size two? Not all men like that. Why wouldn't he like you? You're loyal, dedicated, and tenacious."

"It sounds like you are describing a family pet."

"Beth! You flew halfway around the world to help Maya and you stood up to Luca when he wanted to sideline you. You are compassionate, and you love children, and yes, you are beautiful. Not all beauty comes in a tiny box. You could use a different bra, though. What is up with the both of you?"

"Both of us?"

"Yes, on our second day in Lisbon, I took Maya out shopping and made her buy all new lingerie."

Beth laughed. "Point taken."

"Anyway. A good bra can give you heaps of confidence. What did Luca do? Did he try to have sex with you?"

"Well, no, kind of. He kissed me. I was so shocked I pulled back, but he just smiled, and said perhaps another time, in his crazy accent. When I asked him what he was doing, he asked me why not. He said I was beautiful, and ..."

"And he wanted to make love to you? That is a very European thing."

"Well, yes. But I am not a one-night stand kind of person, and we are in the middle of this whole thing."

"Maybe his timing is not the best. But he strikes me as a man who's very genuine. He's also very good-looking and could have any woman he wants. If he kissed you, it's because he wanted to."

Beth stopped and looked at me again. "You're right. For a first-time friend, you did a pretty good job at supporting your second."

"Second what?"

"Second friend."

"You want to be friends with me?"

"If Maya can forgive you, so can I. Anyway, I think you are much better at talking about sex than Maya. She can be a little prudish."

Unexpected laughter filled the space.

The office door broke open and Ravn came running into the living room.

"Dalley, what is the first thing that comes to your mind when I say toxic waste?"

"Jade!"

14

Stepping Up

Maya

Dakar was done with being "kind'" and if he didn't hear from Cristiano soon, I knew he would make me disappear. Hauling myself off the ground, I climbed on to the cot and curled up in a ball. I had seen a thousand punches landed in far too many movies, but never knew how much it could hurt.

I reached up to the edge of a reopened wound and wiped the blood on my already soiled pillow. Exhaustion and sorrow took over and as I settled into a deep sleep a part of me hoped when I woke, I would find myself back in Portugal at the cottage, Avo would be baking bread in the garden, and Cristiano would be lying beside me holding my old face in his hands.

But no, when my eyes flashed open, I had slept the day away. I was not in Portugal, not at the cottage, and there was no Avo, no bread, and no Cristiano. I reached up, feeling the familiar bandages. Saafa must have slipped in and taken care of me while I dreamt of the life I was so close to having before the gunshot, before the windshield sliced up my face.

As the light faded in my little prison, I pulled out the pen and paper from under my pillow.

Somewhere Hot and Alone
Bandages stick to my skin, like flailing flies trying to detach themselves from yellow paper.
My flesh feels dead, my face is dead. Who am I under this plaster of white?
Am I the same person?
Am I still the fresh adventurer who hopped on the train to find the man I love?
No. I don't think so.
I want to disappear, to get lost in the sea, to sit on a rock where only the fishes are my friends.
Fear of what I will find leaves my heart in spasms.
His voice, he loves me. He loves the old me. Could he love this one too?

The pen landed on the other side of the room, hitting the wall with nothing but a disappointing click. The tears that fell slipped under the bandages, stinging the seeping wound Dakar had opened again. I placed the tragic poem under my pillow, then ran my fingers over the bandages. It was time. I needed to know. I needed to see what was happening and to figure out what to do next. So, I unwound the gauze again. When I got to the last layer, I took my bottle of water and soaked the edge of my sheet against the dried blood that stuck to the skin. As I pressed it against the wound, brown and red seeped into the cotton, staining it forever.

When the gauze finally released, I unwrapped the last of my cloth prison. My face felt stiff and I could feel the ridges as I ran my fingers over the healing wounds. When I touched my cheek, however; a stream of warm blood trickled down my arm. My stomach turned, and I barely made it to the bucket in the corner. The nausea was brief and when I was done, I could feel a halo of sadness trying to blanket my heart. I pushed it away long enough to rip a few strips off the sheet and dab the open wound. It was then I looked down and saw the scar on my arm. The scar left by the for-sale sign so many years ago, the scar that would have been much worse had my father not stayed with me holding the wound together until it would hold itself.

So, I sat in the dark, pinching the two pieces of fragile tissue, hoping for a miracle and relying on my magical thinking. When the bleeding stopped, I knew there was nothing left for me to do. So, I took the bloody bandages and placed them in a pile by the door. If Dakar was going to keep me there, he would have to see what he did to me. I could only imagine what I looked like, and he deserved to see all of it. I would be strong for as long as I needed. Whatever happened after that, I didn't care. I cleaned my face as best as I could with my dampened rag and went to sleep clutching the poem that lay under my pillow.

Cristiano

"She's in pain. I can feel it. How can I feel her pain?" I asked Marcos as the rest of the house slept and I paced back and forth in the living room with my new father.

"Cristiano, come sit down. You shouldn't be walking around so much."

"How can I sit when every part of me aches? I don't know where my pain ends and hers begins."

"Son—can I call you that?"

Seeing the worry embedded in his brow, I decided he might be right and sitting down was a better choice than falling over. "Yes, you can call me son, but I am not sure I'm ready to call you dad yet."

"That's fair." He paused. "I understand your pain, at least I think I do. I've been where you are, when the woman you love is in pain, breaking in half, and there is nothing you can do. This is not coming out right." He moved uncomfortably in his spot, then stopped talking as if he was not sure he should go on.

"Please, Marcos, what do you mean?"

"Your mother," he said carefully. "In the letter Avo wrote, she spoke about that last day in the hospital; that morning when your parents came to get you and we had to say goodbye for what we thought would be forever. As your parents gathered your things and walked out of the hospital, Euphemia shook like a volcano ready to erupt. I wasn't sure what was happening, but I later found out she had gone into some kind of shock; giving you away broke her heart."

I heard the pain in his voice and saw the flush in his cheeks as he held back the tears.

"I didn't think things could get worse for us, for her, but when her parents arrived and saw me with her, they threatened to call the police. She couldn't even fight them. I didn't want her to, but I was not leaving without letting her know it was not my choice. Her parents said some horrible things about both of us, and I left. I left her with those people."

He could no longer hold the tears as he recalled the story. "I yelled to her as security dragged me out of the room, letting her know I would fight for us, that I loved her, and that you were safe. The last image I saw was of her holding your blanket.

"Weeks after the adoption, I felt like I was losing my mind. You were gone, she was gone. I felt sick all the time, and I knew she was in pain. I could feel it every minute of the day."

"What did you do? How did you get through it?"

"I came up with a plan and found a friend of hers who agreed to give her my messages. We communicated in secret for a year. She tried to keep up a brave face, telling me she was alright, but I knew her heart was broken. I was losing her. She was fading away, and I couldn't let that happen. We had to be together if we were going to survive losing you. I often wondered if we should have just run off when we found out she was pregnant, but we were teenagers. We had nothing. We couldn't take care of you."

"You lived her pain and your own, but you kept going. You loved her so much you could feel her pain and her love, even if you couldn't be with her."

"Yes," he nodded.

My thoughts spun over to Maya's letter. "Then, why? If you loved me so much, why did you not even talk to me when Jack figured out who I was? When you came down to see me surf and put all the pieces together."

Marcos hid his hands in his face, then took a breath and looked up. "Honestly, Cristiano, I was afraid if I ever held you again in my arms, I could not let you go. I know it sounds irrational, but you weren't ours anymore. You belonged to someone else. I had given you away to Rosa and Michel."

Another round of tears fell.

"I didn't know they were gone. But even if I did, what right did I have to take you away from Avo?" He paused. "Look at me, I'm a mess."

"Thank you."

"Thank you? For what?"

"For letting Rosa, Michel, and Avo take care of me when you and Euphemia couldn't." I took a breath. "I'm sorry I've caused you two so much heartache."

"Cristiano, heartache goes with loving someone. Your mother and I have always loved you, will always love you. When you feel pain, so do we. We would do anything for all of our children, that includes Maya."

My heart crumbled when he said her name.

"Regarding Phillip, I know he has said and done a lot of things in the last few days, and it feels like the two of you are on opposite sides, but that's not true. You both love her and want her home safely but right now, we can't let fear paralyze us. We have to work together and find a way."

When I looked up, Euphemia was standing in the arched entry to the living room with her hand over her mouth.

Marcos followed my gaze and saw her, then grinned. "What? I can be inspirational when I want to be." Without saying a word, she ran toward us and threw her arms around our shoulders, crushing us together.

"I never imagined I would ever get a chance to hold you and your father again."

Marcos looked over at me, smiled, and slipped one arm out so *he* was holding the three of us. Our forever moment only lasted a minute or two when we heard a hoot and holler and Ravn, Dalley, Luca, and Beth came running in.

"We think we found her! Or more accurately, Sachi's father did the finding," Dalley shouted. "But either way, we know she is in Morocco."

My body swayed. Before anyone noticed, my father had his arm around me. Helping me, lending me the strength I didn't have.

"Where is she?" I heard Phillip's voice boom from behind the crowd gathering in the room.

Luca stepped in. "We believe she is being held at a property in Morocco."

"So, we don't know for sure. What do we know?" Phillip asked with growing impatience.

"With the information Maya gave on the call, and with a little extra help, we confirmed that Jade Axeline is with them and from what Ravn and Dalley pieced together it was she who contacted the Ptolemites and told them where you were. The car crash, the kidnapping, all of it. I have been in contact with Pierre La Nou."

My teeth ground together, when I heard his name.

"He will be flying in from Paris the day after tomorrow," Luca said.

"Why?" I asked with frustration.

"We need his expertise to find out more about the Ptolemites, and his contacts in Egypt could be very helpful."

"No!" I shouted, not being able to hold back my anger. "I don't want to see Pierre. This is all his fault. My parents, Maya, Avo." I screamed. I could feel my body buzzing and my father's hold on me getting firmer as my legs gave way.

❧

When I woke, I was lying in bed and my sister was sitting beside me with a sketch pad in her hand.

"What happened?" I asked, mystified by my new surroundings.

"You fainted, big brother. Had a little hissy fit and fainted. You realize you were in a terrible car crash just a few days ago, right?" Jacinta asked.

"Yes, and my wife is missing and Avo is dead."

"Now you're sounding like Zef. Stop being so mean and snarky with me. I get enough of that from my other brother."

The chuckle that escaped from my chest surprised me. "I'm sorry. I'm being a jerk."

"Yes, you are, but I'm okay. I rarely let that kind of stuff bother me."

"So, I'm like Zef? Or Zef is like me?" I asked, trying to lighten the mood.

"I don't know, but either way, both of you are acting like idiots, actually everyone is right now. I don't feel like being here. I can't help with anything, and I'm just getting in the way. But it doesn't matter how I feel. The only thing we need to focus on is finding Maya. So, if this Pierre guy can help us, then let him."

I smiled, "Yes. When did you become the wisest and most talented person in the family?" I asked, pointing at her sketchbook.

"Wise and talented?" She shook her head. "I should let mom know you are awake. She's been coming in every fifteen minutes to check and see if you were still breathing. I guess she missed out on all that worry when you were a baby."

"Jacinta, is it odd to have me show up like this in your life?"

"Odd? No. Well, maybe a little, but it feels right. Like it felt right for me when Maya came to the house and told us about you and Avo." Then I saw it, the flush of her face.

"You're sad. Sad about Avo but afraid to show it because of everything happening with Maya. And confused that although you just met her, the hole in your heart seems so big with her gone."

She looked at me with shock.

"How did you know? I waited my whole life to have a grandparent. And then all I had was one day."

"One day?"

"I had one day with her before you woke up and then she was gone."

My heart lurched forward, and I could feel the pain she was feeling, but had to keep mine tightly locked away. I was afraid if I started crying, I might never stop, that the little boy holding Avo's hand as we walked home from the Netuno chapel, might crumble and never put himself back together again. I couldn't do that, for Maya and at that moment, for my sister.

"Jacinta, you said you felt like you were in the way right now. Do you want a job?"

"Yes, anything. I just want to feel useful."

"Okay, if your parents—our parents—agree, maybe you could go back to Netuno with Puro and stay at the inn. I know this is a lot to ask. But maybe you could attend Avo's cremation and then take care of her for me until I come back with Maya."

A look somewhere between apprehension and anticipation appeared on her face.

"I'm sorry, that's too much to ask. Forget it."

"No. I won't forget it. You understand. You totally understand. Yes. I want to help. Now we just have to convince mom." She bit her cheek. "Can you ask her?"

"Yes. Go get our mother. Puro will pick Avo up at the hospital today and head straight to the airport. So, if we are going to make it happen, this would be the time. Any suggestions on how to ask her?"

"Straight and honest is always the best way with her. She doesn't like when you try to soften her up. Mind you, I think she would do almost anything for you right now." Jacinta ran out of the room., "Mom, he's awake and he needs a favor."

⌘

Jacinta was correct. Straight and honest was the right move. Euphemia agreed that giving Jacinta a job to do was a good decision. I think she also said yes because Judith agreed to travel with them. The shift in Judith returning to Netuno without Phillip was unexpected and I could only speculate it had something to do with Judith's position on supporting my marriage with Maya.

As the sun rose, people started moving about the house in a sleep-deprived state. I needed to get away from everyone for a moment and searched out a secluded deck and empty railing to lean on. When Puro found me, I was deep in thought.

"Cristiano? Cristiano," he called my name quietly.

Without looking up I knew who it was. "How did I get here, Puro? How did I mess everything up again? When I met Maya, I thought I had a second chance to set things right in my life."

"Set what right, Cristiano?"

"Where do I start?" I laughed as if he should know the answer.

"Tell me. Tell me what you think you did wrong?" he asked.

"I was born."

"Well, it's not like you had any power over that," he said.

"I couldn't stop my parents from leaving for Egypt that day."

"And again, Cristiano, not your decision to make. You were a little boy."

I pushed back. "If I had never picked Maya's journal up, she would be safe right now. None of this would have happened. The blog, the accident, the kidnapping."

"Yes, you're right. If you hadn't picked up the journal, then none of those things would have happened. But let's look at things from another perspective. If you hadn't picked up the journal, you would not have gone on the date, fallen in love, come back home, had time with Avo, learned about your parents and your siblings, got married. Yes, Cristiano, things are horrible right now, but that doesn't make the beautiful things that happened less beautiful."

"What about Avo's death? I feel like it's my fault too."

"Cristiano. She always did what she needed to do. She came for you, but maybe she came for some other reason, too? Maybe she came for herself, maybe she needed you, too?"

I wrapped my arms around my chest trying to hold myself together but lost the battle. "When I think about never seeing Avo again, it feels like I can't breathe. She was the one truth in my life I never doubted. She loved me, no matter what."

"And so does Maya. Maya loves you. Cristiano, you will find her." I stopped, stood up straight, and gave him a push. "You don't have a choice. Right now, in this moment, everything needs to be about getting Maya home, and Avo would have it no other way."

I pulled my chest back and let the grief wash away, at least for the moment.

"Jacinta and Judith and I will take care of Avo and when you bring Maya home—and yes, I said *home*—the cottage will be ready for the two of you."

"How do you know that? How do you know she will make it home?"

"Because there is no other ending you can accept."

I smirked and came in for a hug.

"Puro, you had better head out. Avo will be irritated if you are late picking her up."

We both chuckled, but it was time to go.

"Are you going to be alright?"

"Yes, between my mother, father, brother, almost father-in-law, Dalley, Beth, and Ravn. I should be okay, not to mention Luca and Jack. I think I can manage here."

"Keep us informed."

"I love you, Puro."

"I love you too, Cristiano."

We all stood at the door as the taxi arrived to take Puro, Judith, and Jacinta to the hospital. I caught my mother's eyes as she hugged my sister one last time.

"Call me if you need anything. Do you still want to go? You can change your mind," my mother said, tugging at Jacinta's backpack.

"No," Jacinta said firmly. "I have a job to do."

I saw a flicker of pride appear at the edge of my mother's lips.

15

Avo's Going Home

Puro

WHEN WE ARRIVED AT THE hospital everything was ready. Avo was in the transport vehicle, and I just needed to sign a few papers. Judith stayed with Avo as Jacinta and I walked into the hospital to collect her things. Jacinta stood close to me like Carmo used to do when she was little and feeling nervous.

"Jacinta, why don't you sit down, I'll come and get you when I'm done."

For a talkative teen, she had become quiet, and when a nurse walked into the waiting room holding a plastic hospital bag that had *Cristiana Lazaro* written across it in black marker, Jacinta froze.

"Hello, are you Cristiana Lazaro's granddaughter?"

Jacinta looked over at me, not knowing how to respond. I nodded, encouraging her to accept the bag but I too was feeling speechless and a little embarrassed. I had no idea Avo's first name was Cristiana. How did I not know that Cristiano was named after her?"

Jacinta gathered her courage. "Yes," she said tentatively at first, but as she took the bag, I saw her disposition change, stepping into her new role as Avo's only granddaughter. She hugged the plastic as if she were holding Avo and my heart broke for her.

"Please take care and again, we are very sorry for your loss," the nurse offered as we stepped out the door.

Jacinta was walking a few steps behind me when I met up with Judith.

I whispered to Judith, "I'm afraid this might be too much for her."

Judith tapped my arm. "I've got this, Puro," she said as she waved Jacinta towards her. "Jacinta, do you need help with the bag?"

"No, thank you. I'm okay." She held the bag tightly.

"You could join us in Netuno in a couple of days if you like?"

She shook her head, then lifted her chin and squeezed the bag so firmly I thought it was going to pop.

"I have a job to do."

Judith looked over at me with a smile; there was no changing Jacinta's mind. I nodded back, knowing it was time to go.

Collecting Avo from the hospital was one of the most difficult things I ever had to do. Avo was not my blood, but she was family. She had taken care of me when I had nothing. The bread she gave me as a child kept my belly full and, as an adult, kept my soul joyful and curious. Her heart was one of pure determination mixed with mischief. Being around her made me happy to be alive. She always had a mission and when she had something on her mind, there was no stopping her.

As we settled into the flight, Jacinta only allowed the bag out of her grasp at the insistence of the flight attendant. With reluctance, she let them place it under the seat, where she could still see it.

"Jacinta, what do you know about Netuno?" Judith asked, trying to distract her from staring at the bag.

"I looked it up online and it's beautiful. I'm looking forward to seeing it in person. When we found out about Cristiano and Netuno, my dad and I spent some time looking at the images of the new inn at the vineyard. Being an architect, he gets really excited about design stuff. I just wanted to see where my brother hung out when he was growing up."

Then I saw a shift in her body.

"Where am I going to stay? At the inn? Or Avo's cottage? Oh, I'm sorry, I'm asking too many questions. Sometimes I talk too much."

Judith and I laughed.

"Jacinta, you're asking just the right number of questions," Judith said. The reassurance was just what she needed.

And I added, "I know we'll be able to find a room at the inn for you. Not sure if I can give you a full suite, but I think I might have something you'll like."

"I don't need anything fancy. I'm just happy to help."

"Jacinta, what are you going to do about school?" I asked, changing the subject.

"My parents agreed I could start my term online. My mom contacted the school and let them know I had to go away for a family emergency."

"Well, that's good news. Maggie, a friend of mine from Vancouver, Canada, is here with her son Tim. He is doing his schooling online as well. Maybe you two can study together?"

"I don't know, maybe?" she said tentatively. "How old is he?"

"Tim is eighteen. He's in his last year of school."

She laughed and relaxed back in her seat. "Thank goodness. I thought you wanted me to babysit."

"No, Tim can take care of himself." I paused and thought it best to let her know about CJ. "Tim's twin brother died recently. So, you might find he doesn't want to talk very much."

"Oh, I didn't put all the pieces together. That's right, the whole thing about Maggie's son. The blog had some stuff … that is horrible. I feel terrible. He lost a brother, and I found one," she mumbled to herself.

"Yes, there has been too much tragedy in all our lives."

"Well, maybe it's time for something good to happen then," Jacinta offered, putting a positive spin on things.

"I think you're right. Why don't you rest your eyes? I will make sure Avo's bag is safe."

Jacinta smiled and drifted off to sleep for the rest of the flight.

~

After the plane landed, we waited for Avo's body to be unloaded and then followed the vehicle to the crematorium. It was harder than I thought it would be, and doing it without Cristiano seemed wrong, but he was insistent. I was thankful he had gotten a hold of the priest at the hospital, and final prayers had been completed there. As they wheeled Avo's body into the crematorium, I tried to guide Jacinta back to Frances-co's SUV, but she resisted.

"I'm staying," she said, planting her feet firmly on the ground. "I promised my brother I would stay while they were cremating her, and I will not let him down."

"Jacinta, I can guarantee this is not what Cristiano intended when he asked you to take care of her." I tried to negotiate but could see her decision was set.

"I'm staying. I can do this. I'm strong."

I looked at Judith for some support, but Judith was silent.

"Okay, let's go in. But might I suggest we only stay for a little while. The process takes hours."

Jacinta looked over at Judith to see what she thought.

"Jacinta, I think Puro has a point. Let's go to the viewing room and when you're ready, we will go."

"Okay," she agreed, raising her chin up, trying to keep her tears from falling.

"You and Cristiano are far too alike to have been raised by different people; must be in the DNA," I said with a smile.

She chuckled as we walked into the crematorium and took our seats.

We waited for about thirty minutes and then they opened the drapes. My heart rate accelerated when I saw the furnace. I had never attended a cremation before.

"Jacinta, maybe we should go," I said, straining to keep myself calm. But Jacinta was resolute. She was not moving. Then, from a side door, an attendant appeared.

"Would someone from the family like to push the button?"

"The button?" Jacinta asked.

"To start the furnace. To start the cremation," he said calmly.

Judith gasped. This process was more complicated than I imagined. Cristiano would never have wanted his little sister to go through this.

"I've never heard of this before; offering family the option to push the button," I said with disfavor to the idea.

"It's something new we are trying. Being part of the process is quite natural for some cultures. But no pressure. I can take care of it for you."

"Jacinta, I think it's time to go," I said feeling uncomfortable.

"I agree, dear," Judith stepped in.

Jacinta ignored us both. "I'm family. She's my grandmother. It's my decision."

"Okay then, come with me. The rest of you can watch from here." The man said.

And there she went. After they placed Avo in the furnace and locked the door, Jacinta said a brief prayer, pushed the green button, then joined us in the viewing room. No one said a word. An hour into the process, I saw Judith wrinkle her nose and grab a tissue.

"It's time to go," she said, not leaving any room for discussion.

The drive to Netuno was one of silence and sadness. And when we finally arrived and saw the grape vines hugging the landscape, I let out a breath, knowing I was home.

As we walked into the lobby, Jacinta held Avo's bag like it had become fused to her body.

Maggie approached us at a slow pace. I had texted her, letting her know we had stayed for the first part of the cremation at Jacinta's insistence, but I was worried about the young woman, as she had fallen silent on the drive back.

"Jacinta," Judith said, giving her shoulder a squeeze. "Puro told you about our friend, Maggie. She is going to take you upstairs and get you settled into your room. You did great today; Cristiano and your parents would have been very proud of you."

Judith handed Jacinta over to Maggie and made a quick exit of her own, avoiding the barrage of hugs and questions that were heading towards her.

I watched Judith, Maggie, and Jacinta disappear, wishing I could find my own escape route.

"Have you heard anything about Maya?"

"How is Cristiano?"

"This whole situation is horrible."

"Is there anything we can do?"

"What happened to Avo?

The questions fell fast around me. I held up my hand asking for everyone to stop. "Please."

"Josie, could you go check with Gervais and Tim, see if they can rustle up some food for everyone and send some tea and a sandwich up to Judith?"

"I know what you're doing, Puro. Don't anyone say a word until I get back."

Carmo was standing behind the desk, observing me. "I'm okay dear."

"No, you're not. Go home, Dad. I'll make sure Jacinta is okay."

I nodded my head, too tired to disagree.

Maggie came down the stairs. "She's resting. She'll be down in a little while. In the meantime …" Maggie took my hand and led me out the door.

16

I'm Burning

Maya

WHEN I WOKE IN THE morning, splatters of dried blood lay next to me on my pillow. All I could do was pretend for a moment that the tightness I felt on my face and the ragged edges of open skin under my fingertips weren't real, that it was someone else's face which had been torn apart. When I heard the bolt slide across the door, I turned over, not sure who was coming in, but the boots dragging across the concrete gave him away.

"It appears a few people are poking around to find out where you are. I hope they are putting as much effort into finding the relic."

I sat up without turning around.

"Oh, come on Maya, give me a little peek. I saw the bandages on the ground by the door. Aren't you worried about infection?" he laughed like he had just told the funniest joke.

He stopped laughing the moment I turned around. I saw his body draw back slightly, so I leaned in, trying to increase the discomfort.

"Come on then, why don't you come closer and inspect your hand-iwork? You must be proud of all of this …" I waved my hand around my face, "Do you really think Cleopatra would approve? Just to recover her hair fork?"

"I don't think she would really care. She was quite a selfish creature, must run in the family." He smiled ever so slightly, then pursed his lips. "I can't look at you anymore. Saafa? Where are you? Cover her up. Her face is too distracting." He stood at the door. "I'll be back when you're more presentable."

"Maya," her voice and hand were gentle as she sat beside me. "Turn over, let me see. I'm sure it's not as bad as he said."

I covered my face, but not before I heard a little gasp escape. She tried to hide it, but her reaction was so natural. I could only assume Dakar had not been far off in his description.

"Saafa, where is the mirror?"

"No Maya, we should wait a few days."

"I need to see it now."

"I'm sorry, Maya."

"What are you sorry about? You did everything you could."

Saafa pulled the little mirror from her pocket and handed it to me.

Closing my eyes, I held the mirror up to my face, preparing myself for the carnage. When I opened them though, I did not recognize the person I saw in the reflection. I couldn't cry or get angry. The only reaction I had was overwhelming nausea; I literally made myself sick.

Saafa grabbed the bucket and held me as I retched again and again, my body trying to remove the image I had just seen in the mirror.

"Maya, it doesn't matter. You're the same person. Cristiano is going to love you no matter what. That's what you told me, right?"

"Saafa, I'm not sure love is enough to deal with this situation. Can you please leave me? I need to be alone."

"No, you don't. You need me to clean you up and then sit quietly with you. So that's what I'm going to do."

I didn't have the energy to fight her, so I let her stay. As she lay out some fresh bandages, she also pulled out a small jar.

"I brought a salve my mom used to make. The women in the neighborhood said it worked like magic and could heal almost anything."

"Have you ever tried it?"

"No." She looked down. "I refused to use it after seeing my brother cry like a baby. He said it stung really bad. On the bright side the gash on his forehead healed with almost no scar."

What could I do but try? As she applied the fragrant mixture to the wounds, I felt nothing at first, but then my skin warmed and began to prickle. The discomfort Saafa spoke about was starting, and I needed to distract myself, but all that came to me was painful memories.

"Mental Maya," I spat, trying to outthink the burning sensation.

"Pardon me?" Saafa asked with confusion.

I sucked in a breath. "Growing up, no one knew much about my mom, but when I hit middle school, rumors grew about her stay in the psychiatric hospital. When they found out she had gone for ECT treatment, I was a target for every crazy joke people could come up with; that's when they started calling me 'Mental Maya'."

"That's terrible, Maya. I'm sorry you had to go through that. I don't know much about ECT.

"Let's just say the movie version of electroconvulsive therapy is very different from real life. Truthfully, it helped her deal with her depression for a while." I sucked in a deep breath as my skin ignited in flames.

"Does it hurt?" Saafa asked.

"No, just a little warm on the wounds."

"You're lying. I can see it in your eyes. Please don't lie to me."

"Yes, it burns and yes, I can understand why your brother cried, but …"

"Keep going. Tell me more." Saafa squeezed my hand.

"When they started calling me Mental Maya, I wanted to curl up and die, but Beth, my friend, stood up for me and told me 'If people can't love you for who you are, then good riddance. You don't need them anyway.'" I smiled as I thought of Beth. "She dropped everything and came to Portugal to find me. That's friendship."

We sat for some time in silence as I breathed through the pain. When the worst of the burning was over, Saafa re-bandaged my face.

"Tell me more about Beth. You mentioned she is your best friend. What is that like? I have never had one."

I took a breath and blinked out the tears. "Beth treats me like what I say matters. We can laugh about nothing and cry over everything. We share secrets and stories and will love each other forever."

"Having a best friend sounds, amazing."

"One day, Saafa you'll meet someone and the two of you will click like two pieces of a puzzle coming together and before you know it you'll be tromping across Europe and staying in a youth hostel in Greece."

"Is that where you and Beth went?"

"No." I stopped talking as memories of my cancelled graduation trip pushed their way forward.

Saafa thankfully changed the subject. "Feeling better? Maybe putting it on the open wounds was not the best idea."

"If it works, it will be the best idea in the world and if it doesn't, at least we tried. Thank you, Saafa …" I smiled as the tingle faded to a buzz and then the pain disappeared leaving me with a small thread of hope which I tucked away deep in my heart.

17

Netuno Bound

Cristiano

I WAS RESTLESS AFTER PURO left, between worrying about Maya, saying goodbye to Avo, and wondering if I had done the right thing by sending my sister away, I was in knots. Jacinta said she was up for the task and Euphemia agreed, but Marcos was hesitant. It was not until later in the evening when I got a call from Carmo I was able to breathe a little easier.

"Cristiano. It's Carmo."

"Is everything okay? I haven't heard from Puro and was beginning to worry."

"Everything is fine. When they got back from the crematorium, everyone was exhausted. Maggie helped Jacinta get settled into her room and my dad went back to the house for a rest. Jacinta is a lovely girl. Quiet, but lovely."

"Quiet? Now you have me worried."

"Well, quiet at first. It was a big day. She had to make some grown-up decisions. It was difficult for all of them."

"I shouldn't have asked her."

"Cristiano, she'll be alright. My dad said she was amazing. She's stronger than you think. After she had a rest, she came bounding down the stairs and let me know she was going for a walk. I handed her a pair of pruners and she laughed. About an hour later, I wandered out to the fields and found her with Mateus. He was teaching her the best way to harvest. They stayed out until the sun went down, then meandered back, tired but content. There was this look on her face when she came through the door. It was like looking at you, but not you. I don't know. It feels good having her here." She paused. "I've missed you, Cristiano."

"You have?"

"Yes, I have. Don't be so dense. You are one of my closest friends and after you left to become a flight attendant and start jet setting around the globe, the old you never came back."

"I would hardly define doing seat belt checks and giving nervous flyers a rum and coke, jet setting."

"Well, I think we can both agree *you* never came back. A sleeker, cooler version would show up, and all I wondered was, where did *you* go?"

I stayed quiet as I listened to Carmo; somehow, I had let her down too. "I … I don't know what to say, except I'm sorry. Everything is so messed up right now."

A thoughtful pause filled our space.

"Cristiano, I never got a chance to say it, but I am so sorry about Avo and Maya too. How are you doing? I know it's a stupid question but I'm asking you all the same."

"It's not a stupid question. It's an honest one, because that's who you are, honest and kind and smart. Carmo, I can't believe I'll never see Avo again, and maybe Maya too." I held the tears back, but my voice was betraying me. "I need to come home, back to Netuno and pick grapes.

Everything seems to come into focus when you're picking grapes and right now, I need as much clarity as I can find."

She laughed. "I think it's a good idea. Bento and I fixed up the cottage and …"

"And what?"

"And we have a job waiting for you if you want."

"A job? I didn't know I was looking for a new career?"

"You don't need to make any decisions right now, but Bento and I want you and Maya to have options. Options that will keep you closer to home."

"I thought Sachi was the new owner."

"Sachi has asked us to make all the management decisions moving forward. I know you're going through a lot right now, with Maya and Avo and finding your family, but Netuno and the cottage are home and I know this is where Maya will want to start her life with you, *when* she is back. Because Cristiano, she is coming back. There's no room in your mind for anything else."

"You're right, Carmo."

"I am? Which parts?"

"Everything."

I hung up the phone with a mixture of peace and renewed determination. I had to believe that somehow, I would find Maya and bring her home.

⟣

The rest of the day was like sitting on pins and needles. Luca and Ravn worked with Sachi's father, trying to secure more details about where Maya was being kept in Morocco. I was ready to fly there by myself, but Luca talked me down, explaining how much worse I could make things if I arrived there without a plan. As the hours ticked away and tempers flared, Luca instructed everyone to stop for the night and we would look at the information with fresh eyes in the morning.

Jack stopped by the house to let me know he was heading back to Lisbon. He was worried about Mrs. Dutra with all the Ptolemite business going on. He'd been staying at my apartment for less than two weeks and somehow had won over Mrs. Dutra. She was still the fiercest gatekeeper a guy could ask for, always making sure my parent's apartment was ready for me when I returned from whatever trip I had taken.

"Maya told me you got off on the wrong foot with Mrs. Dutra. You two are talking now?"

"You know me, Cristiano, I can win over any woman with my Texas charm. Putty in my hands."

"She started bringing you food, didn't she?"

"Yes, you got me there, but when I invited her in to eat with me, well, we became fast friends."

He leaned in and hugged me goodbye, holding on just a second longer than I would have expected. Jack was never one to share his feelings, but his extended hug told me everything I needed to know.

After he left, I went back to my room. I was exhausted but my mind couldn't settle. My nerves bristled and I was worried about everything, including how I was going to deal with Pierre in the morning. A part of me knew Luca was right, Pierre's knowledge of the Ptolemites could help, but I wasn't ready to see him and I needed to go back to the cottage. Maybe if I was there, I could figure out where Avo put the package. There was nothing else I could do in Porto and if I stayed any longer, I was afraid Phillip might take care of what the Ptolemites did not. His fatherly pain was palpable and I could no longer bear it. I was sorry to leave Euphemia and Marcos, but I needed to be away from them too. I just needed a couple of days to think.

As I was packing the last of my things, Zef walked by my door.

"So, where are we going, brother?" he asked, filling in the frame. He was going to be taller than I was and, dare I say, even better-looking.

I laughed. "I was going to sneak out of here and head back to Netuno tonight, but you caught me."

Zef's face showed a mixture of hurt and annoyance. "Sneak out? Cristiano, you can leave whenever you want. You have a whole life outside of ours. If you don't want to be part of our family, that's your choice."

"What are you talking about?"

"I thought you were leaving because of the family. I'm sorry. I can be a jerk. Jump to conclusions. I thought—"

"You thought wrong, little brother. But don't worry. I have jumped to some conclusions in the last couple of weeks that got me into deep trouble. But no, you can't get rid of me that easy. I just need to go home. With Maya missing and Avo's death, I need to find my bearings and the only place I can do that is at the cottage. I also thought maybe I could figure out where Avo put the package, find the relic."

"That sounds like a good plan," Zef said quietly.

"What is it, Zef?"

"Do you … want some company? I'm pretty good at solving puzzles, even if our sister thinks I'm just a troublemaker."

My first reaction was to say no. I always thought I had to get through everything on my own, but when I looked at the creases in his young forehead there was only one answer.

"Yes, I would love it if you came along. You can stay at the cottage with me. I would like to hear more about the trouble you caused growing up. We can compare stories. Mind you, I have an extra ten years of troublemaking on you."

Zef took in a deep breath, and I could see the sheen in his eyes, letting me know what it meant to him to be asked. "Yeah, the cottage sounds good."

"Should we head down to Netuno to check in on Jacinta?" I asked.

"No, she'll be fine. We can go see her in the morning."

"Let me book another flight. Um, do you need me to talk to our parents?"

Zef laughed. "I'm eighteen, I make my own decisions now."

I smiled. He reminded me of myself. "Okay, I'll call a cab and meet you outside."

"You know our mother is going to follow us down there, right?"

I felt stunned when he referred to her as our mother. "No, really?"

"Oh, yes, she may let us go, but she won't like it."

"Do you think she would give us a couple of days to spend some time together?" I asked.

"I think Dad will help her see it's a good idea."

"Okay then, you talk to them, and I'll go downstairs to let everyone else know we're leaving."

⁕

"What do you mean, you're leaving?" Dalley yelled at me.

"Dalley, just like I said. I need a couple of days at the cottage to get my head on straight and I have to see if there is something you all missed when you were there."

"We went through everything; they went through everything," she continued to yell.

"Dalley, settle down!" Ravn said, trying to assert a little control in the situation. "That's enough, don't you think?"

"Don't tell me to settle down. And only I know when enough is enough!"

I looked at Ravn. "Luca has my number; you all have my number. If there is anything you need, call me."

"Unbelievable. We are busting our asses to find Maya and you're running away again."

The room froze. I imagined what Maya would do. Would she give Dalley a hug or a punch? I knew I couldn't do either, but a nudge in the right direction might work.

"Oh, Dalley, I know you can keep everyone in line."

"And what about Pierre?" she asked, trying to give me another reason to stay.

"What about him? I know he might be able to help, and I'm glad for that, but … well … I need to go. I believe the answers we're looking for are in Netuno."

Luca, who had been standing in the background, pulled me off to the side.

"Cristiano, are you sure you're ready to go back? No offence, but you look like crap. Please promise you'll call me before you do anything stupid."

"Yes Luca, I have to go, and yes, I promise nothing stupid without calling you first."

"Okay then, follow your instincts, and keep your phone charged. Things could change in a moment and if we find the relic, I have a feeling this Dakar character won't trust anyone but you to deliver it. Assume you are being watched and, most of all, be careful."

As I stepped out into the evening air and waited for my brother. Euphemia was on the balcony, waving. She was trying to smile but I could tell she had been crying. I felt horrible, but I had to go. As the taxi pulled up, Zef came running out of the house and I saw Marcos join Euphemia on the balcony.

The next words surprised me as they slipped from my lips, "I love you, mom and dad."

When we got in to the taxi, Zef laughed, "Well, I bought you two days with a sob story about wanting to spend time with my brother and your 'I love you' should give us an extra twenty-four hours before they descend upon Netuno."

18

Prisons

Maya

"Maya," Saafa whispered, rousing me from my restless sleep.

"What? Is everything okay?" I responded, my heart pounding in my chest.

"Yes, it's early. The sun's not up yet, but Dakar said I can take you for a walk in the garden before the rest of the house starts their morning prayers. One guard has to come with us, but he is not so bad."

"Okay, let's go," I said impatiently as I got up and took a few steps towards the door. For a moment I felt lightheaded but pushed it off with the thought of getting some fresh air.

"Wait, you can't go out without a headdress. Here, I brought you one of my hijabs and a very pretty neck scarf which I thought would look lovely on you."

"Thank you Saafa, that was so thoughtful. Do I need to cover my face completely?"

Saafa laughed a little. "I think we're okay in that department."

I reached up to the bandages and smiled.

"But no, most Muslim women here in Morocco don't do full face coverings, much to Dakar's dismay, so at least for now, no."

"We're in Morocco?"

Saafa paused for a moment confirming with a nod, then changed the subject back to Dakar.

"He calls himself a Ptolemite, claiming the blood of Cleopatra, but also asserts himself to be Muslim, picking and choosing which history and set of rules suits him best in the moment.

When I was first brought here, he told me to switch to a full face covering, but I told him 'no'. It cost me a black eye, but it was worth it. After he hit me, he just laughed and told me to wait until we got to Egypt. At least while I am still here, I have a voice."

"And if you were in Egypt?"

"Far less voice, one might say."

❧

When we stepped outside, it was like a different world. I could see the night hues in the sky changing colors ever so slightly and it reminded me of the morning I watched the sunrise on the veranda at Netuno. I sighed, not sure if I would ever see it again. So, I drank in every beautiful color in the sunrise, while I still had one to watch.

As the day's light hovered just below the horizon, the thought of going back into the dank, musty basement made me nauseous. I tried to take in a few deep breaths, but I still felt sick.

"Maya, are you all right? You don't look well."

"I'm fine. Just getting used to what clean air smells like again."

Saafa said nothing else as we strolled in the beautifully kept garden, stopping and drinking in the fragrant flowers.

"Can I pick a few for my room?"

Saafa turned to the guard, who shrugged his shoulders, and smiled at her.

Although just sixteen, she had a mature face and uniquely shaped violet eyes, which highlighted her perfect skin. She was stunning. I reached up to my bandages and touched my face, wondering if *he* would ever see me as beautiful again.

"Maya, it will heal."

"Heal, yes. Ever be the same, no."

As we began picking flowers, the sun broke over the top of the building and the melodic prayers of thousands of Muslims across the country began.

Smiling faintly, the guard gestured for the two of us to head back towards the villa. "Saafa, it was good to see you today, but Dakar will be out soon. I hope you enjoyed your walk."

"Thank you, we did." Saafa gave my arm a squeeze as she walked me back to my room.

"Thank you, Saafa."

"For what?"

"I know the garden walk wasn't Dakar's idea."

"You're right, but I'm smart enough to make him think it was."

We both laughed and headed inside.

Having to go back into my cell was harder than I thought it would be. But it also made me realize that no matter what happened, I was going to find a way out. I could not stay there for another week or I would certainly lose my mind and I was not ready to earn the title of Mental Maya, not yet anyway.

"How long do you think I should leave this set of bandages on for, Saafa?" I asked, reaching to my face.

"Oh, I think we need to wait at least another week."

Whatever peace I had felt out in the garden was instantly lost. "Saafa, I'm going to rest."

"Okay, Maya," she said, looking distressed. "I'll bring your breakfast in a couple of hours."

I lay down on the cot and tried to stop thinking about my face, tried to recall those few days of happiness Cristiano and I had after our wedding. And it worked momentarily but after the happiness came the next string of memories about the call from my father, the windshield shattering, Cristiano pinned to the seat by the steering wheel, and there I was, right back in my dank hole of suffering. The tears fell and my hand scribed my invisible words in my imaginary journal.

In my own little prison,

My heart keeps going back to those days after my almost-wedding to Steven, when I would sit in the gazebo with a cup of tea. I barely remember getting up and going to work for those few months, but I remember sitting in the garden, watching the season change from spring to summer. The more I think about it, the more I think they were right. I didn't want to admit it but depression had been knocking on my door for a long time, lurking around the edges, always lurking. I wonder if I stop fighting would it just come for a visit and then leave me alone? Or would it decide to stay forever? I don't want to be my mother, always fighting, always pushing it off. Maybe there is hope though? Look at her, she has found a way back to happiness. But right now, I'm not sure I have the strength to fight back.

My hand unfurled and the invisible words disappeared except in some deep corner of my mind. Fight or give in. I would fight to get out, but when it was over, I didn't know what I would have left.

My dad was right, legally I wasn't married to him, and there was nothing keeping us together. I'm not sure what kind of joke God was playing, but I thought it was a cruel one and wondered if it was time to be done with God because bringing him back into my life only appeared to be causing more pain.

"Do you hear that God? I'm thinking about firing you. No severance package or anything."

"Firing God?" I heard her ask.

"Saafa?" I sat up to see her standing quietly in the room.

"Yes, I came back to see you. I was worried."

I smiled. "Thank you."

Saafa sat on the edge of the bed staring up at the window which cast a shaft of morning light into the room.

"Saafa, what did you mean you are as much a prisoner here as I am?"

"Hm, no one has ever asked me that."

"Well then, tell me. How did you end up here with Dakar?" I could see her hesitate. "Please, I would like to know."

And so, she began telling me her heart-breaking story of growing up in Morocco. Of a good life with her parents and older brother and how all that changed the day her brother died. Her brother was a pilot in the Moroccan Royal Air Force and tragically died in a training accident. After his death, her parents were never the same.

In an instant, his death snuffed out their family joy. Her parents stopped working, and she took over their stand at the local flower market. Then one morning, when she woke, they didn't. Their grief had won, and they followed her brother into death.

"They could not continue, not even for me. Their grief consumed them; they left me with no one," she shared. Saafa stood up and began to pace. "I remember the morning I found them dead. At first, I tried to wake them, shake them back to life, but they were already cool to the touch. I was alone, but I knew I had to push past the pain and take care of their bodies—their souls. Twenty-four hours was the time I had to prepare for their burials. I pulled out the burial sheets from the closet— my mother was always prepared," she said, smiling and remembering a relationship of love and admiration, "and began cleansing her body. With my father, I knew I could not do it myself, so I knocked on our neighbor's door and asked her husband. She did not like me, as she knew I had been working in the market and it was against what she believed, but she kept her thoughts to herself and offered me a chair to sit on while her husband prepared my father's body. When he returned, she shooed me out of the house. The next time I saw my father, he was shrouded in white. I looked at their bodies, paralyzed about what to do next, so I left.

"You left?"

"Yes, I put on my white garments to mark that there had been a death in the family and I went to work. I was only fifteen, I didn't know what to do with the bodies, but I knew if I did not get to the market by a certain time, I would miss my best customers, and I could not risk losing them to all the other flower vendors. I knew enough that somehow, I had to take care of things. I had to take care of me."

"How? How did you do all that without falling apart?"

"My faith, and because I had to. I know few Western people believe in God anymore, but for me it is my only path. It is what keeps me alive and helps me find some kind of peace, even here."

I didn't want to talk about God anymore, as I was mad at him and hearing that someone else had a good relationship with him frustrated me, so I changed the subject.

"Didn't the authorities ask questions? What did you do with the bodies?"

She shook her head and smiled sadly. "No, no one asked anything. Dakar took care of it all."

"Dakar?"

"Yes, Dakar had been buying flowers from me on an off for several months after my brother died. I didn't know who he was then, and he never talked to me until that day. I tried to control my emotions when he asked me about my white garments; I cried. He offered to help with the burial and took care of everything else I didn't know how to do. He asked all the right questions, and I told him the truth: that I had no one. That was when he expressed concern that I should not be living alone and he asked me to come and stay here. He said he would sell the flower stand and my house and give me the money. He promised me a lot of things and in my grief and confusion, I said yes to all of them. Then came the day he wanted me to cover my face with the niqab. When I said no, he hit me, and I knew my life would never be mine again. I should never have gone with him that day.

"Saafa, you were in shock. He took advantage of that. I will get you out of here."

"Well, it had better be soon, as he has promised me to someone, and I will have to marry him on my seventeenth birthday."

"He's going to force you to marry someone?"

"Yes, the laws here in Morocco say I have to be eighteen to marry, but with a judge's order, a parent or guardian can insist I marry before that age."

Words failed me as I stared at Saafa, thinking about the freedoms I had taken for granted all my life.

19

Brothers

Cristiano

As we drove to the airport, Zef told stories about growing up in Porto and some of the crazy things he did to get our parents' attention over the years.

"I was not the most diligent student and rarely listened to them. Let's put it this way: if I wasn't grounded, I was doing something that would get me grounded."

"Why? No offence, but you seem much smarter than that," I offered.

"Last year I straightened up a bit, stopped being such a jerk." He paused. "Life with our mom and dad was not always easy. I think I understand better now." He looked at me and smiled. "It makes sense. Mom never got over giving you away and dad felt like it was his fault. He does that you know, takes on the weight of the world and thinks he can solve it."

I laughed. "Yes, I understand. He and I are more alike than I thought."

"You think?" Zef laughed.

I stopped for a second. "Does it bother you? That I'm here? That he and I look alike? That …"

"Cristiano …" He leaned over and pretended to punch me. "Now you're acting like our mother—stop worrying and just be my brother and we'll be okay."

⁂

The flight to Lisbon was short and I could tell Zef was excited.

"So, tell me about Netuno," he said, switching the subject again.

"Well, truthfully, it is quite amazing. When I was growing up, it was just the vineyard, but the brothers who owned it built the inn and retreat center on the property recently. The goal was to create a destination where people could come to rest, learn, and create. It is beautiful."

"How are we going to get there?"

"Oh, I've taken care of that," I grinned.

As we walked out to the curb, Francesco's stretch limo came driving up.

"We're going in that?" Zef asked.

"What, not big enough for you?" I teased.

Francesco came running toward me with open arms and worry on his face. "Oh, Puro and Judith told me what happened. I am so sorry. And you, you look terrible, Cristiano, and Avo …"

"Thank you," I stopped him before he could go any further. Somehow, those few hours alone with my brother had given me a much-needed reprieve from my worries, but when Francesco mentioned Avo, I was flooded with guilt and regret and wondered if I was ready to go to the cottage. "Francesco, this is my brother, Zef."

"Zef, it's late, maybe we should hold off on going to the cottage tonight, we can go to my apartment in town and head out in the morning."

"Fresh clothes and a shower? That sounds great. Wait, isn't Jack there?" Zef asked with a clearer head than me.

"Yes, I forgot." I paused. "You know, Zef, one day you can come and stay at the apartment here in town if you like."

"That sounds awesome but let's not mention that to mom quite yet."

"Deal. Hey Francesco, let's skip the apartment and head straight to the cottage."

"Do you want to stop by Netuno first?" Francesco asked.

My stomach went into knots at the thought of seeing Netuno again. My life fell apart the last time I was there, when I jumped to a conclusion that resulted in the woman I love being taken from me. Maya's kidnapping had caused a desperation to seep into my bones and I was not ready to face that yet.

"No, Francesco. Let's go straight to the cottage."

"You know our sister is going to be mad at us for going there without her," Zef said.

"I'm sure she'll understand."

"Oh, man do you have a lot to learn about our sister."

"Then I'm glad I have a younger brother to deflect the punches."

"To the cottage then?" Francesco asked.

"Yes, take us home."

❧

Zef dozed off on the drive, forcing me to deal with a flood of memories that had been crashing up against me since we touched down. The first one that surfaced was the day Avo taught me to make her magic bread; the day I found out about my parents' death. Avo loved me for who I was, asking nothing from me but an unspoken promise to do my best, to love as she loved, without judgement. I felt like I'd failed her.

The cottage was dark when we arrived, no lights greeting me like before.

I nudged Zef.

"What? Are we here already?" he asked.

I chuckled as he shook his doze off and climbed out of the vehicle.

"This place is so cool."

"Yeah, it is."

"You spent your whole life here?"

"Almost."

"Cristiano, you ready to go in?"

I paused at the front door. My heart squeezed tightly in my chest as I thought about the cottage without Avo. "Yes, I'm ready."

Zef stood with his pack on his shoulder. "So, what do we do now?"

I smiled. "We bake."

20

Tears to Cheers

Cristiano

THE SUN WAS BREAKING OVER the horizon when we took the last of the loaves out of the oven.

"I'm beat, Cristiano, I can hardly keep my eyes open. Who knew baking could be such hard work?"

Avo would have been happy to see Zef and I baking together. "Go have a nap. After that, we'll walk over to Netuno, see our little sister, and share our bread."

"Thank you, Zef."

"Thank you for what?"

"For baking with me last night."

"That's what brothers are for, right?"

We left the loaves to cool outside and stepped into the cottage. Although clean and tidy, the absence of the laughter jars left a deep sadness in my heart. Zef crashed on the couch and I made my way up to my room. When I walked in, I barely recognized it. A queen-size bed had replaced my twin. There was new lighting, and there were some framed photographs on the wall surely gifted by Gervais. On the pillow was a note.

Hi Cristiano, I got a call a couple of days ago that there was a delivery for Avo. She was one step ahead of you again, as she had ordered some new furniture, expecting your return after the wedding. You owe us. We had to pay the delivery guys extra for getting this bed up the stairs. Hope you like it. I'm sorry about the laughter jars. I know they were Avo's pride and joy. Everyone here at Netuno contributed something to help fix the place up and make the cottage feel like home.

Love, Carmo, Bento, and everyone else.

I fell on to the bed and whatever tears I was holding escaped into the new pillows.

Maya

I wasn't sure where the tears came from, but they fell fast and hard. I knew they weren't mine and if they belonged to him, I'd let them fall if needed.

~

Cristiano

Zef's knock on the door startled me out of a deep sleep. The kind of sleep that consumes you and never wants to let go.

"Cristiano? Are you awake? I think we should probably go. There's nothing to eat but the bread we baked and I need some protein. I'm starving."

I shook the fog from my head. "Yeah, Zef. I'll be down in a minute. When we get to the inn, you can have anything you like."

"I had a shower, not sure there is much hot water left."

I laughed, knowing I would have to fix that for when Maya came home. She took the longest showers of anyone I had ever known, but it made her happy and I would do anything to make her happy again. My heart lurched forward, fighting the "if" or "when" scenario that battled in my brain.

"No problem, Avo never let me take showers for more than a few minutes, anyway."

"A few minutes?"

"Oh, there are a lot of stories about my growing up here I could share."

When I came downstairs, the kitchen was too quiet without Avo. Zef had folded the blanket and placed it neatly back on the couch. You can tell a lot about a person by how they take care of the details and Zef was a details guy. I walked outside and saw he had found the bread bags and wrapped the loaves. They were ready to go and so was he. He looked a little anxious, and I wasn't sure why.

"Zef, is there something on your mind?"

"I'm a little worried about our sister."

"I wouldn't worry too much. She's well looked-after."

"I'm sure. I just need to see her."

"Do you want me to call? Avo has a landline inside—I'm sure you noticed; cell service is very sketchy out this way."

"And ruin the surprise?" Zef said.

"I have a feeling there is no surprise. Francesco is not great at keeping secrets, and we didn't ask him to. I imagine he called Puro last night to let him know we arrived safely, not to mention that our mother probably called your sister this morning. We had better start walking. It's about forty minutes from here to Netuno; twenty-five if we pick up the pace."

I tried to lift the bread over my shoulder but winced in pain.

"Here, let me take that for you." Zef offered. "What good am I if I can't help my big brother when he needs it?" With bread slung over his shoulder, we made our way to Netuno.

We walked silently for about twenty-five minutes until I heard his intake of breath.

"Tell me, what was it like growing up here in the country, away from everything?" Zef asked.

"Growing up out here was the best part of my life. I spent the first few years at the cottage with my parents and Avo and then moved into the city when I started school. After they died, I moved here permanently."

"What was that like?"

"The moving or them dying?"

"When your parents died."

I paused, not sure how to answer at first.

"I'm sorry, that was rude."

"No, not rude, a little direct, but that's okay." I paused for a moment, thinking about his question. "I missed them every day. It was not until I went to Egypt and stood where they died that I felt like I could finally let them rest. It was a long twenty years. Truthfully, I'm not sure I could ever go through anything like that again. A part of me feels selfish but if anything happens to Maya, I am not sure how I could keep …"

"We will find the relic and you will bring her home." Zef said the statement with such resolution I believed him.

"Hey, you want to run the rest of the way?" I asked.

"Are you sure?" The smile on his face answered my question.

"Sometimes you have to push through the pain and create the fun around you."

Zef stopped running when we hit the crest of the hill and looked out over the entire valley.

"Wow! It looks different than I imagined."

"I know, right?"

"Race you?" Zef called out to me as he took off down the hill with the sack of bread flopping on his back.

I took a breath, feeling guilty about the momentary happiness, and then I heard her voice, *Run.* So, I listened, or at least tried to until my body made me stop. I watched Zef as he collapsed on Netuno's steps and our sister came running out of the inn, hugging him and then punching him in the gut.

"Cristiano, I could have sent a car to pick you up. You are not well enough to do that walk," Puro scolded me.

"Yes, well, here I am, Puro, and I'm fine. The walk did me good. It was humbling to watch my little brother outrun me. Mind you," I looked over at Zef. "at least I can out surf you."

"Not for long." He raised an eyebrow challenging me. "Can you teach me that, too?"

"Mom won't like that, Zef. You know how she gets." Jacinta added with a sour face.

"What? Our dad surfed. Our brother surfs. It runs in the family. Anyway, mom married a surfer. What did she expect to happen?"

I was happy for a minute, then Judith walked on to the veranda and my heart seized as if I could feel her pain.

Judith tried to smile. "Maya would love this—will love this." She walked down the stairs and gave me a hug, then whispered in my ear, "Maya loves you."

I hugged her back.

"Well, look who decided to show up." Carmo took over where Judith left off.

In quiet tones, she spoke to me, "I thought we lost you. Don't scare me like that. Remember: you may have a new family but, we're family too."

"I know. I may not have been acting like it for these last few years, but I know."

"Well then, you need to help us celebrate. Bento and I had an idea, and we hoped you would agree. Since our wedding was *interrupted,* I thought maybe we could throw something together that was a little less formal and a whole lot more fun. I promised him we would not go ahead if you thought it was inappropriate, but truthfully, I think Maya would love it."

Bento stepped out on to the veranda, "Oh Carmo, just tell him already."

"A grape stomp wedding!"

"A grape stomp wedding? We haven't done a grape stomp in years; didn't Branca ban it?"

Carmo looked at Bento. "Branca is irrelevant now."

"Cristiano, a lot happened after you left," Bento said.

"Yes, that's what people keep telling me. I may need a few more details."

"I think you are going to like this update." Carmo paused. "Reinaldo is divorcing Branca."

"A divorce?" I asked, knowing how much being married meant to Reinaldo.

"Yes, not sure what Maya told you about the attempted takeover, but in short, Branca threw her hat into the ring with the Axelines over a year ago and tried to take Netuno down. Reinaldo refuses to talk to her and shipped all her things to her mother's house in Spain. The extra bonus is that when she found out Bento and I were getting married, she almost lost her mind. The messages she left were rather colorful. I just want to get married before anything else happens."

"Of course, and I think a grape stomp wedding is wonderful. Maya would love it. What do you need to do to get ready?"

"We still have all the vats in one of the storage units. And we have a fresh harvest of tempranillo picked and ready to be stomped. Your sister has been such a big help. She is delightful. Everyone is excited about getting started."

"Everyone?" I asked.

"The brothers believe even an excellent grape can be improved when you stomp some joy into it. And I think we all need a little joy right now."

"You're right. Maya is going to be so sad she missed it."

"The wedding? Or the grape stomp?"

"Both."

"I know she'll be back in time for the second stomp of the season and, with any luck, maybe we could have another wedding?" She smiled mischievously.

I froze, thinking the worst, wondering if we would ever have the chance to marry legally.

Carmo had a gift of reading my body language and picked up on my thoughts.

"Don't go there, Cristiano. You are not allowed the luxury to imagine anything but the best. She is coming home to you. Besides, I like you much better with Maya in your life. You will find the relic, and you will bring her home," Carmo stated.

My heart shook as she spoke with such certainty. "You're right, Carmo, about everything. So, when is this all taking place?"

"Tonight!"

"Tonight? What if I had said no?"

"I would have had to change your mind."

"So, what's first? The wedding or the stomp?

21

The Price of Freedom

Maya

Between the itchy face and strange knot in my stomach, I was too upset to eat. But it wasn't until I heard an unpleasantly familiar screech in the hall when my day got much worse.

"Open it!" I heard her yell at the guard.

Speculating that a person could do horrible things and knowing they have, are two very different things but when the bolt slid across the door and she walked into my dank hole, the strength and courage I hoped for, never showed up.

Jade recoiled when she saw my bandaged face, instinctually I threw my hands up but there was no hiding it. My bandages weren't even off yet, and I was hideous.

"Maya? Is that you under all that gauze?" she asked in her acidic tone.

I looked at her perfectly beautiful face and a part of me collapsed like a delicate house of cards.

"No, Jade, that Maya is gone. You made sure of that."

"Don't be so dramatic, I'm sure it's not that bad, and if it is, at least one more good-looking man will be released back into the pool. Oh," she laughed, "you thought he would take you back like this? You're joking, right? Men are fickle creatures. You were tolerable to look at before, but oh my God, Maya, be realistic."

My shoulders sagged. I kept standing, but my knees were giving way.

"That's right. Now you're getting it. I'm the winner here. You're the loser."

I could feel myself losing balance. Before I knew it, Saafa came blasting in, pushing Jade to the floor.

"Stay away from her," Saafa growled at Jade and caught me before I fell. "You are evil; pure and utter evil."

"You'll pay for that, you little bitch," Jade yelled at Saafa and scurried out of the room like the rat she was.

Although Saafa spoke, all I could hear was Jade's voice. *Men are fickle. You thought he would take you back like this?* and then she laughed.

I lay down and blocked out any thoughts of seeing Cristiano again. We weren't married. He would be free to move on. Who was I joking? He and I only met a month ago. I saved him from himself and now I had to save him from me. I needed a plan to escape from Dakar and my future with Cristiano.

Jade

When I got back to my room, Dakar was sitting, waiting for me.

"Where were you?" he barked at me.

"What? I can't go for a walk? Leave me alone."

"Yes, you can, but you need to ask for my permission first."

"I don't ask for any man's permission for anything. I take what I want, when I want it."

"Oh, dear Jade, that is where you're wrong. I looked into your situation, and you are in quite a bind. Fired by your father, cut off from all your funds. I will solve that for you. When I am done here, you are coming back to Egypt with me, and I will take care of you."

"Go to hell, Dakar. I am not going anywhere with you. Actually, I'm done with this place. I'm leaving today."

"Oh, Jade, and yet again, wrong. You're not going anywhere."

Dakar grabbed my face and squeezed so tightly I could feel his fingers pressing against my molars. Then he began whispering in my ear, "What a beautiful face. It would be so unfortunate if anything happened to it. Oh, how is Maya, by the way? Such a shame." He laughed, "Don't worry Jade, nothing is going to happen to that stunning face as long as you do what I say. It's worth far more to me in one piece than you could imagine."

Dakar laughed and as he left I heard the deadbolt slide through the locking chamber. I needed to find another way out and soon.

Maya

Saafa sat with me.

"Maya, what do you need?"

"I need to leave here, but I can't go home. Even if Cristiano finds the relic and gets me out, I can't go with him. He'll try to be noble and take me back, scarred and literally defaced, but how could he love me like this? I cannot ask that of him. Please help me."

Saafa tried to convince me I needed to go back to Cristiano, but I had made my decision. He deserved more than a broken me. I knew I had to leave and find a place to disappear.

So, Saafa and I created a plan. Our success would depend on Dakar's blind need for the relic and Cristiano's ability to assess the situation and not overreact. Only time would tell who would win, as we were putting our lives in the hands of good and evil. By the time Cristiano had read the letter and discovered it was Saafa and not me at the exchange, I would be gone. I knew he'd do the right thing.

Saafa was very resourceful and got me everything I needed for my journey. I didn't know if trading places at the exchange would work, and if he would accept my choice to leave, but I had to try. And I could only hope one day he might move on.

I told myself I was doing it because I loved him, but most of it was my fear. The fear of seeing that first reaction and never knowing if he was with me out of pity or because he loved me, scars and all.

As the plan came together my nerves bristled. The clothes Saafa gathered would allow me to fit in on the street in Morocco once I escaped from the compound and before I headed out on the next phase of my journey. Our plan was for both of us to dress in the niqab on the compound so Dakar would see us wearing it, and when the time came and Cristiano arrived, Saafa and I would exchange clothing; she would go in my place, and I would disappear. We would both be free.

22

Unexpected Moments

Cristiano

"She's not picking up, Cristiano. That's not like our mom."

"Maybe they needed some alone time," I offered.

"That's just gross."

I laughed, remembering he was still only eighteen. "That's not what I'm talking about. Maybe after you called her earlier today, our parents went for a walk and left her phone behind."

"I guess that's possible, they love to walk," he said, breathing out, but not completely.

After hearing the concern in Zef's voice I discreetly called Luca to check in and see if everything was alright. When he answered, it sounded like he was on the road.

"Hey Cristiano, is everything okay?" Luca asked with his own worried tone.

"Yes, I was just about to ask you the same thing."

He exhaled, then chuckled. "Yes, yes, I didn't want to call you until things were certain," my stomach dropped.

"What? What is it?"

"No, Cristiano. We didn't find her yet, but I decided to move the operation down to Netuno. I spoke with Puro, and he said we could use one of the spare rooms to set up there. In my experience, it is always better to have family and friends closer when they are going through something like this."

"What do you mean, family and friends?"

"We'll all be there shortly. Everyone took an early flight; we arrived in Lisbon about an hour ago."

"Everyone is coming here?"

"Yes, things were getting awkward between your father and Maya's dad. There was a scuffle again; no punches thrown but it was close. I thought it best Phillip be near Judith. She has a calming effect on him. Anyway, they're on their way. Ravn and Dalley and Beth are here with me."

"Did you miss me?" I heard Dalley yell in the background, sounding like she'd had one too many drinks on the short flight.

"How are you doing? Did anything pop up?" Luca asked, fishing for answers I did not have.

"We saw each other only twenty-four hours ago, but I'm managing. I feel like crap, and my wife is still missing, but besides that …"

"Cristiano; I mean … the cottage. Did you get a chance to look around a little more?"

"Always working, hey? But no. As far as the cottage, I went through every cupboard, closet, and hiding space I could remember, but no package."

"I'm sorry, I hoped we missed something."

"No, all I found was a home filled with old memories. If you'll excuse me, I better let my sister know our parents are on their way."

When I got off the phone, Zef looked like he had just eaten something bad. "What? They're coming here already? I can't believe it."

"You called it, when you said two, maybe three days before you thought they would come down."

"I didn't think she would actually do it. Mom swore she would never come back to the area again after what her parents did to her; they live close by."

"What happened?"

Looking down on the ground, Zef began. "They disowned her after she left with Dad. I'm not sure they know we exist, except for you, of course."

An irrational anger emerged. I felt instantly protective of Euphemia and wanted nothing from the people who rejected us both, "Well, they made their choice to kick our mother out of their lives. I don't have any time for people like that."

"I know, but maybe they've changed." I saw a flash of something behind his eyes. "Forget it. It was just a thought," he said.

"No, you're right, Zef," I paused, realizing I may have sounded too harsh, "maybe they have changed, but the decision to reach out to them needs to be hers alone. What about dad's parents?" I asked awkwardly.

"After he left with mom both of his parents passed away without ever talking to him again. I only know about their deaths because I heard Mom asking him if he wanted to go to his dad's funeral as he had missed his mom's. I don't think he went."

Zef stopped and shoved his hands into his jean pockets "Hey, can I stay with you at the cottage over the next couple of days? I came down here to get away from them for a bit, and here they are again."

"Zef!"

"Yeah, I know," he said, rolling his eyes. "But I've had to deal with them and their crazy moods my whole life."

"They're not crazy, just concerned. But sure, I think it would be good."

"Who should tell Jacinta?" he asked, obviously hoping I would take on the task.

"About staying at the cottage or our parents arriving within the hour? Don't worry, I'll take care of both."

"Good, because Jacinta is acting strange. When she saw me, she barely said two words. I think she's out picking grapes with Maggie's son, Tim. She seems to talk to *him* with no problem."

"Just give her some space, her world is upside down."

"Yeah, Carmo said yesterday, after the funeral home dropped Avo's ashes off, Jacinta took them to her room, insisting it was her job to keep Avo safe. Carmo let her know she could take care of the urn, but Jacinta insisted."

"I shouldn't have asked her to look after Avo for me. It was too much," I said.

"Cristiano, I don't think it was too much, just a lot. She's strong like our mom."

"Thanks, Zef, I'll find her and let her know."

∾

As I walked out into the fields, I could smell the grapes ripening and admired the perfection of each bunch as it hung on the vine. Loving Maya with my whole heart left me defenseless and now I had an entire family to be concerned about.

"Is it worth it?" I asked myself out loud.

"Is what worth it?" A voice popped up on the other side of the row.

"Oh, hi, Jacinta, I was looking for you."

"Really? Is there news about Maya?"

"No, not directly about Maya, but I spoke with Luca, and he is moving the command center from Porto to Netuno." I paused. "I also wanted to let you know everyone has come with him."

"What do you mean, everyone?" she asked, peeking through the vines.

"I mean, everyone at your place in Porto is coming to Netuno, including our parents."

Jacinta slid down onto the dirt, facing me through the vines. I could see her, but I couldn't hug her, so I held out my hand.

She took it, smiling.

"Although you look like dad, your personality is like mom's. Quiet, thinking, keeping yourself just one step removed, but kind, with a heart that is ready to jump but hasn't quite decided what direction."

"That's how you see me?" I asked, squeezing her hand.

"So far."

"You and Avo are more alike than I thought."

"We're alike?" she asked with a rush of excitement in her voice.

"Yes!"

"I pushed the green button," she blurted.

"The green button?" I asked with confusion.

"I had to. It was my job." And her tears fell.

"Stand up and walk with me." We moved side by side down the row until we found an opening, and then I took her into my arms. "This is me jumping in the right direction." She hugged me back and cried. "Tell me about the green button."

She hesitated. "When we were at the crematorium, the guy came out and asked if anyone wanted to push the button."

"Did you know what the button was going to do?"

She shook her head. "Kind of, but not really."

My stomach dropped. "Tell me more."

"Not a lot to tell, but I'll try. Puro and Mrs. Wells didn't want me to go in, but I felt like I had to. I didn't want Avo to be alone."

Sucking in a breath as she told the story, I tried to hold the tears back, but I couldn't. So I let them fall. "I'm sorry, Jacinta, that was too much."

She shrugged her shoulders, "Maybe a little, but we didn't stay for the whole thing. It started to smell, if you know what I mean."

An unexpected bark of laughter broke free from both of us.

"Judith got us out of there pretty quick."

"That is awful," I said, still trying to imagine her pushing the button and igniting the furnace.

"Just one thing, Cristiano."

"What is it?"

"When mom and dad die, I don't ever want to do that again."

"Jacinta, I promise you no one will ever ask you to push the green button again in your life."

"I'm glad it was me and not Zef. He would have puked all over the place. He is sensitive to smells. It was weird," she segued back to the conversation, "but I think Avo would have thought it was funny."

She looked brighter after sharing her story. "I love you, Jacinta. You are the best sister a new big brother could ask for."

Then I saw the teenager pop out. "So, are they really coming here?"

"Yes, they're on their way right now."

"How long do I have without them?"

"I would say maybe an hour."

"Well then, I'm going to find Tim and have some fun while I still can."

She ran off, leaving me with the brotherly question of "What did she mean by fun?"

"Jacinta??" I yelled after her. She waved her hand at me, without turning around, and disappeared between the grapes.

"Cristiano?" I heard her yell.

"Yes, Jacinta, what is it?"

"Yes."

"Yes, what?"

"Yes, you dummy. Loving someone is worth everything—love you, brother," she yelled and then was gone.

I stood between the vines, knowing something important had just happened, but how could I feel a moment of peace when the woman I love was in peril?

So I walked, taking the peace I felt and imagining Maya beside me, fingers woven together as we found our way through the forest. In my mind we whispered to each other and exchanged quiet glances as we let nature take us on a journey. I saw us standing at the front doors of Netuno's chapel and walking in together. I picked up my old guitar and played. The music bounced off the stone walls, filling the space with love and comfort and Maya lit the candles. At one point, she turned and offered me the flaming stick, only giving me a moment to decide who I wanted to pray for.

Closing my eyes, I tried to keep hold of Maya's smiling image, but all I could hear was the crack on her cheek and the crumple of her body when she fell to the ground during our call. When I opened my eyes, I found myself standing on the familiar path I had walked for so many years with Avo. Something or someone led me to the chapel because I needed to be there. I hesitated for a moment, then entered.

When I walked through the door, a part of me hoped the candles would be lit and Avo would be there, waiting for me, but all I found was stillness. So, I sat, and then I kneeled, and then I prayed. I talked to God about Avo, my parents and Maya, and then I waited. For what? I wasn't sure. I thought about the first moment I felt Maya's hand on my shoulder in Egypt, when she said yes to being my wife, when we made love for the first time and the second; that red button flying into the air and Avo's instructions to find her, to love her.

Jacinta

Tim and I met up in the vines after I had my big cry with Cristiano.

"Where were you, Jacinta?" Tim asked with some concern.

"Oh, my brother found me and I had a mini meltdown."

"Which one?" he smiled.

"Yeah, right? Now I have two brothers; I thought one was trouble. You want one?" I froze, realizing what I had just said. "Oh crap, that's horrible. I'm sorry."

Tim smiled at my insensitive remark. "No need for sorry. Just because my brother's dead doesn't mean I don't have a brother anymore; it just means he's not here. I have to believe he's somewhere out there, though. We didn't really do the God thing growing up, but ever since my dad died, it is something I have thought about. And now with CJ gone, well, I believe a part of him is still with me. I couldn't go on living if he wasn't."

I didn't know what else to say so I changed the subject.

"This whole thing is a little weird don't you think?" I asked.

"Yes, I would agree this is not a typical summer but I'm glad I met you."

"Really?"

"Yes, you're easy to talk to." He laughed. "Truth is, I just feel comfortable with you. It feels like you understand everything."

"Not sure about everything but I am trying to get my head wrapped around the emergence of my long-lost brother, Maya's kidnapping, and the fact that we are all searching for Cleopatra's hair fork."

We both laughed. "Throw in that my Avo, who I only knew for forty-eight hours, is sitting in a jar on my bedside table, then yes, I would agree this has not been a typical summer." The laughter continued until my stomach ached. I reached out to touch his hand, and he pulled away. The laughter stopped.

"I'm sorry, I was just … I thought that …"

"Oh Jacinta, I'm not … Oh, I'm sorry if I gave you the wrong impression."

"What impression would that be?" I asked.

"That I liked you, like *that*. I can only be friends."

"Tim, I *know*," I smiled and punched him in the arm.

"You know what?" he asked, fishing a bit.

"Okay, if I'm wrong, please don't let it offend you."

"Now you have me very curious," he smirked.

I paused, almost afraid to say it out loud. "That you don't like girls?"

"I like girls. I like you." There was a hint of a smile hidden behind his eyes.

"Hm, not the same way I like guys."

"Why would you think that?" he asked, not with anger but more with curiosity.

"A bunch of my guy friends are gay, so I kind of picked up a few things from hanging out with them and most guys by this point would have tried to hit on me. Not that I'm beautiful or anything." I blushed. I felt awkward thinking I might have gotten it wrong. "I'm not sure. Maybe boys from Canada are different," I said, feeling flustered.

He covered his face, laughing again. "I knew we were going to be friends from the first time I saw you the other day. Don't worry, you are beautiful, and I can assure you if my brother was here, he would have asked you out on a date already, or something as lame as that."

"You think I'm beautiful?"

"Yes, with that hair and smile."

I flushed.

"I know you were twins, but did you guys look a lot alike?"

I could tell he was trying to find the right words to answer my dumb question. "Exactly. We looked exactly alike on the outside. But everything else was different. He was an athlete. I am a musician. He loved to eat food. I love cooking it. He liked girls and …"

"You don't."

"Yeah."

"Did he know? About you?"

"Yeah, he asked me about it last year."

"Was he weird about it or anything?"

"No, not at all. He just wanted me to be happy. He also made a joke about having less competition," Tim smiled. It looked like he was thinking about a memory.

"I wish I could have met him."

"Oh, like I said, he would have *liked* you."

"Does your mom know?"

"No. I don't think so. Maybe? We've never talked about it. I don't think she will freak out or anything. We know a few same-sex couples that have been together for a long time. She may be a little sad because CJ was her one way of getting grandkids—well, the easy way. I don't know, though. CJ thought I should tell her when she got back from Portugal, but he got sick and … and we came here. I'm not sure about anything right now."

"Well, I don't know the answers either, but I'm glad we met, too." I looked at him, hand held out, and eyes wide open. "Friends?"

"Friends," he said, opening his arms and taking me in for the third big hug in a day.

We laughed again but found ourselves distracted by some singing we could hear through the trees and decided to investigate.

Following the song, Tim and I walked in silence, letting the melody guide us to the smallest, cutest chapel I had ever seen. The door was open, and we crept quietly into the building. The singing had stopped. It was then I saw Cristiano crumpled over a pew, half-laughing, half-crying, giving up on the song and letting the tears take over. Tim clenched my hand, motioning for us to back out silently.

When we were far enough away from the chapel, Tim spoke, "Sometimes you have to let go, and for some people, it is easier if no one is watching."

23

Truth

Judith

WHEN I HEARD LUCA WAS moving the police operation to Netuno and everyone was coming with him, I felt a mixture of nerves and irritation about seeing Phillip. We had never fought before, and I was not sure what to say when I saw him again.

I hoped a couple of days apart had given him time to think. Phillip and I had been through so much throughout our lives, never fighting, always making things work. He had done everything for me, giving his heart and soul so I could find myself again after being lost for so long. I didn't ask him to, he just did.

I knew I had to speak to him, to set things right, so I sat on the veranda and waited impatiently for him to arrive. When I saw the car driving down the road, my nerves kicked in but I took a breath, put on a little lipstick, and brushed my fingers through my hair; ready for anything.

⁓

"I'm sorry, Judith," were the first words that fell from his lips when he jumped out of the car, followed by another man I didn't know.

"No, I'm sorry, Phillip," I gushed back.

"Judith, I would like to introduce you to Pierre La Nou."

Taking a step back, I centered myself. "Yes, I believe we spoke briefly on the telephone when Maya was in Egypt," I replied cagily, knowing he had something to do with my Maya getting involved with the Ptolemites.

"Bonjour, Judith," he offered with a pain in his eyes that had an apology attached. My heart softened, and I extended my hand.

"I'm glad you're here, but if you'll excuse us, Phillip and I have a few things to discuss." "Walk with me?"

Taking Phillip's hand, I guided him up the steep and narrow path to the ridge Maya had told me about, never loosening my grip until we reached the top. When we finally arrived, he slipped his fingers from mine and stepped towards the edge of the valley, looking out longingly at the undulating vines.

I reached for his arm, not sure how to start.

"Please let me go first," he entreated.

I smiled and nodded, thankful he had broken the silence.

"I love you, Judith. I'm sorry. I've been impossible these last few days."

"It's true you haven't been yourself. Phillip, what is going on?"

"I know. I want to explain but I'm not sure I have the words."

"I know they're in there somewhere."

He smiled. "I love our daughters. Jordan has always been able to take care of herself in her own unique way, but Maya—it always felt like she was balancing on one foot while trying to convince me she had two firmly planted in the dirt. Then just a few weeks ago, I talked to her and she told me she had fallen in love and was never coming home."

"Phillip, that's not what she said."

"I know, but that's the way it felt. She was starting a new adventure with a man we never met and with the intention to 'live the life she always wanted,'" Phillip paused. "Judith, I could lie and tell you it was fear that caused my reaction, and at first, I tried to convince myself of that. But after you left Peachland to help her, I took a deeper look at what was going on for me. I'm not sure how to say this, but I was jealous of our daughter. I was jealous she had her whole life in front of her and was making a choice to go after what she wanted."

He clasped his hands over his mouth, like he said something foul, when in fact he spoke a truth I had wondered about, but never had the courage to ask him.

"I love you Judith, I'm sorry, I love you."

"Stop, Phillip. I know you love me. And I love you too. I also know that being married to me has not been easy and you had to give up a lot. The depression took center stage in our marriage, our parenting, our careers, and our children's lives. It became like an unwanted guest, and so when we finally kicked it out the front door, you worried if it would come back. In the end though, we cannot let 'what ifs' run our life."

"Yes," he said with tears, "I lost my dream for many years, and when I saw our daughter willing to fight for hers, it reminded me I wanted it back, and …"

"I know. We may never be able to purchase another vineyard, but that doesn't mean we can't buy grapes and make wine. We could convert the back yard, we could—"

"We could, but why do that when we already own the real thing."

"The real thing? What are you talking about Phillip?"

"Judith, there's no easy way to say this. I've been lying to you."

My heart rate spiked, and pricks of anxiety circled around my breath.

"Phillip, you had better explain what you're talking about, and quickly. This is not a time to be teasing me."

"When you got sick again and we had to move from the vineyard—" He stopped.

"Yes?" I could hardly hear him as the blood was rushing to my ears.

"The vineyard," he mumbled.

"Pardon me? Please explain."

"The vineyard …"

I could feel the tension building, but I had to control it. "… what about the vineyard?" I asked.

He turned from me. "I never sold it. Judith, I never sold the vineyard."

I staggered ever so slightly, shocked and surprisingly thrilled by the news.

"What? What are you talking about? I saw the sold sticker. What happened?"

"The financing fell through for the purchase. The Kapoor's were the kindest family who had such magnificent plans for the vineyard and when they couldn't come up with the money they were devastated. So, I did what I knew you would have wanted: found a solution for both of us. I offered them an extended lease while maintaining ownership. They have been living in our house and running their own label for two decades, Living Root Wines."

"Living Root Wines? The wine we have been drinking for twenty years? You told me the winery was a client of yours and the Kapoor's gave you a case every year at Christmas."

"Well, technically that is true. They are a client, as I lease the land to them, and they have been giving me wine every year as a thank you."

"And the five cases you bought for Maya's wedding?"

"Oh, I paid for those. I insisted."

"So, what you're telling me, is that we have been drinking our own wine for the last two decades?"

"Sort of. Wine made from our grapes. I'll be making a couple of changes once we move back."

"Really? Once we move back?" I stared deeply into his eyes and watched the myriad of emotions wash over his face. He pleaded with me to say yes.

"Tell me more."

"In the early spring they contacted me with concerns about the irrigation system. I told them to go ahead with ordering the new system and I would take care of the cost. Over the last few months, I have been working on the weekends to pay off the balance."

I chuckled. "Well, that's a relief, I was starting to wonder about some of the odd hours you were keeping but didn't want to ask."

"Oh Judith. You are the only woman in my life. I'm sorry I made you worry."

"Well, what happened?" I sat down on a rock and invited Phillip to join me.

"I'm not sure about the reasons but Mr. Kapoor reached out just after you left, noting that he and Mrs. Kapoor had been thinking about retiring and going back to India. Then just before I flew out, he called, asking if they could break the lease. They wanted their freedom. I was so excited, but I was also afraid of what you were going to say. Then Maya ended up in Egypt and now with the kidnapping … I have been acting so irrational. I know it needs to stop."

My heart brightened and my body filled with relief as I watched the young man I fell in love with over thirty years ago reveal his truth to me.

"So, when do we move back?" I sparkled.

The next thing I knew, I was swinging around in the air. "I thought you might be mad or sad."

I laughed, "No, not either, but how did you manage to keep this a secret all these years? You don't have any other big mysteries lurking around do you?"

"No, one big secret is one too many in a marriage. It wasn't always easy, especially when their label won awards at several international festivals using my grapes, but I had to believe that one day—"

"Yes, and that day is here. Phillip, I appreciate you having the courage to finally tell me the truth but you made a few mistakes lately and those need to be fixed; starting with the way you have been treating Cristiano."

"Of course."

"Maya choosing to marry Cristiano was her decision. She loves you, don't make her choose between the two of you. We'll lose her. Can you please talk to him today? He's a good man, and he loves Maya with all his heart."

He stared out over the valley and nodded. "Yes, of course. Pierre was singing his praises all the way from Porto." He paused. "Judith, when did *you* know you loved me?"

I smiled and thought back to the first evening we met. "When you gave up your holiday with your friends and came to visit me every day at design school. And you?"

"When you walked into that pub and took pity on a weary Canadian backpacker and invited me to your studio." His brow furrowed. "Over the years I've wondered if we'd not gotten married, maybe you wouldn't have had to suffer for so long."

A deep peace settled around my heart. "Phillip, nothing would have stopped me from being with you. Do I wish we could have managed the postpartum depression better? Yes. Do I regret having our two beautiful daughters—never. I have the most loving husband in the world and—I am just finding out—the savviest, too. Maya is going to be so excited about the vineyard."

"Do you think when we get her back, she might come home?" Phillip asked.

I smiled. "I hope not. Her life is here with Cristiano." I saw a flash of disappointment in his eyes. "Look on the bright side: maybe Jordan will come live with us."

We broke into laughter. "I love her, but no thank you." He rolled his eyes. Taking a deep breath, he straightened his shirt. "Maybe it's time for me to meet our son-in-law the proper way."

"Without fists?" I teased.

"Yes, without fists."

Phillip squeezed my hand as we walked back to the inn.

"Cristiano will get her back, right? She may be his 'wife,' but she's still my daughter."

"Yes, Phillip. He has no choice; he loves her that much. What would you have done if someone had taken me?"

He stopped and stared intensely into my eyes, frustration and anger gone. "Not someone, but something, and it did! And I fought for over twenty years to get you back. I won … and so will he."

"Yes, he will, but for tonight, we are going to have a little fun and regroup."

"What do you mean, regroup?"

"Oh, Carmo and Bento are having a grape stomp wedding."

"Grape stomp? People still do that?"

"They do here. You packed some shorts, didn't you?"

"Yes, Judith," he laughed. "Race you."

24

Two Sets of Tears

Cristiano

After leaving the chapel, I thought briefly about going back to the cottage and disappearing into the sadness tugging at the edges of my heart. But whatever pain I was feeling inside or out had to be shelved. I needed to figure out what Avo had done with the package, but before I could think about it any further, I heard laughter spilling out from between the vines. When I turned around, Judith and Phillip appeared.

Phillip stopped short when he saw me, knocking Judith off her stride and sending her forward. I grabbed her before she fell but could only hold her for a moment before we both dropped to the dirt.

"Judith!!" Phillip cried out.

"Cristiano are you okay?" she asked hurriedly, jumping up and dusting herself off. "Well, that wasn't very graceful of me." She turned and shook her finger. "And Phillip, why did you stop like that?"

Phillip looked at me as I sat up.

"Oh," she said. "Well, I have had enough of this. I'm leaving the two of you to work it out. I'll see you both at the wedding stomp. Phillip, don't forget to wear your shorts."

Judith laughed then her face turned serious. "Phillip, help Cristiano up, and don't come in until you've apologized and worked things out."

After Judith skipped up the stairs and disappeared inside, Phillip held out his hand.

"How are you feeling?" he asked awkwardly.

"Like I was in a car crash, punched and …"

He mulled over my words. "Yes, about the punch. I'm sorry about that." He shook his head. "I've not been myself since Maya left for Portugal, and when she met you, well … I had a hard time accepting the suddenness of the whole thing, and then the blog, Steven and Egypt and …" I saw the strain on his face.

I smiled, "Well when you put it that way, I can understand. I can't imagine what I would do if I had a daughter, and she ran off, got married …"

Phillip and I were having trouble finishing our thoughts about Maya.

"I talked to Pierre on my way here. He explained everything," Phillip said.

"He's here too? What could he possibly explain?" I asked with irritation.

"You, Cristiano. Well, you and Maya. All he talked about was how much the two of you love each other." Things got quiet again between us.

"I know you think we're not married, and I guess in the eyes of the law we aren't, but Phillip, we took our vows in front of God. I'm not sure how much more married I could be to your daughter?" My heart seized like someone was squeezing it tight. "I know we will have things to work through. But I want a chance to build a life with her. If anything happens—"

"Cristiano, nothing is going to happen to her. That's why we're all here, working together to bring her home. I know you love her, and *that* is not an easy thing for a dad to admit. How about tomorrow I start on the paperwork so you two can get married officially when the time is right?" He squeezed my shoulder. "Any tips for the grape stomp tonight?"

I laughed, "Whatever you do, don't use the white towels after you shower."

I sat outside on the steps, fatigue taking over my body and mind, but for the first time in days, it felt like something was going my way.

Carmo joined me. "Cristiano. You look awful."

"Why, thank you. Is that part of the familial honesty I have been missing out on?"

"Maybe you should skip the ceremony and lay down for a little while?"

"I couldn't do that."

"Yes, you can. I don't want you falling over during my 'I do' moment. Get some rest. I'll send someone for you once we get the stomp started. I know you won't be doing any actual stomping tonight, but we want you there in one piece. I left Maya's room just as it was, hoping she would be back for my wedding. Why don't you rest there?"

"Carmo, I don't know what room she's in. She never invited me upstairs."

"So, it's really true," she laughed. "You are such a good boy."

"Only since I met her." I shook my head.

"Here is a key. She's in room 206. I'll have Gervais send up some food."

"That's okay."

"No, it's not. I spoke with your mother when she arrived. She told me to make sure you got something to eat. Go to sleep."

As I stood outside Maya's door, I thought briefly about turning in the opposite direction, but knew I had to go in. Smell her, see her clothes, lie in her bed and put my head on her pillow. When I walked into the room, my knees buckled, and I fell to the floor. The pain in my heart was greater than anything my ribs could offer. She was all around me. I climbed onto the bed and wrapped myself in her sheets until sleep took over and I could almost feel her in my arms.

෨

Maya

I slept on the edge of waking, dreaming of him, but when I woke, I was alone—I needed to get used to that, to stand on my own. I wished it could be different, but I would not burden him with the new broken me. Reaching up to the bandages, I wondered how disfigured I was going to be. The thought made me nauseous and again I grabbed the bucket, retching and spewing up my sadness.

When I heard the heavy boots coming down the hall, I placed the niqab on quickly, so only my eyes were showing. I stood, holding my stomach and leaning against the cot as he walked through the door.

"Well, what do we have here? Saafa finally agreed to cover herself up, but you too? This is a good day for me. Why?"

"You are my host. You let me go outside for some fresh air and I wanted to be respectful of your traditions."

Dakar looked at me with suspicion. I interrupted his thoughts before he could dive any deeper into my reason.

"Have they found it yet?"

"What, the relic? No, but from what I've heard, they've moved their little command post to Netuno. I have not called them since you told them my name, but for your sake, I hope to hear from them soon."

"I'm very sorry about that, Dakar. It just slipped out."

"No, it didn't. You are a very clever girl, smarter than most."

"I'm not that smart. Believe me." I switched to honesty. "I've made so many mistakes and thought for a time I could be something or someone else, but I'm not so sure that is possible now."

Dakar's face almost softened. "Well, I am sure they will find the relic soon and then you can go home and live your life."

I stared at him with disbelief, shocked that he didn't understand how my old life ended the day of the kidnapping. No marriage, no face, no freedom.

"Yes, going home is all I want." I said the words, speaking a truth that could not be my reality.

"If you wear the niqab, you and Saafa can walk the grounds two times a day."

"Thank you. Is there any way I can spend some time in the kitchen? I am very good at baking and thought you might like to have something different to eat."

He paused, thinking about my request. "Yes, that is acceptable, but you will make me Khobz."

"What is Khobz?" I asked.

"My favorite bread," he said looking at me like I had asked a stupid question.

"Of course, Dakar, whatever you'd like," I choked out, hoping he couldn't see the disappointment in my eyes.

⁓

When Saafa arrived, she closed my door and pulled down her face covering.

"So, I hear you convinced him to go on two daily walks and to work in the kitchen. Why would you ask for kitchen duty?"

"I didn't ask for kitchen duty. I was hoping I could bake some bread, my kind of bread."

"Well, now you've done it. The kitchen is the second hottest room in the house."

"What is the first?"

"Laundry. I hate doing laundry," she shook her head and I got to see a touch of teenage rebellion poking through. She made me think of Jacinta. They were the same age, but their lives were so very different. "We had better get that walk in and then I'll take you over to meet the women."

When we arrived in the kitchen, I wondered how I was going to cook and wear the traditional clothing without fainting from the heat. Saafa introduced me and they all smiled politely. It felt good being in a kitchen filled with women again.

There was something about their friendship and combined purpose that helped me settle into the space with ease. When they encouraged me to remove the fabric directly over my face, I was nervous at first, but with encouragement, I took it down, revealing my bandages. The women didn't respond with fear or rejection, but with kindness in their eyes.

They showed me how to prepare several dishes. Gervais would have been so proud of me. It was a wonderful afternoon. I didn't understand a word they said, but I understood the food. Next, they took me out to the garden and showed me the bread oven. I felt calm. It reminded me of my last bake with Avo. After finding out she had passed away, I had not allowed the information to find its way into my heart, but as the wood burned and crackled, it awakened the truth. My tears soaked the bandages, making the wounds sting with memories.

The women brought me back inside and put me to work, kneading and shaping the dough. The Khobz only needed one rise, so I didn't get to pound it down, but I got to watch it bake and taste it as it came out of the oven. I missed baking with Avo. I missed her magic bread.

After finishing the bake, the women looked at me with concern as I sought out a chair in the corner.

"I'm okay, just tired," I said, reading their expressions.

One woman scooted out of the room and returned with Saafa.

"You look flushed, Maya, are you alright?" Saafa asked, fussing over me more than usual.

"Yes, thank you, just heat and memories. Not a great combination."

"My mom always told me remembering was good, but not when you're too tired. That's when the brain plays tricks on you. Not a time to make life-changing decisions."

I smiled, knowing she was right, knowing she wanted me to rethink the plan before it was too late, but I would not change my decision. I couldn't. It was no longer just about me.

25

The Package

Cristiano

WHEN I WOKE A FEW hours later, I heard the sounds of laughter and music floating up from outside. The stomp had begun. I needed a shower before I could face anyone, so I reluctantly let go of Maya's pillow and walked over to the bathroom. Carmo had tidied her space, but I found a couple of her things on the counter waiting for her. I picked up her hairbrush and felt a rush of nervous energy. I needed to find the relic, to find her.

Stepping into the shower, I revisited the details of my last few conversations with Avo before she died. I knew her better than anyone. The answer was close to me. I just needed to clear my head so it could appear.

As the hot water rained down, I allowed my mind to wander. It started with Maya; she would be so pleased to know her father and I were getting along. It did not take long for my thoughts to careen down the path to the morning of the crash and before I could stop the memory I was back in the car. I remember seeing my parents' suitcase out of the corner of my eye. It was covered in blood. Where was the car? A thought burst into my head.

"The suitcase? What happened to my parent's suitcase?"

My mind raced and I wondered if we could have missed the relic when we checked the suitcase the first time. I jumped out of the shower ignoring the screaming pain. Hair sopping, I threw a towel around my waist and ran into the hall, forgetting shoes and common sense. I needed to find Luca, but when I turned the corner, I ran smack into Pierre.

"Cristiano, I was …"

My anger ignited, and Pierre stepped back.

"Cristiano, calm down," he cried. "This is not the time."

"Not the time? What gives you the right to speak to me?"

"Nothing. I'm just trying to help."

"I don't have time for this. I need to find the suitcase that was in my car."

"The suitcase?"

"Yes, my parents' suitcase, Pierre. I think we missed something the first time."

"No," he said, shaking his head.

"What are you saying?"

"No, you missed nothing."

"What?" I could feel my adrenaline fade and suddenly felt cold.

"Let's go back to your room. You can dry off and we can talk."

A numbness came over me as my suitcase idea was extinguished by one simple phrase, "you missed nothing."

Pierre guided me back to the bed, then grabbed another towel and placed it around my shaking shoulders.

"What did you mean when you said we missed nothing?"

Pierre averted his eyes. "I haven't been to a grape stomp in years. They sent me up here to get you. Why don't we head down there? It will take your mind off things."

"Take my mind off things? You mean Maya and the relic? I don't want to take my mind off it. I haven't been able to think straight for days and right now I know what I need to do. So, either help me or stay out of my way. What do you know about the suitcase?"

A sheen of liquid rolled over his eyes. "All I wanted to do was help."

"Save your tears Pierre. You can't undo what you've done."

"That's not fair, Cristiano."

"Fair, what do you know about fair?"

"You don't have the corner market on sadness and heartache Cristiano. I would do anything to have your parents back. They were my family. You were my family. And it all disappeared that day."

We sat in silence while I let his words filter through my brain. I wanted to punch him and hug him at the same time. I wanted to yell at the world, but how was that going to get me any closer to finding the relic and rescuing Maya? It wasn't.

"Pierre, my parents chose to go to Egypt in search of the relic. They loved working with you and lived for their summer adventures. And me? I had to see where they died. There was nothing you could have said to stop me. And Maya, well, she has her own mind and does what she wants—tell me about the suitcase."

"When I heard about the crash, I immediately booked a flight and came to Porto. I snuck into the hospital to see you while you were still unconscious. That's when I found out Maya was missing. No one had put the pieces together yet, but I had a feeling it was the Ptolemites and if it was them, I knew what they were looking for. I started searching for the relic after that."

"You started looking right away?"

"Yes, I wanted to do everything I could to find the relic. To start, I tracked down the car to a junk yard, and when I arrived, convinced the guy I was an investigator from France and had to look at your car."

"Luca is going to be upset with you."

"Yes, Luca and I have met. We came to a quiet understanding. He felt my knowledge and firsthand experience with the Ptolemites could be an asset as we moved forward. I think he just didn't want me poking around without him knowing."

"And the suitcase?"

"It was in pieces. There was nothing there but a few items of clothing. I was going to tell you tomorrow. But then we—"

"Ran into each other. So what do we do now?"

"There's nothing we can do tonight. Maybe a little grape stomp wedding is not such a bad idea, hey?"

Taking a breath, I realized he might have a point. "They do sound like they're having fun. I may not be in a party mood but I can at least support Carmo and Bento."

"Get dressed," he said, throwing my clothes at me. "I need to get downstairs and grab a glass of the French wine before it runs out and all there is left to drink is the Portuguese bottles."

"Don't let anyone hear you say that. We take our Portuguese wine very seriously around here." I smirked. As I slipped on my wrinkled and well-used shirt, I thought about what Pierre said—that my parents were family to him—and realized if I was going to find Maya, I needed everyone's help, including Pierre's. First things first though, I needed to show my appreciation for him talking to Maya's dad. "Pierre, I wanted to thank you for speaking with Phillip about Maya and me. It seems to have helped. He is willing to start the paperwork to make the marriage official.

Oh, there was one other thing I needed to ask you about before we head downstairs. The package."

"The package? What package?" He asked.

"Luca didn't tell you?"

"No. What package are you talking about?

"Before Maya and I got married, I called Avo to let her know. During the conversation, I mentioned your name, and it triggered a memory for her. She asked me to wait as she searched through her cupboards and found a package my parents sent to you before they left Egypt. She had forgotten about it until that moment."

Pierre gripped my arm. "Cristiano, I knew they found it, but I did not know they had sent a package. Could it be?" I didn't know if he was going to be sick or jump for joy.

"Do you really think it could be the relic?"

"I am not a hundred percent sure, but I knew your mother well. She had a reason for everything she did. Rosa must have thought it a safer way to get *something* home."

"Why would she send it to Avo though?"

"Just in case someone was watching me." He hung his head.

"Pierre, I don't know whether it is or not, but it's our only lead. And we haven't been able to find it. Somehow the Ptolemites found out about it and tore the cottage apart before Luca, Dalley, and Ravn were able to get there. I looked too but found nothing."

Then I saw a change in Pierre's face. "What? What is it?"

"Avo came to see you after the crash happened. Who brought her?"

"Puro. I don't know who else was there."

"We need to see him right now."

"He is knee deep in grapes at his daughter's wedding."

"Now, Cristiano!" Pierre screeched.

I ran through the inn and out the front door, replacing my pain with hope.

"Puro, where is Puro?" I yelled into the crowd.

The music stopped, and so did the stomp as everyone stared at me. I must have looked crazed. Barefoot, with my shirt open and billowing behind me. Dalley's voice cut through the sudden silence.

"Cristiano, what did I tell you before about walking around showing your chest off?" she laughed. "Damn, that looks painful." She said, poking at the bruising on my body.

"Dalley, shut up already. Where is Puro?"

"No need to be rude. He went in to get more wine."

Luca stepped up as well as Zef, my dad, and Phillip.

"What is it?" Phillip, my future father-in-law, asked, covered in grape juice and trying to catch his breath.

"Pierre thinks he might know where to find the package."

"It's just a hunch," he said, looking uncomfortable with all eyes on him.

"Always follow the hunches," Luca commented, encouraging him to keep talking.

Puro came out of the inn.

"What is it?"

Pierre moved forward. "Puro, what happened when Avo found out about Cristiano?"

"I don't remember, it was all such a blur."

Judith stepped in to answer Pierre. She appeared calm, not like the rest of us. "After Avo found out about the crash she insisted on travelling with us to see Cristiano. We drove to her place to pick her up. Puro went inside and Phillip and I stayed in the car."

"I remember now. I went inside and helped her pack. While in the kitchen she placed a loaf of her bread in a paper bag. That was it."

"Puro?" Judith asked. "Didn't Avo go back into the house?"

"Yes, you're right, Judith."

"And if I recall, when she came out again, she was putting something in her purse."

Luca shouted. "Where is Avo's purse?"

Everyone looked at me. "I don't know."

"What happened to her things? After she died?" Luca asked.

"I don't know," I said, feeling like my heart was going to explode. I turned towards the gasp to see my little sister knee deep in grapes and looking like she was going to fall over.

"Jacinta," I said calmly. "Can you come out of there please? Zef, give her a hand. Why did you gasp?"

"I have her things," she whispered. "You asked me to take care of her until you got here."

"And you've done a great job, but I need to know where you put her belongings."

She looked over at Marcos and Euphemia and they ran towards her. Then I heard Judith's calm voice. No one would have guessed Judith had suffered with anxiety and depression most of her life as her demeanor that moment showed only strength and courage.

"Jacinta, when we were on the plane, you were holding the plastic bag from the hospital. Where did you put it?" Judith asked, almost in a whisper.

"It's in my room. Have I done something wrong?"

Judith looked at Euphemia.

"No dear, we just need to look through the bag."

"The bag is in the closet. I did everything you asked," she said, looking at me.

"Yes, Jacinta, you did, and you took care of her and her things. Did you look inside her bag?"

Jacinta looked mortified. "No, of course not."

"Mom, can you stay with her?"

"Yes, you go, we'll be there in a minute," she said, putting her arm around my shaking sister.

Luca and I took off toward the inn, a line of people trailing behind us.

When we got into Jacinta's room, Luca pushed past me and ran to the closet. Before I could say a word, he was dumping the contents of the hospital bag onto the bed. I could smell her before I even knew what hit me. I saw her shoes and then her dress.

Pushing the grief aside, we rummaged through her things. Then I saw her purse. I opened it slowly, not sure if I could bear the disappointment of not finding the package, but there it was.

"Pierre, she addressed it to you."

"No, Cristiano, you open it."

Dalley stepped in, "Well, someone open it already," she barked.

"I'll do it," Luca said. He pulled a set of nitrile gloves out of this pocket and snapped them over his fingers.

"Is that really necessary?" Beth asked.

"Yes, it is. Step back." Luca said.

As he sliced open the package, everyone leaned in. It almost felt comical. When he pulled back the last piece of paper, there it was: pure gold, beautifully crafted with jewels encrusted over the surface and two razor sharp points at the end of the hair fork. It was exquisite.

Luca reached in to pick it up and Pierre screeched, "Don't touch it!"

Luca stopped. "What?"

"There are too many tragic tales connected to that hair fork. I wouldn't touch it if I were you."

Luca smiled and closed the box, then placed it into a bag.

"So, what now?" asked Zef.

Luca smiled. "We leak the information and get ready to make a trade."

⤳ 201 ⤝

26

Last Night

Maya

"Open it!" I heard her yell at the guard outside my door.

It had been an unsettled night of dreams about Cristiano and the vineyard, but I pushed it all away as Saafa came running into the room.

"He found it! Or at least I think he did. Pieces of information have been trickling in all night. Dakar was trying to keep it contained, but everyone is online, and he has no control over that!"

"Online? How do we know for sure?" I could feel a queasiness coming on.

"Prices Portugal. That's where Dakar found the information about the relic. Cristiano had your friend Dalley post something on her blog. He wanted to make it as public as possible. Maya, this will all be over soon. Dakar is going to call him, but he wants you to be there. Put on your niqab."

I lifted my chin and stared into her hopeful eyes. "We are one step closer to making the switch."

"Maya, you don't have to do this."

"Yes, I do. It's the only way for both of us to find a way out. Hand him the note first."

"Cristiano will do anything for you. He loves you. What am I supposed to say to him when I take off my niqab?"

"You will find the words Saafa. We talked about this. I don't doubt he loves the old me, but how could he love this?" I threw my hand up to the bandages. "It's not fair to him."

"Maya, he is your husband. Scars or no scars."

"No, he's not!" I said, ending the discussion too abruptly. Saafa shook her head and walked in circles as I finished getting dressed.

"Okay," she finally sputtered. "I'll do the switch, but Maya, promise me you will not make any forever plans regarding Cristiano until after the bandages come off. You owe that to him, to yourself. Don't you?"

"What difference will it make?" I asked, defeat seeping into my heart.

Saafa helped me adjust the niqab without saying another word.

When I heard his heavy steps coming down the hall, I braced myself for the last conversation I was ever going to have with Cristiano.

"Well, hello, Maya. It looks like our time may end sooner than I had planned. What a shame," Dakar said with a note of pleasure in his voice.

As much as I wanted to scream, I clenched my fists and sucked in the anger, leaving all conversation to Saafa.

"Thank you, Dakar, for allowing me to take Maya for a walk yesterday and letting her work in the kitchen. I was told her kitchen skills were very impressive. Did you have time to try her Khobz?"

He stared at me. "Maya, your Khobz was delicious. I am almost sad to see you go." He stood close enough to me that the smell of his breath permeated the fabric and got caught under my veil. "I might have kept you on in the kitchen if Cristiano had not found the relic. But who am I to stand in the way of love? Honestly, it may be the only chance you get, looking the way you do."

I let out the breath I had been holding and could feel my knees shake. "Maya, you know I'm right. You're wondering if he can love you the way you are. Let's call him and see. It has been so boring around here, since you started doing what I want except for my other guest. Now, she is exciting and something special to look at."

As the phone rang, Dakar hissed in my ear, "Listen to me, Ferret. You're very close to leaving. Don't ruin this for me, for us … I'm warning you."

"Hello?" He sounded strange, not himself.

"Cristiano," I said flatly. "Dakar got your message. The exchange will be done in two days. He will text you the address and the instructions."

"Maya? What's the matter? What's wrong? Did he hurt you again?" Desperation seeped through the phone, blanketing me in his worry and sadness.

Dakar ripped the phone out of my hand and walked out of the room. I could only hear a muffled laugh coming from the hall as he walked away.

Hidden tears trickled down my cheeks. "We will both be free in two days," was all I could utter.

Cristiano

I stood frozen with the phone in my hands, waiting for the text from Dakar. Something was wrong. Something was wrong with Maya. People were yelling at me, but I didn't care. I just kept thinking about what Maya didn't say. *She didn't tell me she loved me. She didn't even try. What has he done to her?*

"What's the matter with him?" Dalley asked.

"Things happen when people are held against their will. I think Maya—".

I interrupted Ravn "Yes, Ravn, I really don't care what you're thinking." I thundered back at him. The room went silent.

"Cristiano there is no need to—" Ravn tried to calm me.

"Yell? What better time is there to yell? Everyone wants me to stay calm while my wife is locked away and I don't know what he's done to her!" I held up my hand and took a breath. "I'm going for a walk. Take my phone." I threw it at Luca. "Dakar will text the information shortly. The exchange will happen in two days."

"Cristiano, what did he say? What did Maya say?" Judith approached me, looking frantic.

Then I saw it, the panic, the deep-rooted anxiety of a mother wrestling with the idea that something terrible has happened to her daughter. As much as I wanted to be alone, I couldn't leave Judith wrapped in her fear. Maya would never forgive me if she knew I could have helped her mother and didn't.

"Judith, would you like to walk with me? I'm not great company but …"

"But nothing. Of course. You don't have to say a word."

Judith walked with me through the vines and over to the olive grove.

"This is one of Maya's favorite places," I finally said, breaking the silence that had settled between the two of us.

"Cristiano, please tell me. Is she okay?"

"No, I don't think so. She didn't say anything, but I felt it."

Judith took hold of a tree branch and, with several deep intakes, slowed her ragged and worried breaths. "Cristiano, we must have faith. Maya will come home and the two of you will work through this." She smiled just enough to help me take a breath of my own.

"Judith, I asked you along, thinking you needed me, but it was *me* who needed *you*."

"Cristiano, we all need each other. That's what family is for, except maybe Jordan, Maya's sister. She has a mind of her own. Listen to me going on."

"No, it's alright. I enjoy hearing about Maya's life. She knows almost everything about me, but truthfully, she only told me snippets about her life back in Peachland."

"Yes, Maya has always held her cards close to her chest. I assume she told you about my depression and what a terrible mother I was?"

"Depression yes, terrible mother, no."

Judith grinned. "I think I know why she fell in love with you."

"And why is that?"

We heard Judith's name being called from a distance.

"Cristiano, I had better go. I was in a state when we left the group. I'm feeling better though. How about you?"

"A little better, yes."

"Remember, Cristiano, *when* she comes home, she may not be the same person you married. Circumstances can change us. Your only job will be to love her and help her pick up the pieces; no matter how many."

I waved to Judith as she walked back to the inn.

"Have faith," she had said to me. "How do I do that?" I looked up, "Avo? How do I do this?" I turned when I heard a twig snap.

"One step at a time," Euphemia said as she wrapped her arms around me. I was stiff at first, unsure how to accept the love from a woman I had only recently met, but she was not giving up. She would not let go.

"It's okay, son," she whispered as we sat down in the grove. My mother's arms tightened around me as my tears fell and did not loosen until they stopped.

When I finally looked up, she was smiling. Filled with strength and purpose, something had changed from the first time I saw her standing on the balcony.

"I thought I needed to do this on my own," I said, as she wiped the tears from my face.

"You never need to do anything on your own again. I'm your mother. You're stuck with me."

⁂

Maya

"Make sure you hand him the letter before you remove your niqab," I said.

"I will come visit you as soon as I can," Saafa tried to comfort me.

"Promise me you won't tell him where I am."

"I promise," she said hesitantly, "but if he guesses, I won't lie."

I spent the next two days baking bread and avoiding writing the letter to Cristiano, but when Saafa came into the kitchen the night before the exchange and handed me a pen and paper, I knew it was time.

"You need to write this tonight. They will be here at dawn."

As I was leaving the kitchen, one lady came up to me and laid her hand on my cheek. I shifted away from her touch and ran back to my room. Saafa followed me several minutes later, staring at me.

"Write the letter," was all Saafa said with a painful look in her eyes.

⁂

Jade

I heard him in the hall before he barged into my room.

"Don't you ever knock?"

"Why? It's my house."

"Well, I'm your guest, and this is my room."

"You're right, you are my guest, and you should remember that. If you continue to be rude to me, I could easily put you down into Maya's room after she leaves tomorrow."

"She's leaving? You're letting her go?"

"Yes, they found the relic and if it's true, I will keep my word. Besides, I broke my little ferret. She's no fun anymore."

"Well then, you have what you want; it's time for me to go."

"Go? You're not going anywhere, except maybe back to Egypt with me. I'm done with Morocco. Besides, where do you think you're going with no money or identification?"

I saw him holding my passport and smiling.

"She was a ferret, but you're more like a feral cat. You're going to be much more fun to break."

"Feral. Interesting description. I hope you know what you're getting into."

Dakar laughed. "I have been waiting for one like you." Then he stopped laughing. "Pack your things. We will leave the moment I have the relic in my hand."

I thought Axel would have negotiated a deal to get me out by that point, but once again, it was up to me to save myself. "Thanks Dad, always the doting father."

I would have to keep my ears open for the perfect opportunity. Dakar may have taken my cash and passport, but I was sure the little trinket he liberated from Maya's neck would pay for anything I needed once I escaped.

27

The Switch

Cristiano

AFTER BETH CAME BY TO help me gather a few things for Maya, I tried to get some rest as Luca had instructed but my stomach was in knots and sleep was impossible to find. So, I sat on the bed, with her PJs laid out as if she was sitting beside me and waited. I jumped when the knock came and opened the door to a sleek looking Luca, hair pulled back and jaw set with determination.

"You ready, Cristiano? Beth said she came by earlier to help you gather some of Maya's things.

"Yes. Where is she? I thought she would be with you?"

"No, after she finished helping you, she came back to my room and broke down. I usually know what to do to help people, but that woman has me completely turned around, so I sent her to see Judith."

"Turned around, hey?" I commented, thinking about the first time I saw Maya at the airport. "Yes, I know all about that."

As we walked down the stairs, it felt eerily quiet until we stepped into the lobby and then there they were: all the women Maya had come to love since she arrived at Netuno. Josie, Petra, and Maggie held hands while Sachi paced back and forth and Dalley shot back what looked to be an espresso.

"That is coffee, right?" I teased.

She shook her head. "Watch out for goats," she said, referring to our adventure in Egypt. "Oh, I have something for you to give to Maya." Dalley dug into her purse and handed me a handkerchief. My stomach flipped as I ran my hand over the carefully embroidered flowers Avo had so lovingly stitched into the fabric, and I could feel the tug at my heart.

"This was Maya's? When did Avo give this to her?"

"You're going to have to ask her about that," Dalley said, holding back her tears.

I folded it carefully and placed it into my pocket. "If only goats were the worst of our problems." I turned to Luca. "So, what's the plan?"

"A simple exchange: Maya for the relic. Dakar insisted it was you who does the hand off. He knows what you look like, so there is no way I could take your place."

"No offence, but there's no way I'd let you. She's my wife, and it's my responsibility to bring her home."

"Our responsibility. Remember, I'm the police officer. Don't do anything stupid. This guy is volatile. Don't give him an excuse to hurt Maya or you."

"Fair enough." I gritted my teeth, knowing full well what Dakar was capable of doing to Maya.

"Once we have completed the transaction, we will head back to the airport. Everything will go smoothly. You'll see," he said almost convincingly. Luca moved in closely to me so only I could hear him "Cristiano, you look pale. You okay?"

I swallowed back the bile. "You don't have to worry about me."

The ladies in the room waved goodbye. No one said a word as we stepped toward the door.

"Okay then, let's go."

When we walked out into the cool night air, Phillip was standing near the stairs.

"Bring her home, Cristiano, just promise me you'll bring her home."

My mouth was dry, but I forced the words out. "I promise."

As I got into the car, I held my head in my hands. "How could I promise him, Luca?"

"How could you not?" he asked, shaking his head.

He sent me my flight information, letting me know we would be sitting apart on the airplane and that we would rendezvous at the hotel in Casablanca.

When I arrived in Morocco, I saw Luca for a moment, then he disappeared into the crowd, and I was on my own. Travelling on my own had never bothered me before, but this was different. My nerves were on high alert and I could feel my anxiety seeping through my pores.

My French barely got me through security and at one point I wondered if they were going to stop me. After checking in at the hotel, I sat in the room, waiting. Luca's knock on the door startled me out of a strange slumber I'd fallen into and sent my heart straight to my throat.

"Open the door, Cristiano. We need to talk." His voice was strained.

I opened the door and saw two Moroccan police officers in the hall with him. He pushed me inside the room.

"There's been a complication," he uttered in hushed tones.

"How could there be a complication? We haven't left the hotel."

"I received a call from my superiors. They are telling me we need to stand down, at least for a couple of hours, regarding Maya's exchange. Axel Axeline is talking with the Ptolemites in Egypt about getting his daughter back. It appears Dakar has gone rogue and they are willing to help get Jade Axeline back if Moroccan and Portuguese authorities send Dakar back to Egypt. They've made a deal."

"Jade? Saving Jade is more important than Maya? She's the one who went willingly with them, told them where they could find us. She's not innocent in this. NO! I'm not sacrificing Maya so some rich guy can get his bitch of a daughter back. That's not the deal I made with Dakar, and he is not a man you break a deal with."

"Shh. Keep your voice down. Cristiano," he whispered. Then said loudly "I can't disobey a direct order." Luca raised an eyebrow. *What was he trying to say?* "Cristiano, I'm going to my room to get some sleep. I will be there for several hours. I'm sorry that we need to delay. Everything will be okay," he said, then slipped a piece of paper into my hand. He walked down the hall with the officers. As soon as they were out of sight, I opened it.

Go now. There is a car waiting for you downstairs. He has it.

Leaving through the emergency exit stairs, I saw a car idling across the street. As I got closer, the driver rolled down the tinted window.

"Get in!" He yelled.

"What are you doing here?"

"What? Are we stopping for coffee? I've already had enough, thank you." Dalley yelled across from the passenger seat. "Get in."

I crawled into the back seat.

"Hard to believe we are back in the middle of it. First time you, now Maya. You guys are impossible."

"How?" I asked trying to put the pieces together.

Ravn sped around the corner and stopped short.

"Just wait …"

The next thing I knew, the door was opening and Luca climbed in, smiling.

"You think I'm going to let you guys have all the fun?" He punched me in the arm.

My hands shook, and my breath quickened.

"I can hear you back there. Cristiano, no heart attacks today, we don't need any additional drama," Dalley spouted off.

"I don't know what to say."

"Nothing needed right now, but if they shoot at me again?" Ravn said, half-joking.

"No one is shooting at anyone," Luca said. "It's just a simple exchange."

"And what about the *other* matter?"

"I slipped the Moroccan police, but we had better go. Now! By the time they figure out I'm not in my room we will have Maya back."

"Thank you." I held out my hand to Luca.

"Oh, Cristiano, we are way past that, old friend." And he leaned in for a hug.

☙

Maya

Saafa and I exchanged our garments and wrapped her face in bandages, leaving her eyes looking just like mine. She packed me some bread along with my identification and placed it in her pocket and I handed her the letter.

"Tell him it is the best for everyone. You are going to love Netuno. It's beautiful."

Saafa looked scared for the first time. "I don't know …"

"You don't have to know. Everyone there will help you find your way."

We finished getting ready and when we left the room; I was her, and she was me.

When we arrived at the designated stairwell where Saafa was told to leave me, we held hands.

"I will stand here and wait for Dakar. As we spoke about, you need to follow the path onto the road from the other side of the villa. Wait in the bushes until the first bus comes by. Your documents are in the inside pocket. Whatever you do, don't turn back. My parents' friends will meet you at the ferry in Crete in two days."

I smiled and hugged her goodbye. "Tell him I love him, and I'm sorry." I slipped away, leaving Saafa standing on the stairs, her eyes filled with a mixture of fear and anticipation.

❧

I made it through the halls and into the yard, but before I could cross the lawn, the guard Saafa knew waved to me. I waved back, then turned around and dashed up the path into the villa, ducking into the nearest closet. I stood frozen for about five minutes, afraid to make a sound, to be discovered. Then I heard a yelp and a door slam. Sometime later, when everything was quiet, I slipped out of the closet. The sun was rising, and I knew Cristiano must be on the beach waiting to do the exchange.

Everything was going to plan. It was time to run, to get as far away from that place as possible, but I couldn't. I needed to make sure Saafa was safe and to see Cristiano one last time. So, I snuck down the hall and found my way to an open room that had a view of the beach and I saw them. Dakar was holding 'me', and Cristiano had the box with the relic. I gasped when I saw Ravn and Dalley and Luca there with him. My heart was beating so fast, I could barely catch my breath.

Cristiano gave Dakar the box. He opened it, picked it up, and walked back to Saafa. He stared at her for a moment, and then she walked towards Cristiano with her hand hidden in the niqab. I hoped she could find the letter. I couldn't see his reaction, only that he staggered when she took off the headdress. She wasn't supposed to take it off yet. Ravn caught him. Dalley grabbed the letter from her roughly. Where were her bandages? What was going on?

It didn't matter, Saafa was safe, and I needed to get out of there. I headed back through the house but stopped short when I heard someone crying. What if another young girl was being held against her will like Saafa? I had to at least look and see. The crying was coming from a room down the hall.

As I stepped inside, I saw a Prada bag sitting on a table. It looked like Jade's; I remember her holding it that morning when she left Netuno. It was Jade's room, except there was no Jade. Then I heard the whimper and the tears. When I looked behind the couch, all I saw was a scared sixteen-year-old girl, gagged with a towel and tied with a lamp cord.

"Saafa? Oh my God, what happened?" I hurried to untie her.

"That Jade lady happened. She heard us talking in the hall and after you left she grabbed me, took my clothes, and tied me up. She said I didn't deserve to be free, and that she looked forward to seeing his face when she took off her garment." Saafa cried. "She was laughing, Maya. Laughing at you and me."

I despised Jade for what she had done to me, but that was nothing compared to what she had just taken away from Saafa.

"We need to go right now. Grab some of Jade's clothes and get dressed."

"No Maya, I'm staying, you go."

"No, Saafa, I am not leaving you behind."

Saafa looked at the clock on the wall. "Then we had better hurry." She changed and removed the bandages. Morning shadows covered the path as we made our way through the brush and out to the road. The bus was coming, and we had to run, but suddenly we heard footsteps coming quickly behind us.

We stopped, and he was there, Saafa's guard friend. He stared at her. She tried to speak, but he held up one hand, shook his head, and walked away.

28

I Love You, but ...

Cristiano

I held her letter in my fist, unable to speak, unable to process what had happened. Every time Jade attempted to open her mouth, Dalley shut it for her, but it was Ravn who finally got her to stop all together.

"I don't know who you think you are. And who cares about a stupid teenager, anyway?" Jade snarled at Dalley.

"Jade!" Ravn roared from the driver's seat. "If you don't shut your mouth right now, I will stop this car and leave you on the side of the road. I swear!"

"Cristiano," Luca tapped me on the shoulder, "at least we know she is safe."

"But we don't. We don't know for sure that she got out."

"I'm sure she's fine. From what you've told me Maya is a resourceful woman. She just needs time to process the trauma of the kidnapping and everything that happened to her. Let's give her a few days," Luca said trying to console me.

"Maya?" Jade snapped. "What about me? She should count herself lucky. I'm the one who is traumatized after seeing her. She looks like some kind of monster with all those bandages. Honestly, Cristiano, you should thank her for leaving you; she's doing you a favor."

Ravn slammed on the brakes and erupted, "Get out! I told you what would happen if you opened your mouth one more time."

"You can't just kick me out. I have no money, no ID," she yelled back at him, not believing he was serious.

"Not my problem. Is Jade anyone's problem?" he asked, looking around at the rest of us.

"No!" was the unified response.

Luca smiled. "Cristiano, the honor is all yours."

I turned around in my seat. "Get the hell out!" As she reached for the door handle, I saw it. "Jade wait!" I screamed.

"I knew you had more sense than to get rid of me."

I leaned over the seat and yanked Maya's tear of bravery from Jade's scrawny neck.

"You can't take that. It's mine," she pouted.

"No, it's not. It belongs to Maya." Dalley happily pushed Jade out of the car, but not before Luca added one last thing.

"Oh, and Jade, whatever you do, never set foot in Portugal again or I will arrest you for kidnapping and unlawful confinement."

"You can't—" she whined snarkily.

"Yes, he can!" Dalley said, laughing at her. "Now get lost!"

We left Jade standing on a street corner in the middle of Casablanca with nothing but a scowl embedded on her face.

❧

I stared out the window, holding onto the letter, hoping that somehow I misunderstood her intention; none of it made sense.

"Cristiano, would you like me to read the rest of it?" Dalley asked with a tone of unrecognizable compassion.

"Why? What difference does it make? What am I going to tell her parents? Beth? It doesn't matter to me what she looks like under the bandages. It just doesn't matter. I love her. She doesn't trust me anymore."

"Cristiano, this is not about trust or love, but more about trauma," Luca tried to explain. "She loves you, but right now, she's scared. She doesn't know what the future holds, and we don't know what she has been through."

"No, we don't," Dalley broke in, "but she's not the only victim in this situation. If Jade took Saafa's spot, what happened to Saafa? Maya said she was only sixteen and needed to get away. Give me the letter."

"Dalley, there is nothing we can do for Saafa right now. We can only hope she is resourceful enough to find another way out," Luca offered.

"That's easy for you to say. You're not sixteen, alone, and ready to be married off into a life of marital slavery!" she screamed, filling the car with her anger and indignation.

"Dalley," Ravn said, trying to calm her down. "This is not helping Cristiano."

"We should go back for her," she tried again. I wasn't sure if she was talking about Saafa or Maya, but I saw the pain in her eyes. Dalley had changed.

"I'm sorry, Dalley, but we can't." Luca tried to explain to her. "I'll look into her story when we get back to Portugal. Maybe I can do something from there."

For the first time since I met her, I agreed with Dalley. I wanted to save Saafa, as I knew it's what Maya intended, but the truth was I couldn't even speak. I could only stare at her handwriting on the letter. *How could she just leave me?*

Dalley reached for the letter, and I didn't resist.

Dear Cristiano,

I'm safe, or at least I will be by the time you're reading this. I need you to take Saafa. She's sixteen and all alone in the world. She needed to escape from that place, or they were going to marry her off to an old man. I know you can make sure she has a good life. So please, give her a hug right now as if it were me. They are all watching. I'll already be gone. Saafa helped me find a way out, so just turn around and leave. You can read the rest of the letter in the car. Go right now, I am begging you. Please. I know you don't want to, and you have a million questions, but you have to go right now.

You must be in the car feeling confused. I will not try to convince you I don't love you. That would be futile. But loving someone and sharing a life with them are two different things. I guess in some ways, not being officially married makes it easier for us.

"Cristiano, are you okay?" Ravn asked, interrupting Dalley. "No, I'm not. My wife just told me it would be easier not to be married to me."

"That's not what she said, Cristiano. Do you want me to stop reading?" Dalley asked.

"No, if she could write it, the least I can do is listen to it."

They told me about Avo. I'm not sure what I can say, except my heart breaks for you. I wish it could be different, that I could be with you during this time, but your new family will help you through her death. Euphemia and Marcos are such wonderful people. They will know how to help, and Puro, well, he has always been there for you. Avo was one of the most important people in my life. She taught me so much while we were together.

I reached into my back pocket and pulled out the handkerchief and placed it to my nose. I could smell her, feel her. Oh my God, where is she? Where is Maya?

You're still asking "why?" And you're right, it wasn't just about Saafa. This is about me. She didn't want to do it, to take my place, but I made her.

I could never ask you to take me back the way I am. I'm not the same person you fell in love with. I'm broken and not sure if I will ever heal. In the crash, when the windshield shattered, it sliced my face up. Saafa helped me as much as she could and I am forever grateful to her. It was because of her I survived the entire ordeal.

Saafa helped me find a way out. I owe her my life.

Cristiano, please know that coming to Portugal and meeting you changed my world. I never thought I could love or be loved with such passion and respect, but you proved me wrong. During my time at Netuno, I found my voice, and this is me using it.

I hope one day I will find the peace to learn how to love my new self, but I cannot ask you to wait for a day I don't know exists. I need to figure things out on my own. Please apologize to my parents and Beth and tell Carmo I'm sorry. I promised her I would never hurt you or break your heart, but I don't have any other choice.

Maya

I love you. Goodbye.

"Yes, you had a choice, and you made the choice to run. Run away from me and the life we could have had." I looked at Dalley. "Whatever happened to her face, it doesn't matter. How could she think I wouldn't love her, after everything we've been through? Ravn, stop the car. I'm going to be sick."

29

Fear

Maya

SAAFA AND I ESCAPED THE property and made it to the bus stop in time. My heart was still racing when the bus arrived and did not slow until we slid into our seats. Saafa squeezed my hand and whispered into my ear.

"Maya? How are you doing? Your hands are cold."

"Really? I feel so hot I could vomit. Saafa, I have to take the niqab off. My insides are churning and the morning heat is already unbearable."

"Maya, you cannot take it off on the bus. That would be terrible for us. How can I help you?"

"Saafa, are you sure I can't at least take the bandages off? My breath quickened and my palms became clammy. I grabbed the seat in front of me.

"Maya? What's the matter?"

"It's coming." I said, pulling at the fabric that was sticking to my body.

"What's coming?"

"A panic attack." I found a single screw to stare at on the back of the seat.

"What can I do?" she asked. I heard the worry in her voice, but I couldn't take my eyes off the screw.

"I'm too hot, I feel like I'm suffocating. Distract me. Tell me more about Crete? Tell me what it's like."

"It's part of Greece?" she blurted out.

"Yes, that much I know, Saafa." I was agitated and being unfair.

"I don't know what to say. I've never been there. Why are you mad at me?"

I took a long breath in then started to blow the air out slowly. I had to get this under control before the panic took over, I had to be the grown up, she was depending on me.

Breathe in. "I'm sorry about the Crete thing." I blew the air out. "When I was in grade twelve my graduation gift from my parents was a trip to Crete, but the trip was over before it even began." I took another breath in and blew it slowly, putting me in charge of the panic that swirled restlessly under the surface of my skin.

"What happened?" Saafa asked, leaning in.

"The usual. My mom got sick again, and I had to cancel another trip and look after my sister."

"Another?" Saafa asked with a break at the end of the word.

I blew out a long-protracted breath. "Yes, another. The first was Paris, two years before that. Back to Crete, tell me what you do know."

"My parents went when they were first married and stayed for two months. My mom said Crete was like stepping back in time, that it was breathtaking. After my brother died, my mom once told me if she had another life to live, it would have been on Crete, walking free by the ocean, smelling the salt air and picking wildflowers all day long."

Saafa paused. I could hear the sadness in her voice and could only imagine how much she missed her mother.

"I had one other story to tell. I think you'll like this one. My mother talked about a mysterious wild woman who lived near the sea. How she let her curly hair fly around her face in the ocean breeze, and how by just being near her, people started to breathe again. You can't find her if you are looking, but she will find you if it's meant to be."

As Saafa spoke, the panic passed, and I imagined the ocean breeze flowing over my skin, letting the salt air fill my lungs and allowing me to breathe, in and out. I could feel my temperature decrease and my heart rate slow. I imagined myself sitting with the wild woman on the edge of a cliff, watching the waves crash into the rocks again and again.

I unclasped my fingers from the seat in front of me and sat back. "Have a rest, Maya, I'll let you know when we arrive in the city. We are going to be okay. We have each other now." I saw relief in her eyes reinforcing that I had done the right thing for her and that was enough.

꧁

When we arrived in the city, Saafa raised me from my awkward slumber then pulled my tired body behind her through the increasingly busy streets. "Where are we going?"

"The market. My market. We will find everything we need there. Clothes, food, and help to get out of the country."

I felt sluggish, and my body resisted each step. I gave up trying to be in charge and let her take over.

"There are many good people there who will help us. Let's get you changed first."

When we arrived at the market, Saafa smiled and took a breath. "It's like coming home. It's been too long. I didn't think I'd miss this place."

Saafa waved at vendors as we walked through the market.

"I have never seen so many olives in my life," I said, laughing out loud.

Saafa chuckled along with me. "Well, that is good to know, as this is The Great Habous Olive Market," she said cheekily.

"What should I do about my face?" I asked, feeling suddenly uncomfortable about removing the niqab.

"Nothing. It's the city. It shouldn't be a problem. Maya, I know you're not ready to see Cristiano, but you can't hide under a veil forever. That's not what it's for. I know this is not what you had planned for your life, but we can't worry about what other people think right now. I'm scared too, but for different reasons. I don't know what is going to happen, either. I'm sixteen, my parents are dead, and I'm running away so I don't have to get married."

The reality of her words stung with frankness. She was right, if I was going to make any kind of life, scars or not, I had to get healthy again and make some good decisions. I dove into my thoughts as Saafa led me into a little shop where we were greeted by a friendly face. Saafa spoke in hushed tones to the man. He nodded and directed me to a little changing room. Saafa grabbed a few items of clothing and passed them to me to change into. I sucked in a breath. Saafa was right about feeling scared, but it was now my responsibility to make sure she was going to be safe and I had to find the strength.

After changing out of the niqab, I came from behind the curtain, attempting to wrap the hijab around my head.

Saafa laughed. "Here, let me help you with that."

The shopkeeper looked at me and then at Saafa with concern. Saafa and I both understood that things might be more complicated than she first thought about wearing the facial bandages in public. The shopkeeper handed me an extra scarf, and as I wrapped it around my face, I could feel any threads of confidence slip away with each turn of the fabric.

Before Saafa could say another word, two customers walked in. But not just any customers—Dalley and Ravn were standing directly in front of me.

"Bonjour," she said clumsily. I froze, not sure where to turn. Saafa tried pulling me over, but I was stuck.

"Excusez-moi, s'il vous plaît," Ravn said to me, assuming I was a local. He didn't know who I was. My heart was pounding and I could hardly breathe. If they were here, then Cristiano was too.

"Dalley," Ravn said with annoyance. "We promised Luca a brief stop. Luca is worried about him and suggested we get some food for him. He's completely empty after vomiting on the side of the road."

I gasped and they both looked at me without recognition, then continued their conversation.

"Yes, I am thankful you stopped just in time. That would have made things so much worse."

"Honestly, Dalley. I love you, but sometimes you have the compassion of a flea. We need to go."

"Ravn, I'm just mad at her right now. I wish I knew what Maya was thinking. How could she do this to him?"

"Don't be so hard on her. We don't know what's happening. Give her time, she'll come back." Ravn stated firmly, like he knew something I didn't.

A vice grip hold replaced Saafa's gentle tug on my sleeve, letting me know the pieces had just come together as she identified all the names that were being spoken. Eyes wide open, she pleaded with me to say something. I would not.

Dalley continued in her snippy tone, "Well, I hope so. I'm sure she would be interested to know that her father and Cristiano are *actually* working together now." She shook her head, disappointed in me. "And that was the saddest call I've ever had to listen to …"

"I know. I could hear Judith crying through the phone," Ravn said, blowing out a deep breath.

"God, I hope they don't blame Cristiano for this." Dalley moaned. "And then the rest of them yelling in the background, wailing about what was going on. I thought Josie was going to lose her mind."

"Yes, Maya obviously needs some time," Ravn said, shaking his head.

"Really? I thought real friends wouldn't give up. Beth's not giving up on her. I can guarantee you that," she said, punctuating her comment with her hands on her hips, rendering Ravn into smart silence.

Dalley picked out a few trinkets, paid the vendor, and they left without saying another word.

My heart was beating so loud I could hardly hear Saafa when she tried to talk to me.

"Maya, we should go after them. It is a sign."

"I don't believe in signs."

"I don't believe you."

"No, I can't," I said, ending the conversation.

She stopped pushing back and shook her head in disappointment. "What do you need?" she asked as we walked out of the stall and into the market, which was now busy with people.

"I need to be away from everyone." Saafa led me through the throngs of shoppers and out the main entrance.

As we stepped through the gate, I saw him immediately. He was standing against a car, head in his hands, dark curls falling around his face. My heart slammed against my chest and all I wanted to do was run to him.

"Maya," Saafa whispered in my ear. "We have to keep moving. We need to meet the shopkeeper's wife."

Something shifted in Saafa's face from focus to fear. Then I heard it. His bellowing voice, calling out her name, "Saafa!!!" Dakar shrieked. "Don't you dare move, you ungrateful whore."

I looked over to where the voice came from and saw Dakar running straight towards us, then looked back at Cristiano; as he lifted his head, our eyes met. I dropped the scarf, revealing the bandages and his face filled with confusion. "Maya!" he screamed.

"Run, Maya, run!!" Saafa yelled.

Saafa took my hand and dragged me back into the market, weaving us through the crowds, looking for a place to hide as an enraged Dakar screamed her name. When we finally stopped to take a breath, my mind flooded with images of Cristiano's eyes, staring at me, calling my name. He was horrified by me.

30

I Found Her

Cristiano

IT WAS MAYA. SHE SAW me, so why did she run? She needed help, I was right there.

Luca ended his call with Beth when Dakar screamed Saafa's name.

"We need to move, Cristiano. Maya and Saafa need our help!"

Within seconds, adrenaline replaced pain as Luca and I chased Dakar into the market. I could only hope we found Maya and Saafa before he did.

"Call the police!" Luca yelled to Ravn as we passed him near the entrance.

Luca slowed because of the busy crowds but kept inching forward. "Cristiano, Saafa and Maya got out together. You know what that means, right?" he yelled back to me while tactically scanning the crowd but answered before I could even open my mouth. "She waited for you. She waited to see you."

"How do you know her waiting was about me?"

"Because I do. Cristiano, she threw practicality out the window when she fell in love with you. The woman followed you down to Egypt to find you. People wait their whole lives for that kind of love. Don't give up on her. We have to keep moving."

"If she loves me so much, why is she running from me?"

"Maybe she thinks she's protecting you."

"From what?"

"Weren't you listening to Jade? Or when Dalley read the letter? Didn't you notice the bandages on her face?"

"What are you talking about?"

"Her face, Cristiano. *I* only knew it was her because Saafa called her name. How did *you* know?"

"Her eyes. She looked right at me." I searched my thoughts for the image. I could only see her eyes. Then I remembered Dakar's lackey at the hospital mention her being like a mummy … and the images came flooding back. We were in the car. There was blood all over her face. "It doesn't matter … I … I don't care about any of that."

"You may not, but she obviously does. Cristiano. Listen to me, we have bigger problems right now. If Dakar gets them out of the market, he will make it impossible for us to find them. We have to separate but be careful. He will be armed."

"Oh, I know all about the Ptolemites' shoot-first-and-ask-questions-later policy."

"If you find him, don't engage. Wait for the police and call me on my cell. Promise me. Do you know how much trouble I'd be in if you got shot?" He smiled and then was gone.

"What color hijab was she wearing?" I paused briefly, trying to figure out what direction to go in.

Then I heard Dalley's panicked and breathless voice behind me. "Maya is here?"

"There isn't time to explain, except that we have to find them before Dakar does."

"Them?"

"Yes, Maya and Saafa are here together, but he is after them. Dalley?"

"Ravn called the police. Now go! Find her!"

❧

Beth

"Beth, what did he say?" Judith shouted at me, demanding more information.

"Beth," Maggie put her arm around Judith. "Tell us what you know, and we'll figure it out."

I took a breath. "They stopped at a market on their way to the airport. Cristiano had gotten sick and Luca wanted to get him something to eat. Luca stayed with him by the car while they waited for Dalley and Ravn to return. During our conversation, something happened, and Luca dropped the call."

"What do you mean, something happened?" Judith asked. She grabbed on to Maggie's hand.

"They found her, they found Maya," I tried to say without giving false hope.

"Oh, thank God! Are they on their way home?" Judith searched for answers.

I looked at Maggie, letting her know with a headshake that was not the end of the story. She grabbed Judith more tightly. "No, something has happened," I said almost in a whisper.

The room went silent.

"What do you mean?" Judith roared at me.

Euphemia jumped in. "You said Cristiano got sick, is he hurt?"

"I don't know."

"What *do* you know?" Marcos raised his voice, too.

"Marcos, that tone is unnecessary," Puro stepped in. "Beth, please continue."

"Luca and I were talking about Maya and then suddenly, I heard yelling in the background. Cristiano called Maya's name, and a man started screaming 'Saafa' and Luca was gone. I know nothing else. I called him back, but his phone went to voicemail. The best I can piece together is that Maya and Saafa escaped and Dakar found them."

Jacinta walked into the room with Tim, just as everyone started peppering me with more questions. She looked at me for answers.

"What is going on now? Where is my brother? Maya? Did I hear you say they found Maya? Why are you yelling at one another? You're supposed to be the grownups. Do something!" she cried.

She was right; it was chaos. I could feel a wave of emotion building again, so I raised my teacher hand and silenced them all. Walking over to Jacinta, I placed my hand on hers ever so gently.

"Jacinta, look at me. Maya is very resourceful. She got Saafa out of the compound ... Yes, it appears something else has happened, but your brother is there," I paused, "and so are Dalley and Ravn and Luca. You didn't get to meet Dalley for long, but she is fierce and would do anything to help Maya. And Luca, well, it's his job to bring people home and from what he has told me, he's very good at his job." I took a deep breath. "Tim, why don't you take Jacinta out to the fields? Mr. Wells is out there with his pruners. I bet he could do with some help."

"Jacinta?" Judith stepped over to catch her before she left and whispered in her ear. She smiled and gave her a hug.

"I can do that for you, Mrs. Wells."

"Oh, dear, please call me Judith."

I saw the unspoken exchange between Euphemia and her daughter and the defiance in Jacinta's eyes. "Thank you, Judith. I'll let him know."

Euphemia shook her head. "Thank you, Beth, for getting them out of here. I feel like a terrible mother. I don't know how to help her right now."

"Oh, I have lots of practice dealing with upset hearts. I think we're all very much like the six-year-olds I teach. So much passion and drama, but in the end, all we really want is to feel safe and loved."

Euphemia's fear was palpable, "They are coming home, right?"

I didn't know how to answer the question, so I continued to wear my teacher hat and pivoted. "Like I said to Jacinta, Maya is resourceful and from what I know, Cristiano has had to fight for everything in his life, so between the two of them I don't imagine either of them will give up until they are home."

"Yes, Maya and Cristiano will come stay with us in Porto as soon as they get back," Euphemia stated with no room for discussion.

Then I saw Judith shift into a defensive position. "Thank you for the offer, Euphemia, but it's too early to decide where they might be staying. Who knows, it might be best if Maya comes back to Peachland with us. Cristiano can come and visit when the paperwork gets sorted. It's going to be some time before the marriage can happen."

"What is there to think about? They love each other, and they *are* married, at least in *our* eyes. I can't believe you're thinking about separating them. How could you do that? After everything they have been through?"

"I think Maya will need some time away from your son to figure out what she really wants."

"When did you change your mind? You're blaming this on my son?"

The conversation between Judith and Euphemia was becoming increasingly tense. I looked over to Maggie for help, but before she could intervene, Euphemia broke down into tears and ran out of the room, with Marcos close behind.

Judith ran out a different door and Maggie shooed Puro after her.

At that point, the room cleared, leaving only Sachi, Petra, Maggie, Josie, and me.

"Well, what an interesting turn of events. This has been quite the morning. I think we need something to drink, or at least I do," Josie quipped, sitting on the edge of levity and brevity.

Having time to get to know the group of women Maya now called her friends, I found myself intrigued by the bond they had formed. I was happy for Maya, but truthfully, a little jealous too. I was her best friend, yet it was being there, with those people, which helped her take the next step in figuring out who she wanted to be.

My selfish side wondered if Judith was right that bringing Maya back to Peachland could be the answer. With Phillip and Judith moving back to the vineyard, Maya could start a new chapter of her story.

"Beth, are you okay?" Sachi asked with concern. "It looks like you are physically in pain."

"Oh, thank you Sachi. I'm worried about what's happening, and hope Luca can bring Maya back safely."

The tears brimmed around my eyes. "I'm sorry. I feel like I'm intruding. I'm not sure where I fit in here. Everything has been a bit much these last few days." I rubbed my eyes, catching the tears as they fell.

"I think this conversation would go better with wine. What do you think, Beth?" Petra asked, handing me a tissue.

"I'm sure it's five o'clock somewhere," Maggie said, squeezing my arm. "Maya would not object. Let's open a bottle of that Vinho Verde she loves so much. Did she tell you about the Vinho Verde night our first week here at Netuno?"

"No, she never had the chance."

"Oh, let me tell the story," Josie jumped in.

And then I saw it, felt it. Their friendship circle opened and embraced me. Each person shared stories about their time at Netuno and one could hardly believe they had only met a few weeks before, but somehow life and circumstance had bound them together—bound us together.

"So, what's up with you and Luca, Beth?" Josie asked with a wink.

"Nothing," I said, feeling a blush hit my cheeks.

They all laughed.

"Oh Beth, you'll have to do better than that," Josie insisted. "This lot won't give in until you share the story."

"Is this really the time to be talking about this?"

"This is exactly the time. Maya's in trouble and there's nothing we can do to help her. The only thing we can do is talk about good things. Things that would make Maya smile. And learning about you and Luca would definitely make Maya smile." Josie's answer removed some of the pressure I was feeling.

"There's not much to tell. He's helping Maya and I'm helping him."

"Oh, so modest," Petra teased. "What kind of help are you giving him? From what Carmo told me, he thinks you are something else."

"He said that? That's flattering, but not practical … I live on the other side of the world, and I'm not here for that."

"For what? A little fun? To connect with someone who is risking their life to save your best friend?" Josie asked. "Come on, Beth, let go just a little."

I started fussing with my hair. "Truthfully, if you're right, I'm not sure what he sees in me."

The group stopped and stared. I obviously had said something that was against their women's friendship rules.

"What are you talking about, Beth? You're spectacular," Josie said.

"Yes, you're beautiful," Petra confirmed.

"That's what Dalley said. I thought she was just trying to make me feel better about that part of myself."

"Which part?" Josie asked. "The bigger part? The more voluptuous, round parts. These are the best parts. Or, that's what I've been told over the years," she said, holding herself and laughing.

"We shouldn't be laughing right now; Maya's in danger," I protested again.

Maggie stepped in, "You're right, she's in danger, and the Axelines almost stole Netuno and my son died tragically just a few weeks ago. And yet here we are. Is the pain real? Yes. Does having a glass of wine and a few laughs make all the bad days go away? No. But it gives us a chance to take a breath so that when the next phone call comes, and it will, we are a little more grounded and can reduce the chance of breaking in half. I know all about being broken and right now one of the few things keeping me together is our friendship and all of you."

Sachi approached us, holding two bottles of wine.

"Well then, I guess I made it back just in time. There is no problem a good bottle or two of Vinho Verde can't solve. Yet another life lesson I've learnt since arriving at Netuno," Sachi smiled.

"I can see why no one wants to leave here," I breathed out.

"Yes, at this rate, the brothers will have to build us our own house on the property," Josie laughed. "Oh, wait, you own the place now, Sachi. Can you build us a clubhouse?"

"Yes, let's start drafting the plans today."

Sachi poured the green sparkly wine while Josie grabbed a napkin and started to draw.

31

Stretched Too Thin

Maya

I KNEW SAAFA AND I could not outrun a bullet, and if Dakar found us, we had incinerated any pretense of kindness. He was angry. He lost what he believed was his and wanted her back.

Saafa and I ran back to the kiosk where we had met her friend. One look at our faces and he knew we were in trouble. Within seconds, he had us hidden away behind reams of fabric.

When we finally took a breath. I was rubbing my side, trying to get rid of a cramp.

"Are you okay? Maya, who were those people by the car?"

I didn't answer.

"One man, he was staring at you. He recognized you. He called your name."

Of course he recognized me. He had studied every inch of me and stared enough times into my eyes to know who I was, bandages or not.

"It was Cristiano, my husband."

"He's here? Maya, what more do you need?"

"Are you kidding me? This is a nightmare. All of it. Did you see how he stared at me? He was terrified."

"You don't know that, Maya. You don't know what he was thinking. Maybe he was shocked to find you. He thought you left him. I read the letter and he must have, too."

"What does that matter? Right *now*, we are hiding from a crazy man who wants to marry you off—if you are lucky—and has no use for me except as a kitchen worker."

She pursed her lips.

"I grew up with a pouty sister. Saafa, say what you need to say."

"You are being selfish," she whisper-yelled at me.

"Selfish?" I remembered Jordan sputtering the same words at me the morning I cancelled the wedding. "Yes, Saafa, sometimes you have to put yourself first. Does that mean I'm being selfish? I don't know. I just know we must find a way out."

I cast the dank fabric off my head, as the heat was too much to bear, but regretted my action immediately. My timing in life had often been flawed and, once again, I did not disappoint the universe.

"Oh, you think so, do you?" Dakar laughed as he leapt forward, trying to grab Saafa. I stepped in front of her, blocking him.

"She is not going anywhere with you. She's free now."

"You tricked me, Ferret. I am not sure how, but you took my two best prizes."

"I thought all you wanted was the hair fork?"

"Yes, but I also like to keep what is mine. I understand about Saafa, but Jade?"

My face deceived me.

"Oh," he smiled. "That wasn't part of the plan. I will miss her, but she *was* a troublemaker. You and Saafa will be very useful to me."

"Dakar, we are not going anywhere with you."

"Really?"

It all happened so fast. I thought he was trying to go around me, but before I could react, he twisted my arm and had a knife to my throat.

"Don't hurt her!" Saafa shouted at him "… she's pregnant."

"What?" I sputtered.

"You're lying. You are such a liar!" Dakar yelled at her.

"I'm not lying." Saafa said, coming forward. "She is pregnant. You are a lot of things, Dakar, but not a killer of children."

I placed my hand on my stomach. *Was she lying? Was she just saying that to free me? The nausea, the vomiting, the fatigue—all of it. Could it be true? How would she know before I did?* Just then, I saw Saafa's eyes widen and her body stiffen, like she had seen something behind me. Dakar was so consumed with anger he didn't notice her reaction.

A small smile flashed across her face. Saafa looked at me with hopeful eyes and took a breath. I yelped as the knife pressed deeper into my skin and a trickle of blood dripped over my collarbone.

Saafa took one step closer. "Dakar, I'll come with you. You're right. I'm a liar and an orphan and I need you. I thought I could make it in the world without you." The pressure on my neck decreased. "Please let her go. You have no reason to harm her. You got the relic. She is of no use to you; you made sure of that. Look at those bandages. She could not be married to anyone but a blind man and from what the women in the kitchen told me, she is useless there too."

I knew Saafa was baiting him, but hearing her words stung, knowing there was truth in what she said. Dakar pulled the blade back and Saafa offered me her hand. I took it and she instantly ripped me from Dakar's distracted arms, flinging me off to the side against a wall of fabric.

I landed with a thump, leaving me conscious but unable to move as the scene unfolded.

"Put the knife down!" Luca screamed, gun drawn.

Dakar's rage exploded. "You're a liar and don't deserve to be anyone's wife," he screeched, plunging the knife into Saafa's chest. Before he could lunge at her again, Luca took the shot and ended his life. Saafa reached to her chest, then crumpled in a heap.

"Help her, someone please help her, you can't let her die," I screamed as I scrambled over and held her hand.

Then I saw him; Cristiano came barreling towards me, a look of frenzy and fear shining on his skin. He knelt down putting pressure on my cut, then pulled me out of the way as Luca and the police rushed in to help Saafa. It was not until I saw Ravn and Dalley staring at me did I become conscious of the bandages again. I hid my face in my hands.

"Maya, I need to get you out of here," Cristiano entreated.

"I am not going anywhere without Saafa. I promised to protect her."

"And I promised to protect *you*," He pleaded.

"You don't need to protect me. It's not your job. We're not married."

He reacted as if I had punched him in the gut. "What are you talking about? Of course we are, don't you remember? 'Because God said so.' That's what you told your father on the phone. I didn't understand it then, but I do now. We are married in all the ways that count. We are married enough for now."

"What does that mean? Married enough. Either we are or we aren't. And we are not."

"Yes, we are, and it means we need to get the two of you to the hospital."

"The two of us?" I looked over at Saafa.

"No." He put his hand on my stomach.

Then it hit me. "The baby? I'm not pregnant. Saafa made that up." Then I felt an irrational burst of anger. "Saafa is bleeding out and all you can think about is this?" I pointed to my stomach, not wanting to say the word. "There is no this!"

"Maya, stop. Why are you yelling at me?" He asked with confusion.

But I couldn't stop. The dam broke and every feeling I had came flooding out.

"So, you are going to just take me back hacked up and mangled? Of course you are, now that you think there is another reason to keep me around." I pointed again to my stomach.

"Take you back? What are you talking about? You make it sound like you left me willingly, that I did you a favor coming down here to get you."

"Didn't you? Didn't you do it because you felt obligated? I followed you to Cairo and you followed me to Morocco. We're even now."

"Maya, you're being ridiculous."

"Now I'm disfigured and ridiculous. Why would you ever want to be with me?" I saw the pain in his face, but I couldn't help myself.

I tried to step away but lost my footing. He grabbed me. "Let me go, Cristiano." The anger dissipated. "Please let me go."

The paramedics were strapping Saafa to the gurney and insisted I come to the hospital, too.

"Dalley, come with me."

"Maya, I think Cris—"

"No, you want to be my friend. Then this is being my friend. Do what I say. Ravn, please go with Saafa. We will see you at the hospital."

❧

Cristiano

"What just happened?" I asked Luca as we stood amidst a growing circle of police and onlookers. "We need to follow the ambulance to the hospital."

"No, Cristiano, we don't. She's safe now, but she's not ready to see you."

"Why? What happened to her, Luca? Why is she being like this?"

"I'm not sure," Luca said warily. "I think we need to go back to the compound. It might give us a clearer picture of what she has gone through."

"No, I need to go to the hospital."

"She can't see you right now. You need to give her some space. Dalley will make sure she is taken care of."

"I can't believe she pushed me away. She needs me, doesn't she?"

"Cristiano, with Dakar dead, the compound is the only place we are going to find any answers about what happened to her."

I let him lead me to the car and we began making our way back to the compound. When we arrived, the urgency that filled my body before had disappeared; I felt numb. The property was beautiful and for a moment a fleeting thought occurred that she had been exaggerating. As we continued to walk around, a young officer approached Luca.

"Come with me," he said to us. As we followed the officer, my stomach churned. By the look on his face, I knew he was going to show us something terrible.

As we stepped into an outbuilding, we descended. When we hit the bottom stair, we turned and walked down a long, dark hallway. At the end of the hall, I saw a heavy metal door with a large sliding bolt that clanged noisily as the officer slid it open. It was where he kept her, where he hit her. The place where …

Luca stepped in and then exited quickly.

"Cristiano, I don't think you need to see this. I was wrong to bring you here."

"No, no, you weren't. I need to see where she was. If I have any hope of understanding what she went through, I need to see."

When I stepped into the damp room the smell of urine and vomit hit me like a wave. But instead of running away, I stood, letting it crash over me. I knew feeling her fear and desolation was the only way. I walked over to the cot she slept on and picked up her blood-stained pillow. Under the pillow I found a little slip of crumpled paper. My stomach turned again and I swallowed back the bile. I carefully unfolded it, finding a version of Maya's handwriting which I had not seen before. If letters could be filled with fear, then each stroke of the pen revealed her true state of mind. My hands trembled as I read the poem.

Somewhere Hot and Alone

Bandages stick to my skin like flailing flies clinging to yellow paper.

My flesh feels dead; my face is dead. Who am I under this plaster of white?

Am I the same person?

Am I still the fresh adventurer who hopped on the train to find the man I love?

No.

I want to disappear, to get lost in the sea, to sit on a rock where only the fishes are my friends.

Fear of what I will find leaves my heart in spasms.

His voice, he loves me. He loves the old Maya. Could he love this one too?

Her words tore me apart.

"Don't give up, Maya, on yourself, on me, on us," I whispered. Rubbing my hands over my face, I could feel exhaustion take hold. My ribs ached and my body rebelled.

Luca's gentle hand landed on my shoulder, letting me know it was time to go. "Cristiano, there's nothing left to find here. We should go to the hospital. She needs you, even if she can't ask for it right now."

As we drove back into town, neither of us spoke until Luca's phone rang.

"Hello," he paused. "That's good news. I'll let him know. Thank you, Ravn."

My heart leapt. Good news? "What?" I asked, not sure how anything could be good.

"Saafa, is out of surgery. She's still critical, but they think she'll pull through."

I was happy about Saafa but had to hide my disappointment. I hoped Luca had heard something about Maya. But I was too afraid to ask, and he didn't offer. So, I closed my eyes and pretended for just a moment that I was standing barefoot in the nuns' garden, watching my beautiful bride jump into the labyrinth and make her way toward me. Each step she took was like watching someone float on air.

When I opened my eyes, Luca wasn't in the car anymore and Dalley had taken his place.

"Cristiano." Her voice was too soft, too kind. Something had happened.

"What? What's the matter? Maya? The baby?" I grabbed for the door handle, but she was quicker than me.

"Cristiano. You need to hear every word I'm saying." She took a breath and let go of the door handle, setting herself back in the driver's seat.

"Maya received a couple of stitches on her neck and they gave her something to settle her nerves. She is not acting herself right now."

"What about the baby?"

"We don't know if there is a baby. She refused to have a pregnancy test."

"Refused. What's the matter with her?" I felt angry. Why was I angry?

"Cristiano. Maya wanted me to let you know that as soon as she is able, she's leaving for Crete."

"Crete? By herself? Is she crazy? I'm right here." I felt like she was stretching my heart, just waiting for it to tear in two.

32

Broken

Maya

I THREW A SHEET OVER my head just before he burst through the door.

"What are you doing Maya?"

"Go away, Cristiano." The words tumbled from my lips.

"No, I'm not going anywhere."

"Yes, you are. I don't want you here."

"Why? You think I wouldn't love you? Couldn't love you because of your face?"

I tore the sheet off. "You think you can love this?" He jumped back.

"Get out, Cristiano! Leave me alone."

"Leave you alone? So you can take off to Crete by yourself? No way! I'm not going anywhere. I love you," he said, shaking a piece of crumpled paper in his hand. "You can't doubt that. How can you doubt that?"

"Yeah, sure you love me. That's why you jumped a foot off the ground when you saw me. No one could love this," I yelled again, throwing the sheet back over my head. "I'm going to Crete, and you can't stop me."

"Maya, please."

"Just go away, Cristiano," I cried with desperation.

Cristiano

Dalley arrived in Maya's room just as she told me to leave. I was heartbroken. Dalley led me down the hall and out to a rooftop garden.

"Why was she allowed to love me when I was broken and falling apart, and now she won't let me love her back? What is happening with her face?"

"I don't know, I'm no psychiatrist. I'm still trying to wrap my head around it too. She is refusing to look in the mirror. She doesn't believe us and is insisting the doctors wrap her face back up."

"Dalley, what is going on?" I knew she didn't have the answers, but hoped by asking it out loud, we might figure it out. Then I saw the crack in Dalley's veneer. She cared about Maya, but we were helpless to understand what was happening and why Maya refused to believe the injuries on her face were healing. I saw the multiple scars, but there were no angry wounds, just healing skin.

"Luca mentioned the kidnapping could have long-term effects, that it can mess with a person's mind," she offered.

"Dalley, tell me what happened when she arrived at the hospital," I said, feeling guilty. "I should have been here."

"No, you shouldn't have. It would've made it worse for her. She was quiet while they stitched up her neck. Then, someone suggested they do the pregnancy test. She flat out refused, saying it couldn't be, and then started crying something about her mom. They had to sedate her. While she was out, they removed the bandages, but they discovered her wounds were healing at an accelerated rate. After consulting with the plastic surgeon, he said there was nothing else he could do, suggesting they let the injuries heal on their own. It baffled everyone. When she woke up, they told her about the wounds and how things were healing. She refused to look in the mirror. I tried to explain the situation to her, but she didn't believe me. She's refusing to listen to anyone."

"You should've told me in the car."

"I tried, but you ran out before I had a chance."

I paced back and forth, then handed her the poem Maya wrote while at the compound. As she read, I saw her lips tighten, holding back her own tears.

"Well, if this is the case, we should talk to Beth. She'll know what to do. She knows her best. I'll call her right now," Dalley offered. "I need to talk to her about Saafa anyway."

"What is going on with Saafa? I'm sorry, I haven't even asked about her. When Ravn called, he mentioned she was out of surgery. Is she doing better? God, Dalley, I feel like I'm falling apart."

"This is no time to fall apart. There's too much going on for everyone *else* this time," she raised her eyebrow.

How could someone be so irritating and correct at the same time? "Tell me, what is happening with Saafa?" I asked.

"It looks like she's going to recover. But she has no family, nowhere to go. She can't stay in Morocco; it is too dangerous for a girl her age to be on her own."

"What are you thinking?"

"Ravn and I talked it over and think we can give her a home, or at least offer her a place to stay while she recovers and figures things out."

I paused, not sure if I could respond appropriately, but then saw a flash of something in her eyes. She needed me to agree, to say yes, "Well, I think that—"

"It's a bad idea? That I'm a horrible person and can't be a good role model?"

"I wouldn't say that, anymore." I paused. "Actually, I think you'll do great. She'll need a strong woman in her life."

"Oh," she backed down, surprised by my response. "I'll call Beth to see if she has any ideas."

"Okay," was all I could muster.

"Cristiano! I almost forgot; the psychiatrist wants to talk to you."

"Psychiatrist?" I asked, feeling another layer of discomfort fill my body.

❧

"Hello, Mr. Lazaro, can I call you Cristiano?"

I nodded hesitantly. I would not have guessed he was a doctor if he had not been wearing the ID badge that swung around his neck.

"Oh, yeah, I'm not one for standing on formalities," he tugged at his linen shirt and shorts, "but I can guarantee you I am a doctor, or so my mother continues to tell all her friends," he laughed a little at his own joke, then got more serious. "As you know, your wife has been through a horrible ordeal. The other doctors are still trying to assess the extent of her injuries. Thankfully, the knife wound was superficial, only needing a few stitches, but the facial wounds from the car accident have created an uproar around here … I tried to speak to your wife earlier, but she would not take the sheet off her head for me."

"You're not the only one. Well, she let me see her for a second, but it all went badly. I was so surprised not to see the bandages, I jumped. She thought it was because of the injuries, but it was the opposite. She looked like my Maya."

"Please come sit down, Cristiano. She is showing signs of some post trauma after the accident and the kidnapping. We won't know the extent of the effects it had on her for a while, but you can expect some erratic behaviors. As you know, they removed the bandages, but she is refusing to look in the mirror or believe her face is healing. From what we understand, the plastic surgeon said it shouldn't be possible, but I have to tell you I have seen some miraculous things over the years."

"Well, if you have any spare miracles …"

"Miracles happen, but it's not a miracle that is going to get Maya through this part." He placed his hand on my shoulder. "Her friend mentioned her mother suffered from clinical depression and anxiety most of her life."

"Yes, she experienced severe post-partum, which turned into a clinical depression and took years to get under control."

"That makes sense then, her hesitation about the possible pregnancy. Are you aware if Maya has been through any depressive episodes of her own or has experienced any other anxiety-provoking circumstances in the last six months besides the most recent situation?"

I sat back in the chair and nodded. "You mean like breaking off a wedding, falling in love with someone else, being publicly flayed on social media, getting shot at, escaping, getting married without her family present, and getting kidnapped?" My head fell into my hands as I uttered the train of events out loud.

The psychiatrist sat quietly. "Yes," he answered, taking a thoughtful breath. "That, plus the facial injuries and the possibility of a pregnancy, could all be factors which have pushed her into this state of denial."

We sat together for another hour, him asking me questions about Maya and me realizing how little I actually knew about her. He believed her brain was compartmentalizing to protect itself, finding its own way to cope.

"Sometimes the mind does a better job of taking care of us than we do."

The one piece we both continued to puzzle over was the accelerated healing of the wounds.

"Our medical team doesn't understand how it happened. There is nothing to explain why her face is not the way she believes it to be. She mentioned to one nurse that while being held, she had an opportunity to see her reflection and described every cut in detail. I believe her version of the story but the situation still continues to mystify our entire team. The only clue was the remnants of a salve found on the bandages. I was told that the young stabbing victim was the person who tended to her while she was being held but she is not well enough to fill in all the missing pieces."

"Will the wounds heal completely?" I asked, trying to prepare for the eventual conversation I would have with Maya.

"I'm not a plastic surgeon, but like any other scar in life, it doesn't have to become your entire story. Be patient with her. I will monitor her over the next couple of days, but once she's well enough to leave the hospital, she'll need to go somewhere quiet to heal, inside and out."

"Crete?"

"Yes, Crete would be good. If that's somewhere she wants to be," he sighed and leaned in. "Cristiano, what makes her feel positive?"

"She likes the garden! She loves flowers and trees, and nature helps her feel calm, and the ocean, she loves water and … she just learned how to bake," I said, thinking about the story she told me of her and Avo in the garden. I felt my chest tighten.

"Hm, that's good. Leave it with me. I may have a way to get her started."

Wandering around the hospital, I tried to figure out what to do. I needed to talk to someone. I probably should have called my parents first, but Puro was the closest thing I had to a father growing up, and I needed *him*.

33

Regrets

Puro

WE HAD BEEN WAITING FOR hours to get more information. We knew Saafa had made it out of surgery, but no one was talking about Maya. It plagued her parents with worry and everyone else at Netuno was holding their breath, waiting for the next call to come.

Beth talked to Dalley, but she was not sharing anything except that Maya was managing. Then my phone rang.

"Puro, it's me," he said, whispering my name, as if he was hiding somewhere and didn't want anyone to hear him.

"Cristiano, where are you?"

"I'm in Maya's room. She is sedated and sleeping."

"Sedated? What's going on? Beth hasn't said a word."

"Dalley made her promise. Don't be mad at her. Are you in the lobby?"

"Yes, everyone is here. Did you want me to put you on speakerphone?"

"No!" he shouted into the phone. "Please go somewhere private where you can talk."

I quickly entered the back room and closed the door. "Cristiano, is everything okay? Is Maya alright?"

"No, Puro, she's not. The doctor told me she is experiencing symptoms of PTSD. It is very confusing. I don't know what to do," I hesitated, "And … she might be pregnant, Puro."

"Pregnant? She's pregnant?"

"We don't know. She has been having symptoms, but she won't get tested."

"Why? What did she say?" Puro asked.

"She won't talk to me. The doctor thinks it has something to do with a combination of her mom's history of depression and the recent events. She thinks she would be a burden to me because of the facial injuries and that I would only stay with her because of the pregnancy. She told Dalley she's going to Crete as soon as they release her from the hospital."

"If she's going to Crete, you are too," I said.

"She doesn't want me to." I could hear the sadness in his voice and wished somehow I could take the pain away.

"Well, then you need to convince her that if she lets you go with her, you'll give her as much space as she needs. The two of you cannot be separated again. Three times is too much. You were both lost before you met each other. Then she found you in Cairo and you found her in Morocco. Nothing should separate the two of you ever again." I felt myself choking up. "Tell her I said that. Tell her I said she has to let you come to Crete with her."

"I'll try, but she's not listening."

"Find a way to make her listen."

"Oh, Puro, before I go. Please don't tell anyone about the potential pregnancy."

"I won't say a word." Just as we were finishing, Maggie stepped into the room.

"Is that Cristiano?" she inquired.

"Who's there with you?" he asked.

"It's Maggie."

"Can I talk to her, please?"

Reluctantly, I handed her the phone. As much as I loved Cristiano and Maya, I felt protective of Maggie; it had only been a few weeks since CJ's death and although she had been presenting a brave front to everyone else, I knew what was happening at night.

She was staying in my extra room at the house, letting Tim have his own space at the hotel, but it was she who needed her own space. It was she who needed someone to hold her every night without question as she cried herself to sleep. So, as she took the phone, I breathed deeply and hoped Cristiano would not make things worse for her.

As she held the phone tight to her ear, all she kept doing was nodding her head. Then I saw a tear, and another. I went to grab the phone from her, but she tapped my hand away and smiled at me.

"We will find a way, no matter what. Just take care of her and, when she's ready, come home. Yes, he's standing right here. I know. I do too."

She hung the phone up and looked at me, tears slipping out slowly.

"You know what? What do you know?" I asked, feeling anxious.

Maggie took my face in her hands and smiled. "I know you love me, and I love you too."

I didn't know what to say, but before I could form a word, she placed her finger on my lips. "But that isn't the news. We already knew that didn't we?" She leaned in and whispered, "Imagine, Maya might be pregnant," then she looked at me, laughing and crying.

⁓

By the afternoon, our burden had lessened by some degree. In her excitement, Beth let it slip that Maya might be pregnant and before I knew it, everyone was celebrating the possibility of the good news. It was clear though, the possibility of a pregnancy was not a gift to everyone.

So, when Francesco pulled up to the inn and Judith and Phillip walked onto the veranda with their luggage, my chest tightened. They were leaving and I could only assume their travel plans included a direct flight to Casablanca.

"Judith?"

"Puro, we have to go to her. I cannot just sit here and wait."

What could I say? I'm not sure anything could keep me away if Carmo was in trouble, but they didn't know the worst of it.

"Thank you, Puro, thank you for everything," she said, running over and giving me a quick hug before she climbed into Francesco's SUV.

While Phillip was on the phone talking with Maya's sister, I thought about the news that Maya intended to go to Crete and wondered if I should say something.

"Yes Jordan, we are on our way there now … I don't know if she's coming home … I know you are … I'll tell her … I'll send you a text when we get to the hospital. She'll be okay."

As he spoke, I saw Marcos, Euphemia, and several others migrate out to the veranda. News travelled fast that Judith and Phillip were leaving, and it was clear tensions were growing.

Phillip continued on the phone, not realizing an audience was forming. "I don't know what's going on, but she could be pregnant." There was another pause. "I don't think this is like mom. Honestly, I don't know. We'll figure it out. Goodbye." Phillip turned and saw me standing there.

"Jordan, Maya's little sister. She's like a hurricane and a tornado mixed." Phillip half-laughed, trying to break the growing nervous energy that hung in the air.

It was then I had the feeling, the kind parents get when breaking a confidence might be the best thing you can do for your children. Cristiano was like a son to me, but Phillip needed to know what he was walking into before he arrived.

"Phillip, there's something I need to tell you."

"Puro, we have to go. Judith is waiting."

"This can't wait."

"Just tell me then," Phillip barked.

"Maybe we should take a little walk."

"Look, Puro, just say what you need to say."

I looked over at Maggie, but knew the decision had to be mine alone— I could not let him arrive at the hospital without knowing.

"Puro, just tell me already," he blurted.

"Cristiano called a few hours ago."

Phillip was momentarily stunned. "Why didn't you tell us? What did he say? Is Maya okay?" Phillip stepped uncomfortably close to me. Marcos jumped off the stairs and was standing beside me within two seconds.

"Phillip, maybe it's best if you just go," I said, changing my mind.

Maggie spoke up. "Puro, you need to tell them already."

Judith got out of the vehicle.

"What is going on?" Judith asked Maggie. Maggie put her arm around her as I began. She was resistant at first, but Maggie would not let go.

"No, Phillip, she's not okay." I said as gently as possible. The words hit Phillip hard.

"Who's not what?" Judith asked awkwardly.

I looked over at Judith and Maggie.

"Cristiano spoke with the psychiatrist, and he believes Maya is experiencing some symptoms of post-traumatic stress and is currently denying her current circumstances regarding her facial injuries and the possible pregnancy. It's still early but …"

"Is she talking?" Phillip asked as if he was a doctor.

"Cristiano said she yelled at him."

"That's good," Phillip said, rubbing his hands over his face.

"Good?" Marcos chimed in.

"Good for her," Phillip said, looking around. "If they can keep her talking, keep her from falling, I will have a chance to get to her in time."

"Falling? In time? What are you talking about?" I asked fearfully.

"Look Puro, I have lived with Judith in and out of hospitals and doctors' offices for twenty-five years. Trust me when I tell you, we want to keep her talking, no matter what she is saying."

I reached for him, and he motioned for me to stop but not before I saw the crack in his armor and a glimpse of a broken father and husband.

"Phillip. There's one more thing you and Judith need to know."

"What, Puro? What else could there be?"

"As soon as the doctors will allow it, Maya has decided she is going to Crete."

"Crete?" He looked at Judith and then back at me.

"I don't know. Cristiano said she is determined. I'm encouraging him to go with her."

Phillip's nostrils flared. "No one is going to Crete, not with my daughter. I'm going to Morocco today to pick her up and take her home."

"You mean bring her back here, to Avo's cottage," Marcos interjected. "That's Cristiano's plan."

"Plan or no plan, I've decided I am taking her back to Peachland. She needs to be somewhere familiar where she can heal."

"You can't. That's not your decision to make. What about Cristiano and the baby?" Euphemia broke in desperate to convince Phillip.

"We'll deal with *that* later. Right now, Maya needs to be with her family."

"Cristiano is her family, we are too," Euphemia implored.

Phillip was running out of patience. "Please, Phillip," I begged him.

"Don't 'please' me … I walked through a life of depression with my wife and watched my daughter suffer the consequences. The anxiety, the overwhelm. If Maya is pregnant, we'll have to assess if that's going to be the best thing for her."

Maggie wrapped her arms more tightly around Judith, as she could no longer hold her own weight.

"Phillip, you can't mean that? You're talking nonsense now."

"Puro," he said with gritted teeth. "I appreciate everything you have done for *all* of us, but I think I know what is best for my daughter."

"You are being rash, Phillip. Please," Euphemia tried to negotiate with him while holding on to her husband's shaking fist. "Judith, I know we've had our differences, but … you know how much they love each other. You can't separate them."

Before anyone could say another word, Phillip grabbed Judith by the waist and escorted her to the SUV.

"Don't let him do it, Judith," I yelled to her as he slammed the door, leaving me filled with regret.

34

Stepping Up

Beth

I STOOD ON THE VERANDA, flabbergasted by what I had just seen. Feeling horrible, I wondered if I had just kept my mouth shut, would Phillip have been able to hold it together?

"I can't believe any of this. Mr. Wells—Phillip—is not like this." I tried to explain Phillip's rash behavior and threat to take Maya home to Peachland.

"Beth, I don't think this is the time to defend Phillip," Petra offered wisely, but I didn't listen.

"He would never make Maya do anything she didn't want to do."

"That's not very comforting right now," Marcos growled at me.

But I continued: "Before Judith and Phillip left, I was on the phone with Luca."

"What did he say?" Euphemia asked, worry seeping into her already tired face.

"Luca said Maya doesn't want Cristiano around her. He's trying to be patient, but he's in pain. He doesn't know what to do. But he's not giving up."

Euphemia became agitated. "I've had enough of waiting. If Phillip and Judith can head down there to help Maya, then we should be there to help our son."

"I'm not sure that's such a good idea, Euphemia," Puro tried to reason with her.

"Puro, he may have called you when he needed to talk," Marcos bit at him, "but Cristiano is our son."

Things were getting heated. Then I saw Euphemia take back the space.

"Marcos, listen to me. Puro has been a stable part of Cristiano's world since his parents died. It makes sense he would turn to him, ask him for help when he was feeling distressed. And Puro, thank you, we are so relieved he has you. But Marcos and I still need to go, or how is he going to learn to trust us? He needs us, and I need to be with him," Euphemia insisted. "Besides, somehow we have to convince Phillip not to take Maya back to Canada."

"Canada? He can't," Jacinta yelled as she came running into the conversation, holding a set of pruners in her hand. "He can't just take her away. They're married. Mom? Dad? What about the baby?"

"Jacinta, we don't know for sure about anything," Marcos offered to his distressed daughter.

"Home for Maya is with my brother. The cottage is her home. Avo's cottage is her home."

Jacinta ran back into the fields, with Tim following close behind her.

Euphemia moved to run after them, but Maggie held her back. "Euphemia don't worry. Tim can help her. They could both use a friend right now."

"As long as that's all it is," Marcos added with a distrustful tone.

Maggie sighed with frustration and uncharacteristically snapped back. "Marcos, that's all there is between them." She paused for a moment.

"How do you know that? Jacinta is vulnerable right now, and I saw him holding her hand earlier. I'm not taking any chances with my daughter on a boy I barely know," Marcos began to boil over.

"Marcos, please stop," Euphemia entreated.

Maggie paused as if weighing out whether she should keep talking, then took a breath and continued, "My son is gay, so *no,* you have nothing to worry about," she volleyed back at him, shaking her head.

"Oh, I … didn't …"

"Know? He barely knows. And I am sure is going to hate me now for outing him in front of a group of strangers."

Puro tried to step in. "Maggie we're not …"

"Puro, this moment is not about me or Tim, or even Jacinta. We need to focus on what is happening with Maya and what she needs."

Everyone was silent for a moment until Petra jumped in. "Well, what about Dalley? She's down there. There must be something *she* can do."

I breathed in deeply. "None of this is helping anyone. Besides, Dalley has her hands full right now. She has stepped up and taken over as temporary medical decision-maker for Saafa; she's only sixteen and has no family."

"Oh," Petra said, looking shocked. "Good for you, Dalley."

Zef cleared his throat. "Sorry to interrupt, but I might be able to help, at least a little."

"What are you talking about, Zef?" Euphemia asked.

"The house in Crete. You said Crete, right Puro? Mom, I'm talking about the one dad bought last year."

"Zef, it still needs to be renovated, it's …" Marcos was trying to find the words.

"It's not fancy, but it's livable. I may not have known my brother for long, but I don't think he's someone who worries about things like that."

"Yes, of course if it could help; I will make sure it is ready. I'll fly down there myself," Marcos offered, looking flustered.

"No, Dad, I'll go. I can do this. You need to be with Mom. Puro, can you please send Cristiano a note and let him know we have a place for him to stay when he gets to Crete?"

Pierre La Nou had quietly joined the group outside, listening intently to all that was going on. "Excuse me?" Everyone turned to Pierre. "I would be happy to fly down with Zef and help prepare the house," he offered.

Marcos nodded, and Pierre and Zef stepped back into the inn to begin making plans.

So, what do we do now? I'm not going home until I know Maya is feeling better, but I can't just sit around here doing nothing." Petra said.

Then Sachi spoke. "Well, if you want something to do. I'll put you to work."

"Sachi is right." Puro added. "There is nothing we can do for either of them right now. But if you're all looking for something to keep your hands busy, we are behind in our harvesting and could use your help."

Josie stepped forward. "Take me to your pruners."

35

Is Love Enough?

Maya

WHEN THE NURSE WALKED INTO my room pushing the wheelchair, I turned over in my bed and tried to ignore her, but she refused to accept my rudeness. "The doctor insisted it was time for you to get some fresh air," she said.

"Which doctor?"

"All of them."

The nurse rolled her eyes, and I wished the young nurse who had been in earlier was there, I didn't need anybody giving me attitude. "My legs aren't broken; I don't need a wheelchair."

"Then get up and I'll walk with you."

"What if I don't want to go with you?"

"Then I'll get someone else."

The nurse walked off in a huff but left the wheelchair. I slid out of bed, intending to push the wheelchair out into the hall to prove my point but my legs felt weak. It felt like the weight of my heart was crushing down on my bones. Shuffling over to the chair, I plopped down and placed a scarf over my face to hide my scars. Everyone kept telling me my face was healing, but *I* could feel the wounds and the broken skin under my fingertips. They were just saying whatever they needed to make me feel better. Why wouldn't they let me feel awful? Cristiano was the worst though, he kept telling me I was beautiful. Why was he lying? I knew the truth without having to see my reflection.

A wave of exhaustion overtook my body, and I closed my eyes for just a minute. When I woke, I was in the garden. No one was listening to me; I didn't feel well, and I didn't want to be there.

My one-sided argument soon ended as a wave of nausea hit me again.

"Excuse me, excuse me!" I shouted with irritation at the young nurse who was sitting nearby. "I feel sick and need some crackers! Why don't you make yourself useful."

The nurse ran out of the garden, leaving me alone, or so I thought.

"Wow." Dalley stepped out from behind a planter. I could see her shape facing me through the sheer fabric. "I might almost think you're channeling the spirit of Jade. But how could that be?"

"Shut up, Dalley. Never mention her name again."

"Maya! What the hell is wrong with you?" She yelled back at me no longer teasing. "Why are you treating people like crap? That young nurse has been bending over backwards trying to help you and you're just, being mean." She paused. "And that's not you."

"Maybe it's the new me. Maybe I've had enough of my *new* stupid life and don't want to be positive. I gave the hope thing a chance, and it didn't work out. I'm a disaster, I've always been a disaster. Who was I fooling that I deserved a better life?"

Dalley came closer to me, and I wrung my hands together under the fabric.

"Maya," she said calmly. "I'm going to take the scarf off your head. Don't argue with me. It's just you and me and I can't talk to you like this."

I tried to speak, but the words got caught in my throat. As Dalley slipped the fabric off, I quickly covered my face with my hands.

"Good, at least now I can hear when you try to insult me. Go ahead, give it your best shot, but no matter what you say, I'm not going anywhere and I'm not letting you put that scarf back on your head."

"Why?"

"Why what?"

"Why didn't my plan work?"

"Yes, tell me about your plan. I still don't quite understand what you were thinking. So, you and Saafa were *supposed* to change spots, we were *supposed* to take her back to Netuno and look after her, and you were *supposed* to get on a bus and go to Crete? And then what? Live on a beach somewhere? While Ravn and I chase Cristiano around Europe looking for you? Because you know, Maya, he would never stop until he found you. You've heard it before and I will say it again. He loves you."

"But is it enough?"

Dalley pried my fingers from my face and held my hands in hers. "How will you know if you don't even try?"

"But look at me!"

"Maya, I'm looking at you! What is it you think I'm seeing?"

I rubbed my hands over the ridges on my skin. "Ugly. I am ugly."

She folded her arms across her chest. "The only thing ugly about you right now is the way you've been acting." Flecks of anger shone in her eyes. "I'm tired of being nice to you. You're being selfish. You haven't even asked about Saafa, and Cristiano has been beside himself since you were taken. Did you even stop to ask him about his injuries and how he's doing since Avo's death?"

I felt the shot to my stomach, as if I had been kicked by a horse but she did not relent.

"Maya, I understand you've been through an ordeal but if Maya 2.0 is in there, somewhere, can you please bring her back? I liked the feisty Maya that showed up in Paris and dragged us to Egypt not this new, bitchy version. There's only room for one bitch in this friendship, and that spot is mine. Thank you very much!"

She turned and walked away. I was surprised to feel a small smile forming on my lips. I wasn't sure there were any left in me. Taking a deep breath, I looked around at the plants in the garden and wheeled myself over to the largest cactus I had ever seen.

When the nurse returned, the look on her face startled me. "What? What is it?" I asked defensively.

"Your face," she said innocently in broken English.

"Should I put it back on? Am I offending you with my scars?"

She shook her head back and forth and her eyes welled up. I knew I had gone too far. Dalley was right; who had I become?

"No," she said, trying to hold her tears back. She handed me the crackers and ran into the building.

"That went well. I have now driven away two people, and apparently it has nothing to do with my ugly face."

There was a sound on the other side of the cactus.

"Hello?"

"Bonjour." A soft and gentle voice responded.

I wheeled myself around the plant and saw an elderly woman also sitting in a wheelchair. She had dark glasses on and leaned forward in her chair like she was waiting for something to happen. On her lap lay a pencil and sketch pad. She was reaching out to the cactus.

"Be careful."

"Yes, thank you. I am trying to get a better feel for the plant before I draw it." I looked down at her paper and saw a plethora of plants and leaves. The images were beautiful and detailed. But it wasn't the hospital garden.

"Did you draw those?"

"Yes, I draw everything. Some from memory, others from real life."

"You said you were trying to get a better feel for the plant."

"I draw by touch."

She reached up and removed her glasses, revealing two dark blank, beautiful eyes.

"I only see shadows now, but I still have my memory, so for that I am very thankful."

"You draw, even though you can't see?" I stared deeply into her weathered and peaceful face, knowing that only days before I sat with bandages over my eyes, wondering if I would ever be able to see again.

"I draw because I see something different now. Come closer. I won't bite."

I wheeled my chair closer to hers until she and I were side by side. When she reached out, I was not sure what she was looking for until her fingers found my forehead. I pulled back.

"Come here, I cannot reach you," she commanded. With one hand, she turned to a fresh page in her book.

"No, thank you." I shook my head.

But she would have none of it. She reached for my arm and clasped it more firmly than anyone her age should be able to and squeezed. She squeezed so hard, in fact, it felt uncomfortable. I couldn't pull away.

"Don't move!" was all she said as she released my arm and gently touched her finger to my cheekbone. Her touch was soft, but the skin on her fingertips was rough.

"*Tranquil, mon ami, tranquil, fremez les yeux.*"

I closed my eyes as she directed, letting her trace every part of my face. I couldn't explain why I was doing what she said, but as I sat with my eyes closed, I could hear her pencil on the paper, the scratching, the sound of graphite pushing into the page. With every stroke of the pencil, my heart felt lighter, and as her rough fingers travelled over my skin, I fell into a slumber.

It was not until I felt the soft touch of a different hand and the scent of a certain perfume my eyes flew open. And there before me was my mom—my mom and dad to be exact—with Cristiano and Ravn and Dalley standing close behind.

"Hello, my dear," she said, whispering into my ear. "How are you?"

I could say nothing before my dad pushed past her. "Judith, let me see her." He looked grey, like he had aged ten years since I'd seen him. He was unshaven, and when he hugged me, his scraggly beard scraped my face.

"Mom and Dad, what are you doing here? Dad, when was the last time you shaved?"

"I haven't seen you for over a month. You wander around Portugal and France, then take off to Egypt, get married, and you are asking me about my scraggly beard?"

I could tell he was moving into full lecture mode and there was nothing I could say to stop him, but thankfully he stopped himself.

"One day when you have your own children—" He froze and went red in the face.

"That's enough, Phillip. Maya's not used to seeing you look so rustic," my mom interrupted him, trying to shift the conversation away from his awkward and possibly very true comment.

Realizing I had no face covering on, I reached down for my scarf and a piece of paper fluttered to the ground.

"What is this?" Judith asked.

Cristiano stepped forward and picked up the drawing, his eyes widening, but he didn't say a word, he just showed the paper to my mom.

"I think it's the drawing a patient did of me. I don't want to see it. It must be ghastly."

"No, Maya, it's not. She caught a peaceful side of you. It is hard to describe. Are you sure you don't want to see it?" She turned to Cristiano for the drawing, but I shook my head.

I looked over at everyone, and they stared back at me. "No, Mom, I just want to go back inside, please."

I could see the anguish on Cristiano's face. I didn't understand if it was for himself or me. He struggled to speak, but before he found the words, I insisted again my mother take me inside.

✧

Cristiano

"Cristiano. She needs more time. It's only been a couple of days," Ravn said, trying to remove the sting of rejection.

Phillip walked toward me with a disgruntled look on his face. "Cristiano, I'm sorry for just showing up here, but it might be best if you head back to Portugal. Your parents are worried."

I could feel my body tense and Ravn grabbed hold of my arm, reminding me who was speaking to me. So, I swallowed the patronizing tone he dished out and responded as best I could.

"No, Phillip, I won't be going anywhere. I have a responsibility to my family here."

"Maya's not your—"

"Phillip, I'm not sure this is the time to step into that conversation," Ravn interjected before I said something I regretted. "Cristiano, Luca asked you to meet him downstairs in the café. He has wrapped things up with the Moroccan police and is heading back to Netuno tonight to deal with some fallout about Jade."

"Sure, Ravn. Thank you."

"After you say goodbye to Luca, go to the hotel down the street. I booked several rooms under my name. You look like you could do with a shower and a couple of hours of sleep."

I stepped towards Phillip. "Promise me you will not talk to Maya about Peachland."

"I never—"

"Phillip, don't take me for a fool. We both want what is best for Maya. We just have different versions of what that looks like."

"Cristiano," Ravn continued in a calm voice.

"Oh, and don't talk to her about the pregnancy either. She's not ready to think about that."

"I am her father!" Phillip erupted, trying to get me to back down.

"And I'm her husband." I leaned in. "Do not push me, Phillip."

"I don't know who you think you are, but—"

"But what? I'm the man who loves your daughter. I would do anything for her. She's not well right now but she will get better and when she does, we'll deal with everything else."

"What if she never gets better?" he blurted out. "What will you do then?"

"Phillip, Maya is not Judith. I will find a way. I have to."

Phillip went red in the ears; I had gone too far.

"You're wrong. Stop being so naïve. We need to prepare her for the possibility she is pregnant and make some decisions. We need to know right now."

"No, *she* doesn't. This is not your business. She is my wife." I thundered back at him, breaking my arm free from Ravn's hold.

Phillip raised his fist as if he were about to hit me.

"Try it, Phillip. This time I'm not lying in a hospital bed, and I can fight back."

He stopped.

"Phillip, Maya and I need to work this out. Your daughter is the love of my life. I may not have a piece of paper that says we are married, but I have taken a vow, and I will not abandon her."

Phillip left the garden without saying another word to me.

"Well, that is one way to get on the good side of your father-in-law." Dalley teased.

"Really, Dalley?" Ravn snapped at her, shaking his head.

"What?" she looked at him, daring him to say another word to her.

"Cristiano, Dalley and I have to look after Saafa right now, but after we're done we'll check on Maya and her parents." He paused. "Cristiano, if you keep pushing Phillip like that, you could do irreparable damage to your relationship with him and he could convince Maya to go back to Peachland. Then what would you do?"

"He can't just take her," I said defiantly.

Dalley interrupted, "No, but she could go. If she decided to, she could just get on the plane and leave. Because right at this moment, the two of you are not legally married and we don't know if there *is* a baby. So go, talk to Luca, then get cleaned up and get your shit together. Stop feeling sorry for yourself and be the man she needs you to be."

✎

Luca was waiting for me in the café.

"Cristiano, you look like crap."

"Yeah, well I feel like it too. I'm not sure what I'm doing here. It feels like everyone is mad at me and no matter what I do, Maya keeps running from me. Hell, I almost punched Phillip just now."

"Yeah, I heard about that. Ravn gave me a quick call after you left the garden. Cristiano, this is one of those times when listening to your friends might be a good choice. I know you're used to doing things on your own, but you're not alone anymore. There are people who have your back and want you and Maya to be together, but you can't help anyone if you get arrested in Morocco for punching someone or end up in the hospital yourself. Maya is safe and the bad guy is dead. It's time for you to take a breath and give yourself and Maya some time to process all that's happened."

"When did you get so wise?"

"Oh, last year my bosses sent me to do some courses so I could learn to be more compassionate and empathetic in these kinds of situations. Is it working?"

"It was until you asked me that question." My heart lifted a little and a part of me knew he was right. The truth was, all I prayed for was for Maya to come back alive and that prayer was answered. The next step was up to her. I would follow her anywhere and wait until she was ready. Luca placed his hand on my shoulder and brought me back from my thoughts.

"Cristiano, you okay?"

"I will be. What about you? Everything okay with the Moroccan police?" I asked him.

"Yes, we worked it out. They're happy to be rid of Dakar. He'd been on their radar since last year for some other illegal dealings."

"What about the hair fork? Anyone know where it is?"

"I have no idea whose hands its fallen into. I can only hope it goes back to Egypt and stays there where it belongs. Cristiano, I'd better get moving. My superiors back home have questions about Jade Axeline. They're happy we got her away from the Ptolemites, but let's just say there's been a complaint made about how I *left* things."

We both chuckled.

"What are you going to do about Maya?"

"I know she'll need some time, but I'm not giving up on her."

"I would hope not. She's counting on you."

"Will the Moroccan police need anything from Maya before we leave for Crete?"

He smiled ever so slightly at me and shook his head.

"It's stupid, I know. She hasn't even started talking to me yet."

"No, not stupid, just optimistic. It must run in the family."

"What do you mean?" I asked.

"Oh, I almost forgot. I got a call from Puro. He called me when you weren't picking up. After Phillip and Judith left Netuno, your brother and Pierre flew down to Crete to fix up a place your parents own there. They wanted to make sure you had somewhere to stay if things moved in that direction for you and Maya. Like I said, optimism runs in your family."

"That is amazing." I could feel myself choking up with emotion.

"Family. Oh, speaking about family, Puro said your parents are heading down here too."

"What? My parents? Luca, this is too much." I stopped and took a deep breath, trying to think through all the moving parts of the situation. "Can you call Puro back and tell them to stay put, at least for a little while? I need some space."

"I think their plane has already taken off. I can confirm with Beth if you like?"

"Beth? So, is that a thing?"

"Cristiano, my love life is not up for discussion right now; we were talking about your parents."

"Love life? So, it is a thing. You better not hurt Beth, or Maya will kill you." I smirked. "Don't worry about calling her, I'm alright. I'll manage it somehow. I'm just not sure it's the right thing for Maya, but what do I know."

"Don't worry, you'll figure it out. You love her."

"Yes, but sometimes love's not enough."

Luca got up from his seat and stared at me. "Yeah, and sometimes it is. That's up to you."

36

Garden Love

Cristiano

AFTER MY SHOWER, ALL I could do was sleep. When I woke, the sun was setting. Frustrated that my body betrayed me and made me sleep through my alarm, I rushed back to the hospital, knowing I had some apologies to make. The fight with Phillip was still ringing in my ears.

When I arrived at Maya's room, the space was empty. She was gone.

"She left? They took her? How could she just leave?"

I ran to the front desk, but the staff were in the middle of a shift change and no one could answer my questions. I texted Dalley.

Relax C. They have moved her to Room 724, was all she texted back.

As I sprinted down the hall, Phillip was outside her door, but something had changed. He was different. The anger and fear were gone, replaced with humility. The father, the man who talked about helping Maya and me, had returned. Then I saw something else …

"What is it, Phillip?" I asked, my heart in my throat.

"Cristiano, I'm not sure where to start, but my dear wife has instructed me I was not to move from this spot until you arrived. So, I'm glad you're here. I'm sorry, Cristiano—about everything."

"Phillip, what is it? Did something happen? Why did Maya change rooms?"

"Oh, no. Maya is a little better. The room change was Judith," he whispered with a headshake and a chuckle. "While you were out, the psychiatrist came to see Maya, and Judith stayed during the appointment. Maya seemed better after talking with him. During their conversation, he told them about a research project they were doing at the hospital on trauma recovery and the use of plant material and nature in a hospital room environment. Last year, they received funding to build four garden solarium rooms which back onto the rooftop garden. Judith believed Maya would do well in the program, and the psychiatrist agreed. Maya said yes, and here we are."

"Research? Garden Solarium?" I was confused.

"I know. I was curious, but you should see it. She has not hidden under her scarf once since she moved into the room."

"Can I see her? Does she want to see me?" I asked, hovering around the door.

"Judith is working on that right now. She loves you, Cristiano. I know that. I'm sorry again, for everything. You were right when you said Maya isn't Judith. Fear, no matter your age, can push you to do and say some idiotic things." He placed his hand on my shoulder. "It's getting late. I'll take Judith back to the hotel so you and Maya can spend some time together. Don't let her give up on herself—or you." As he rubbed his hand across his forehead, I could see he had one last thing to share. "I've been where you are, Cristiano. I just couldn't see it before. No one could have separated me from Judith, especially when she had fallen into her deepest depression. I was so protective of her. I remember one time her father, a police officer, tried to step in … let's just say it did not go well." He paused again. "After our *chat* and a tongue-lashing from my wife, I realized what

I was doing. I'm sorry that taking her away ever crossed my mind." He leaned in and hugged me tightly, then let me go and wiped his eyes.

He knocked on the door. "Judith love, it's time to go."

She stepped outside, sporting a quiet smile. "Is everything taken care of?" She looked at me as she asked him.

Phillip nodded.

As she was leaving, Judith opened the door and called back to Maya, "Remember what I told you, dear," she paused. "I'll see you in the morning."

Judith gave me a kiss on the cheek and wove her arm through Phillip's.

I walked after them down the hall.

"Judith, how is she?" I asked, trying to figure out what I needed to do next.

"A little better. She loves the room; it's very peaceful. She's not ready to look in a mirror, but she will eventually. She is, however, quite fascinated with the blind woman who drew the picture of her in the garden earlier. Do you have the sketch?"

I pulled it out of my pocket and smoothed it open.

"Cristiano, she needs you to love her just the way she is. No talk of her being beautiful yet, not until she can believe the drawing is accurate. She's worried about burdening you."

"What do I do?" I asked, feeling rudderless.

Judith walked back to me, placing her hand on my cheek. "Love her. And at least for tonight, don't worry about finding solutions. Enjoy the nature together."

"I'm glad you're here Judith. She needs you."

"She needs you too, Cristiano. Good night."

Nerves shot through my body like pinballs in an old arcade machine, whizzing and dinging against all the point plates. Then, with one final breath, I pushed the door open, holding on to the sketch, praying she would let me stay.

⁂

Maya

When he stepped through the door, he didn't say a word but placed the sketch on the bed and sat beside me, holding out his hand. I thought about saying something, but I didn't want to ruin the first calm breath we had taken together since the crash. We sat quietly as the remnants of the day dropped away, giving into the night. That was when I saw him stir, and he began stroking my hand with his thumb.

Gently, rhythmically, our skin rubbed together, but still he said nothing. The burbling fountain was the only sound in the room. The water gave our hearts something to focus on as we settled into the silent conversation. At some point I fell asleep and when I woke, he was standing near the window looking up into the sky.

"Cristiano?" He jumped when he heard his name, then turned and smiled as I stood beside him. "Would you like to go to the garden?" I asked, feeling strangely shy.

"Yes, that would be lovely. Should you be standing, walking yet?"

"Yes, I can walk. There was never anything wrong with my legs. The doctor said it's time for me to start moving again. I think he was speaking in code about moving forward." I paused and waited for him to say something. He just smiled and gave me the space to keep going. "I'm not quite myself right now but I'm working on it. This room is quite amazing. It's only been a few hours and I already feel like I can breathe easier. My mom and I sat on the cushions in the corner and had a nice long chat. It was the first time she ever talked to me about her depression and the steps she took to get well again.

I think everyone is worried that I'm going to fall into a depression like my mom. Truthfully, the thought has crossed my mind. You know Cristiano, before I came to Portugal I was a very sad person. Was I depressed? Maybe. When I called off the wedding to Steven some people thought my sadness was about breaking up with him, but it wasn't. It was about saying yes to him in the first place because I couldn't say no. I didn't have the courage to start looking at who I was and who I wanted to be. Not until I met Remi, Rembrandt."

"Remi?"

"Remi was someone I met back home. He sculpted wooden chairs. He kind of, saved me."

"Saved you?"

"Yes, he taught me how to sand. And no, I can see what you're thinking, it wasn't like that."

"Just to be clear. I didn't ask."

"You didn't have to. I saw it on your face."

"So now you can read my mind?"

"Maybe a little. As I was saying, he just appeared in my life at the right time and taught me how to use my hands to make something. It was like waking up from a deep sleep. It's funny, sanding kind of reminds me of kneading dough. You have to put your whole heart into it."

"I understand. Maya, I've missed your smile."

I threw my hand up to cover my face, he didn't stop me, but I managed to stop myself.

"Is it true?" I asked as I stared out at the sky.

"What's that?"

"Do I really look like the sketch?"

He nodded his head, then stepped closer and ran his finger over the slightly raised scar where Dakar had hit me and reopened one of the many cuts from the accident. I pulled back, and he froze.

"Cristiano?"

"Your mom told me we don't need to find all the solutions tonight. Let's just go for that walk in the garden."

He motioned for my hand, and a surge of warmth radiated across my body. It felt like a hundred years since his heart was near mine. My head was confused though. I wondered how we were going to get through it all. What was going to happen next? Could I really start dreaming about the future and all that was possible for me?

"You're thinking too much again. I can see it in the wrinkle on your forehead. I'm here for you. No questions tonight, remember?"

"Didn't my mom say no solutions?" I looped my arm through his and stepped out into the garden. The lights had long since turned off and all that lit the space was a crescent moon and a plethora of stars. The night temperature had dropped and I could feel the goosebumps on my arms. In one swift movement, he gently lay his fleece coat over my shoulders. I felt safe.

"Cristiano, what are we going to do?" I asked, breaking the rule we had just set.

He paused, clearly not sure if he should answer.

"That's not a fair question, is it? You're probably asking what's the matter with me. I don't really know. I think it's everything and …"

"What do *you* want, Maya?" He gave in.

"I could ask you the same thing."

He smiled. "I know what I want. That's simple." His eyes glistened.

"You're not making this easy."

"I'm sorry. I'm just doing what Luca told me to before he left."

"He left?"

"Yes, he had to get back to Porto."

"What did Luca say?"

"He said that love sometimes *is* enough."

A sudden gust of warm wind blew through the garden, whipping our hair around and sending his curls into his eyes. He reached to move his hair and I stopped his hand, wanting to do it myself. When my fingertips brushed the side of his face his body shook.

"There's so much to talk about. Where do we start?" I asked.

"I don't think we need to start right now, do you?"

I smiled at him, taking him up on his offer.

We sat in silence again, enjoying the night until even the moon and the stars disappeared, leaving only the wind and an indigo sky.

"How are you?" I asked. "About Avo, I mean. Dalley reminded me I had not even stopped to ask you how you were doing? I feel terrible. You don't have to talk about it if you don't want to."

He adjusted his body. "She came to see me in the hospital after the accident. She and Puro and your parents. I was unconscious for several days."

I could feel my body seize as I imagined him lying there, not able to wake.

"I remember being in a state of semiconsciousness and hearing people talk, but I couldn't respond. Then, suddenly, a familiar scent filled my senses. Maya, she brought me a loaf of bread. Her last loaf."

His tears landed on my hand. "Her bread brought me back. When I opened my eyes, she was there but you weren't. I panicked. I was only awake for a moment before your father started yelling and then he …"

"Yes, and then he hit you and your father hit him and I heard Zef saved my dad, from getting his jaw broken."

"Zef? Really? I didn't hear about that part." He paused. "When I came to, she wasn't there and neither were you. My mom confirmed that you had been taken and then told me about Avo's stroke. My heart ripped in half as the two women I loved most in my life were in trouble and there was nothing I could do to help. I did managed to get down to the ICU twice before she died."

"I know."

"What do you mean, you know?"

"I mean, I saw a recording of the second visit. I couldn't hear it, but Dakar had a camera in the room and I could see you with her, holding her hand. He made me watch while she …"

"Died? I'm so sorry you had to watch that."

"I'm not. I'm glad I could be there for you, even if you didn't know."

"It must have been terrible for you; all alone in that horrific hole."

"What do you know about that?" I could see from the flash of pain in his eyes, he had been there. He found the stink and saw the blood I left behind. "Cristiano, I can't talk about that place, not yet anyway. Tell me more about Avo."

I could tell he wanted to reach out to me, to hold me, to make the bad memories go away. But instead he did just as I asked. "Her heartbeat was strong right up until the moment it stopped. Before she died she tried to say something. In the end I think she was telling me not to give up on you or me, or at least that's what I told myself."

Just then, another gust of wind whipped around us, and I laughed. "Well, it looks like you got the right answer. Avo is that you?"

He smiled. "I have a feeling she'll always be with us." He took a deep breath. "Oh, I have something of hers, of yours—Dalley gave it to me before I came down and thought you might like to have it with you."

He reached into his pocket and smoothed out a wrinkled handkerchief, my handkerchief. It was perfect: the stitching, the flowers; it was Avo. I sucked in a breath as he tied it gently on my head.

"I'm so sorry I wasn't there for the funeral."

"I didn't have a funeral. Not yet anyway. Jacinta and Puro and your mom brought Avo back to Netuno and then I had her cremated. I was holding off on doing any kind of service until you came home."

"Home?" I asked, trying to make sure I understood what he was saying.

"Yes, home, the cottage is ready, when you are, if you want. No pressure. I just wanted to let you know."

I paused for a moment, thinking about what the word home meant to me after everything I had gone through. A look of worry grew on his face when I didn't respond right away. I wanted to choose my words carefully. "My mom and dad told me about the vineyard in Peachland. Imagine that. After all those years. What a secret to keep. My mom wasn't mad at all." I held my breath knowing he needed to hear me say the words. I wasn't sure how everything was going to work out, just that it would. I had been wrong. Cristiano loved me unconditionally, scars and all but it was me who was still learning to love myself. "Cristiano, Peachland is not home. Home is where you are." Reaching over, I touched his cheek and felt him shake again under my touch. "I'm just feeling a little lost and fearful right now."

Unexpectantly, his eyes sparkled with mischief. "Fearful and lost? Then I may have found just what you need to help you find your way."

"And what is that?" He dipped into his pocket and pulled something out that glistened even in the dark of night. "The chain is broken, but I'll get it fixed as soon as possible."

"My tear of bravery." I took the diamond and held it tightly in my hand, making it mine again after its brief stint around Jade's neck. Aunt Olive gave me the necklace on my non-wedding day to Steven as a gift for putting myself first and walking away from a life I didn't want. The words in her note were seared into my memory.

'When we embark upon our true journey, there is both tremendous heartache and joy. Our bodies give us the gift of tears so that we can shed the heartache and share the joy when the time is right. Be brave and let yourself cry. Then stop crying and get on with it.'

Aunt Olive was right. It was time for me to get on with it already and be brave.

Cristiano's face suddenly became contorted and he looked like he was going to break in half. "Oh Maya, I am so sorry."

"Sorry for what?" I was genuinely confused by his apology.

"For everything."

"Cristiano, you can't be sorry about everything. You made your choices. I made mine, Jade made hers, and Dakar, well … I know I have a lot to work through and I realize my initial plan to run away to Crete was flawed, I now know I can't do it by myself. I need you with me, I want you with me."

"What changed your mind?"

"Having a loving family can be more persuasive than I ever imagined."

We both laughed.

His face lit up. "I have some good news about Greece. I just found out my family owns a place there—and have offered us the chance to stay there as long as we need."

"On Crete?"

"Yes. Marcos bought it last year as an architectural project. Anyway, Zef and Pierre are on their way to fix it up for us, just in case you started talking to me again and agreed to let me come along." The smirk on his face melted my worries momentarily.

"Pierre? You're talking to him?"

"Yes, he was the one who helped me find the relic."

I sat quietly for a moment, trying to understand the mixture of anticipation and nerves which filled my body. He felt my hesitation. "If that doesn't work for you, I'll find you something else. I'll stay at the house and come visit when you choose." He paused. "I just need to be near you and need you to know I'll be there when you're ready."

I took a breath and squeezed his hand.

Cristiano and I talked until the sun came up. He told me stories about the grape stomp wedding and baking bread with his brother at the cottage and I told him about learning to bake Khobz at the compound.

When the nurse came with breakfast, she met us out in the garden.

She smiled. "The stitching on your handkerchief is exquisite."

"Thank you our Avo made it." I squeezed Cristiano's hand.

My eyes were heavy as Cristiano walked me back into my beautiful room. "Rest well Maya. I'll be back in a few hours and we can pick up where we left off."

37

Reflection

Maya

After Cristiano left, I curled up in the hammock chair that hung from the ceiling and tried to sleep, but all my body wanted to do was write. So, I climbed out and picked up my journal from where my mother had left it.

In Morocco at the hospital

What do you hear, Maya?

The gentle sound of the fountain cascading over the rocks, blocking out what I know are busy hospital halls filled with doctors, nurses, and patients. But in this room, I am not a patient; I am just Maya. Maya who? I'm not sure yet but If I listen closely enough, maybe I can figure it out. I can also hear the peaceful soundtrack of ancient instruments finding their way into my heart. What do you smell? I smell the plants, the flowers, the earth. The room is filled with vines woven up the walls and different tropical plants that remind me of the oasis where I found Cristiano slung over the airplane wing

... broken and needing me. I searched until I found him and then he let me in.

Was I really so arrogant to think I cornered the market on compassion and unconditional love? And that he could not or would not help me?

I didn't answer him about Crete and yet he didn't pressure me. We just talked until the sun rose.

It is time to decide. Yes. I need to tell him yes and then it is time to look into the mirror.

Maya

⁓

Cristiano

I walked back to the hotel, knowing she had not said yes or no to staying at my parents' place in Crete with me. Sleep did not come easy, so I finally gave up. On my way back to the hospital I got an idea and stopped at a few boutiques along the way.

⁓

"Maya?" I shook her gently from her sleep and closed her open journal, pen still in her hand. "Are you okay?"

"Yes, I will be. She touched my face and stared at me. Last night when I told you about Remi, I forgot to tell you one important lesson he taught me."

"And what is that?"

"He told me that no matter how perfectly you sand a project, it's always important to leave one rough edge. Just to remind you that life doesn't have to be perfect to be beautiful." She took my hand and ran my finger over her scars.

"Yes, I want to stay at your parents' house with you in Crete and yes, I want to build a life with you, no matter how messy things get."

I scooped her up from the hammock chair and held her in my arms. "You just made me the happiest man on the planet."

When I finally put her down I followed her gaze over to the shopping bags I had dropped by the door.

"What do you have there?"

"On my way here, I picked up a couple of new outfits for you. Thought you might be ready for something new."

"Cristiano, it's too much," she said as I handed her five different bags.

"Maybe a little, but when we go to Greece, you'll need something to wear, right? I always want you to have a choice."

"Yes, having choices makes all the difference in the world. Thank you." She wasn't talking about clothing anymore.

"Do you need help getting changed?" I winked at her hoping to lighten the mood a little. She looked like she was going to be sick. "I'm sorry Maya. I didn't mean to push you. I was just teasing."

"No, I'm okay. Really. I'm still all bruised and battered. Not quite ready for you to see me yet."

I saw the beads of sweat on her forehead and felt her panic rising.

"Take your time. Whatever you need, Maya."

My phone buzzed, but I didn't want to pick it up.

"Go ahead, it could be important," she said, looking thankful for the distraction.

Looking down I saw Beth's name pop up on the text message. I had only known Beth for a short time, but she was the definition of a best friend and that is what Maya needed in the moment.

"Good call about checking. It's from Beth, and it's for you." I said handing her the phone.

Maya, Luca stopped into Netuno before heading up to Porto. He explained everything you are going through. My heart broke and I wanted to do something that might help. So, I got creative, let me rephrase that. We, as in your Netuno Wine Club, stayed up late and made something to remind you that your reflection is a gift. You are beautiful no matter what a mirror may tell you at first glance. It should arrive by courier soon. Hang in there. We are all around you. I love you, B.

She handed me the phone, sporting a small smile. "Do you know what they are sending me?" she asked with a hint of anticipation, which squashed the panic in its tracks.

"No clue. We could call Luca. I'm sure he would spill the beans if you asked him directly."

"No, I don't want to spoil their surprise."

"You're probably right. Josie and Petra would have my head if I ruined whatever they were planning."

We were both smiling.

Maya opened one of the bags and pulled out a flowing wrap made with sheer fabric. She placed it around her shoulders and sighed.

"El Escorial seems so long ago," she said, shifting our conversation. "Can you confirm we actually got married?" she laughed nervously.

I watched her carefully then took a few extra moments to answer, as I thought back to our wedding and the days that followed.

"Cristiano? It was real, right? I'm not going crazy."

I smiled, then took a breath. "Yes, of course it was real."

"Then what was that dramatic pause all about?" she asked, sounding distressed again. "You can't do that to me!" she uttered suddenly, on the brink of tears.

The psychiatrist warned me there could be some dramatic mood fluctuations during the healing process. He said I needed to be patient, slow in my movements and let her tears fall. Essentially, he told me I had to create the space where she could feel safe enough to let it out when the emotional bursts occurred. So instead of rushing over to her. I walked slowly and spoke softly.

"Maya." I said, touching her arm. She pulled away. I felt the fear and panic so I slowly removed my hand.

"Cristiano, you can't do that to me while I'm trying to pull my brain back together."

"I'm sorry. You're right."

She breathed deeply and the panic receded again. "The doctor told me to expect some mood swings, but this is ridiculous. I feel like a ping pong ball being wacked around by my emotions. I am so frustrated. Now that I can think again. Why did you pause?"

I hesitated, but she looked insistent, and I wasn't going to lie. "Maya, I was thinking about the morning I tried to convince you to stay off the grid for another day. Maybe this wouldn't have happened if I had."

She took my hands, then guided me to the chairs near the fountain.

"Cristiano, Dakar would have found us eventually. He wanted the relic and was willing to do anything to get it, but it's done now, right?"

"Yes, Dakar is dead, and the relic is gone."

"Good, then it's time for us to move forward."

I knew there were still things that needed to be discussed but it was clear she was not ready.

"I think I'd like to take a shower. I need to leave Morocco as soon as possible. The doctor said I'd know when it was the right time. I think I'm close but …"

"But nothing. If you need me, then I'm here," I said.

I saw a wrinkle in her forehead. "Cristiano?"

"What is it, Maya? I'm sorry, I interrupted you."

"No, that's not it."

"Then what is it?"

She sucked in a breath, then sputtered, "The pregnancy test."

My mouth went dry. "Yes, that is something we need to discuss, but we don't need to do it right now."

She continued. "Cristiano, you need to know, it's not that I don't want to find out. Well, maybe a little. I'm scared about the postpartum happening to me too, but more than that, I don't want to find out while I'm here." She paused. I wasn't sure if she had anything else to say, so I waited.

She breathed in, "I had this dream. Well, it was more like a daydream, a story I wrote just after you left for Egypt. I want it to happen more like that."

"You wrote a story about us starting a family?"

She bit down on her lip and so did I, and she started again.

"Life isn't a fairytale. I know more than anyone, but when we find out we are having a baby, I want it to be just us. I don't want that memory skewed with hospital sounds and people walking in."

I smiled. "We can do this however you want, on your timeline. Bottom line, either we have all the time in the world to figure this out or just under nine months, but maybe we should start with that shower."

"We?" She looked at me questioningly.

"Maya, I have a little more self-control than that. We have the rest of our lives together. And when the time is right, we will make love again and find our rhythm and be stronger for it. But for now, go take your shower so you are ready for your surprise."

Maya

Cristiano placed a towel over the bathroom mirror, as I still wasn't ready to see my reflection. He stood outside the door, checking in on me every minute, making sure I hadn't fallen over.

When I stepped out of the bathroom, he had laid several outfits for me on to the bed. As I dressed, he settled into a chair. Exhaustion soon won out and he fell asleep.

While I sat on my bed watching his chest rise and fall, the young nurse I had been mean to when I first arrived knocked on the door.

"Excuse me," she whispered, I'm sure for fear of me yelling at her again.

"Yes, please come in."

She was holding a parcel and wore a smile on her face.

"That was faster than I thought. How did it arrive so quickly?"

The nurse only nodded and walked toward me.

I heard her voice before I saw her face. "It might have something to do with the delivery service the ladies chose."

I turned toward the door, tripping over my feet. The nurse threw the parcel into the air, grabbing my arm to stop me from falling.

"No!" I heard Beth yell out, then saw her run toward the flying package.

Before it could hit the floor, Cristiano came to life, lunging towards the parcel, catching it with one arm but not without doing some harm to himself in exchange. He tried to cover it up, but I saw him wince and grab his ribs.

"Oh, the things people do for love," Beth teased.

I took Beth's lead and tried to make my own joke.

 "Well, I'm glad to see the parcel took precedence over me."

Cristiano's brows creased for a microsecond, assessing if I was joking or not.

"You had your own guardian angel. I needed to make sure the package was secure."

The nurse held me, not sure if she should let go. Then Beth came over. "Don't worry, I've got this," she said to the nurse, then turned to me. "Hug first, then I'll yell at you for all the stupid and amazingly brave things you've done since you left home."

Cristiano placed the parcel carefully on the bed. "I think I'll grab a cup of coffee and try to find out where my parents are. Luca said they're flying in too."

"Really?" Maya looked so excited about the thought of seeing my parents.

Beth broke in. "Cristiano, you don't have to go."

He smiled at us. "Yes, I do."

After Cristiano left, Beth hugged me again. It started as a gentle squeeze, but soon changed to something else. In all our years as friends I had only seen her cry a handful of times, always pushing the tears away with a tissue and a laugh, but that day, well …

As she sobbed in my arms, I led her over to a colorful wicker floor mat, punctuated with elaborate cushions. Plopping down, we splayed ourselves on our backs like when we were children, lying on the grass under the peach trees.

"I'm sorry, Beth."

"You should be!" she said. "You leave me almost six weeks ago, travel the world, get shot at, get married, get kidnapped, and now you're not coming home! What am I going to do without you?" I was stunned as the words fell from her almost angry lips.

"What are you going to do without me? Ah, that would be simple. Live your awesome, happy life, teach your students, fall in love, and come visit me during the summers."

She laughed through her sniffles. "You scared the crap out of me. I thought you were dead."

"Yeah, there were a few days when I thought God was done with me. But apparently, I still have something important to do, or so my mother keeps whispering in my ear."

"Where are your parents? I thought they would be camped out, saving you from the big, bad Cristiano. Looks like he's not so big and bad anymore?"

"Never big and bad, that was all me and my temporary broken brain. Not that it's completely fixed but I'm working on it. And yes, my mother made my father apologize to Cristiano and gave us some time together. We stayed up last night talking and not talking, but the good kind of not talking."

Suddenly, I remembered my face, not sure how she had been looking at me without a single reservation or reaction.

"Maya, what is it?"

"You … you didn't ask me about my scars."

"Maya, can you please open the package? I think this would be a good time. And I imagine in about thirty minutes if we don't contact the ladies back at Netuno, Josie and Petra are going to jump on the next plane down here, too."

Beth got up and grabbed the parcel off the bed.

"What is it?" I asked hesitantly as she held it out to me.

"Where is the fun in me telling you what's inside? There were a few of us leaning toward a care package, but Carmo's logic won out. One gift to remind you of how beautiful you *are*."

I felt the heat rise in my face and when Beth saw the shift, she simply ripped the tape off the box and handed it to me.

"What could you have made that would help me feel better about the way I look?" Fumbling with the tissue paper in the box, my fingers told me the story before I even saw it. I could feel the rounded edge with the unmistakable smooth surface letting me know what it was. Then as I pulled away the last piece of tissue, I saw something sparkle, shine, almost glow. It was like Athena's jewels had migrated to the large, handheld mirror. I carefully picked it up, avoiding the mirror, as I was not ready to see my reflection. I was, however, captivated by the intricate patterns of multi shades of blue sparkles and beads placed ever so carefully on the unique canvas. My friends had created a gift of beauty, and as I ran my hands over the gems, I could feel their love. The tears that sprung were those of happiness and appreciation.

"Okay," Beth jumped in, wiping away my tears. "You need to know this was a labor of love, made for you by the hands of women who care about you and see you as beautiful." Beth grabbed my face in her hands. "Maya, at some point when you are ready to look, I'm here for you. We all are. And no, I will not cajole or trick you to do it now, but encourage you to take the step soon so you can move forward with your life. You deserve that."

Knowing she had never lied to me, I risked asking her. "Is it horrible? I remember it as being horrible."

"No, it's not horrible," she answered unflinchingly.

"Are there scars?"

"Yes, there are scars, but Maya, every scar tells a story and yours will too."

"What if I don't want them to?" I asked stubbornly, a tear slipping between her fingers.

"You can pretend the scars don't exist, avoid every reflection, but if you do that, then the bad guys win."

"What part of this conversation is not cajoling?"

"The part where I offer to take the mirror back until you're ready."

"No, I want to keep it here. I know everyone keeps telling me the healing process has been almost miraculous, but … can you do me a favor?"

"Anything!"

"I need to see Saafa. She needs to be here when I look at myself."

"I'll be right back." Beth leaned in for a hug, then ran out of the room.

38

I'm Ready

Dalley

WHEN I SAW HER COME around the corner, a sense of relief flooded my body. I found myself curious how one person could have that effect on me. We had only known each other for a short time. My heart jumped and so did I, as I surprised myself and went in for a big hug. Beth never flinched, reaffirming we had chosen each other correctly in our friendship.

I could not believe I had spent my whole life avoiding friendships, avoiding that kind of love, and now that I had it, I never wanted to let it go. Briefly, I thought about my mom and how she had convinced me that friends only weighed you down. What a miserable human being she was. If Saafa accepted my offer to come stay with Ravn and me, I would do anything to protect her from that woman.

With an extra squeeze, Beth brought me back.

"It's so good to see you. It feels like forever, but it's only been a couple of days."

"What are you doing here? Did you have time to see Luca before you left?"

"I did, but I'll have to deal with that when I go back. I needed to see Maya, and some things are more important than boys."

"Really? And what would that be?"

"Friendship."

We both laughed.

"So, you saw Maya?"

"Yes, the ladies made a special gift for her. It was a joint effort, but the idea was Maggie's. She is so worried about Maya." Beth paused. "Oh, I almost forgot. Maya asked if Saafa could come upstairs to help her with the present."

"What is this mysterious present that only Saafa can help with?"

⌘

"Saafa, this is Maya's best friend Beth."

Beth ran over and hugged her. "I cannot thank you enough for everything you did for Maya. It is such a pleasure to meet you. How are you feeling?"

"I am healing, thank you. Did something happen to Maya?"

"No, nothing new, but she's still having some challenges about the injuries to her face." I glanced at Beth, encouraging her to squelch Saafa's worry.

"She needs our help, and she asked for you specifically."

Saafa took a breath. "It is so good to meet you, Beth. Maya spoke about you often. She talked about climbing peach trees and riding your bikes through the orchard when you were children. I don't know how to ride a bike, but I would like to one day."

"I bet there's someone here who would love to teach you." Beth looked over at me.

"Ravn may need to teach both of us as I never learnt either. Saafa, do you feel well enough to help Maya?"

"I am not sure how I can help. But I will try."

Beth jumped in. "Don't worry, Saafa. I think she just wants you nearby when she looks at her reflection for the first time since the bandages came off. The present is a mirror, but not just any mirror. You'll have to see it. But imagine sparkles and jewels coming together in an explosion of color."

I laughed, as all I could think about was Athena, Maya's pen, and the first sparkly miracle when Cristiano found it and returned it to her.

"What's your plan with this mirror Beth?" I couldn't hide my skepticism.

"The goal is to support Maya as she takes her next steps to accepting what she sees."

"Oh, is that all?"

"Dalley." Beth's tone pierced my cynical bubble, making me pay more attention to what she was saying. "Maggie saw an art therapist for a long time after her husband died. She did a project similar this to help her move forward. She thought it might help Maya too, and I believe it's worth a try. Maya already loves it, and she has only seen the sparkly part."

"Art therapy?" Saafa asked Beth.

"Art therapy is a different kind of counselling that invites the making of art to become a bridge in the therapeutic relationship when someone needs more than just words to express themselves."

Saffa looked over at me as if asking a question.

I nodded. "I'll look into it. Do you feel up to seeing Maya?"

"Yes, I'll do anything I can to help her. Dalley, I'm feeling hungry, though. Can you get me something to eat from the cafeteria? Ravn said the food is delicious. Beth, are you hungry?"

"Famished. I haven't eaten since I left Netuno," she answered. "Are you ready to see Maya now?"

"Saafa, please don't push yourself too hard. Only a little while." I could hardly believe the motherly tone coming out of my mouth, it almost felt natural.

I caught Beth's eye again as she smiled at me and wheeled Saafa out of the room. "It's nice to see this side of you," she slipped in before leaving.

Saafa rolled her eyes. "I'm not twelve. I know what you're talking about. Let's go, Beth. I can't wait to see that mirror."

⤳

The cafeteria was quiet and I instantly felt overwhelmed, as I did not know what Saafa liked to eat. So, I started ordering, hoping I picked out at a few items she would enjoy. As the scent of cumin and paprika filled the air, I sipped on a spiced Moroccan coffee and enjoyed the unique taste of ginger and cinnamon mixed in with the freshly ground beans.

"Oh, there you are," Ravn said, grabbing me from behind and kissing my neck. "I missed you. You smell so spicy."

"It's the coffee," I answered, turning and allowing our lips to touch while I held a drop of liquid on my tongue.

"It has been too long," he sighed, slumping down into the seat beside me.

"Well, you may need to wait a little longer." I shook my head, then kissed him deeply.

After I finished, he shrugged his shoulders. "You're worth the wait," he said slyly. "Hey, I ran into Beth and Saafa on their way up to Maya's room. They said you were getting food. How much did you order?"

I looked at my receipt and counted twelve items. Then handed the slip of paper to him.

He laughed. "That's a lot. We might need a little help with this. I'll text Cristiano and Phillip and let them know we have lunch covered."

My stomach sank when he mentioned Saafa's name.

"What is it, Dalley? Are you not feeling well?"

"Just nervous. Ravn, what if she says no? What if she says yes? Can we really do this? Can we really look after a teenager? I don't know about you, but my adolescence was very messy. I don't know anything about setting up a stable life."

"Oh, Dalley. We have lots of people who can help us."

"What if she doesn't want to come with us? I can't leave her. She has no one."

"Dalley, stop spinning. She just survived a knife wound to the chest, escaped being married off to some old guy, and has been asked to come live with people she doesn't know. Give her some time to think about what living with us might look like. Maybe show her some pictures of your place? Or we could go to mine in Finland. It's remote and we might have to homeschool, but I'm game if you are." He paused. "In the end, it doesn't matter where we are, as long as we're together. That's what makes a family."

"A family?" I squeaked out.

"Yes, Dalley. The bonus is, if Saafa says yes, we'll have avoided the terrible twos, twelves and I hear fourteen is the worst."

My heart relaxed as I thought about the idea.

"You're right. I know we can do it."

"Ghidha!" a young man called out, holding up two bags and pointing at three more that sat on the counter.

Ravn collected the bags, juggling them in his arms. "Yes, I believe we'll have enough for everyone," he chuckled.

"Oh, stop giving me a hard time."

Ravn bent down and gently kissed me on my cheek. "I love you, Dalley Price, and you're going to be a great mom, friend, or whatever she needs."

302

39

Taking a Chance

Cristiano

"Mom? It's Cristiano."

"Hello, son, I'm so happy to hear your voice. How are you? How is Maya? I'm putting you on speakerphone. Your father and I are at the airport ready to board a flight."

"You're not in Morocco yet?"

"No, we would have been there sooner, but all the flights were booked. We've been on standby since yesterday."

"You stayed overnight at the airport? Trying to catch a flight to see me?"

"Yes, of course. You need us, and we didn't want you to be alone. You're our child."

It took some time to convince my parents that things with Phillip and Judith had improved and there was no need for them to fly down. My mother was not happy until I suggested that if they wanted to help, they could fly over to Crete and work with Zef and Pierre to prepare the house for us.

"Mom and Dad, I need to go. I'm getting a text from Ravn letting me know he has just picked up a feast for lunch."

"Oh, that sounds wonderful. I can't wait until we're all together." My mother's voice cracked.

"We love you son," my father added. "I'll make sure we're out of the house before you and Maya arrive. We'll find somewhere close to stay for a couple of days."

"Thank you. Maya was so excited to hear she was going to see you."

"I think we'll need to bring your sister down too, just for a day or two."

"I wouldn't want it any other way. Thank you. I love you both."

∢

"Hi, Phillip, it's Cristiano. Are you okay?" He was breathing hard.

"Yes, I'm fine. We just got the text from Ravn about lunch and Judith made a run for it back to the hospital."

"What's the rush?"

"Judith said she's starving, but I think she just wants to see Maya."

"Phillip, I need to talk to you."

"What is it, Cristiano? Did things go well with you and Maya last night?"

"Yes, it did. We are all set. She agreed I can go with her to Crete. We just have to get the okay from the doctor and then we'll leave." I paused.

"Cristiano? Is there something else you need to talk to me about?"

"Phillip, I love your daughter."

"I know."

"I love her with all my heart. I'm sorry about everything that's happened, except for the part about falling in love with her. I can't explain it but having her in my life makes me better. I know we'll have an amazing life together. She loves Portugal and wants to make it her home."

"Cristiano, I think she already has." Phillip's voice cracked but he chose not to say another word on the topic.

"I also know she needs to go back to Peachland, to the vineyard. It *will* happen, just not right now. Maybe once we get back from Crete."

"Crete." Phillip said the name of the island like it was filled with a story. He paused. "Cristiano, do you know *why* she chose Crete?"

"No, I don't. Do you?"

"Yes. I do. Maya was supposed to fly out to Greece immediately after her graduation ceremony, as her trip to Paris had been cancelled two years before but the day went terribly wrong. Judith woke up anxious about attending the ceremony. Then she had a full-blown panic attack, worried about letting Maya down. Judith was beside herself and ended up in hospital again. After having to walk across the stage without us being there, Maya voluntarily cancelled her trip to be with her sister while I took care of Judith."

I could see Maya standing in her graduation gown, with her plane ticket burning a hole in her pocket and having to abandon her dreams again.

"I knew Maya was desperate to go but pretended it didn't matter. She was great at pretending." He paused. "On the day she left for Portugal I instructed her to find some joy. Did you know she texted me before she left Montreal? Telling me she found 'it', she found her joy. It had only been eight hours, and it terrified me. I'm assuming you were the joy she was referring to?"

I smiled to myself. "Actually Phillip, as much as I would like to claim that title, no, the first joy she found was her journal and pen. I might have been a part of her joy that day, but only just a part."

"Thank you, Cristiano."

"For what?"

"For loving my daughter. I think it's time for Judith and me to go home. I have a vineyard to run and a house to renovate."

⁂

Maya

When Beth wheeled Saafa into my room, I was excited to see her beautiful smile, until she started to stare.

"Maya, your face!"

I made a move to cover it.

"No, don't! Beth, can you bring me closer to her?"

I fought back a wave of unwanted anxiety as Saafa reached out and touched my cheek.

"The salve it worked! I was hopeful, but I had no idea it could do this!"

"Yes, everyone keeps telling me how miraculous the healing has been."

Saafa shook her head looking perturbed. "This isn't about miracles Maya, it's chemistry."

"Sounds like we have a budding chemist on our hands."

"Beth, do you really think I could become a chemist?"

"Saafa, you can be anything you want to be. Dalley and Ravn will make sure of it."

I looked at Beth and smiled, knowing all the choices I made to get Saafa away from Dakar were the right ones. Sometimes ordinary people have to take extraordinary risks. I ran my fingers over the back of the mirror again, feeling each sparkly bead; it was time.

I looked at Beth.

"I think I need to give Luca a call. I'm just going to step out for a minute." Beth waved, then disappeared.

I saw a twinkle in Saafa's eyes. "Beth said you needed my help with something your friends made for you."

"Yes, it's something very special, that's for sure. I wanted you to be here when I turned it over." I picked up the mirror and carefully handed it to Saafa.

"They made this for you?"

"Yes."

"I look forward to making those kinds of friends one day."

"You will."

"Stop stalling, Maya." She handed me back the mirror. "I know you're having a hard time believing people but it's true. I told you my mom's salve would work."

"No, you didn't. You said you weren't sure."

"Well, a part of me believed it would. It's time."

"You're right. I need to do this now." I ran my fingers over the intricate design of sequins and gems, then took a breath and turned it over. But before I could see myself, I saw them, dozens of words written in tiny letters reflecting back at me, '*I* am beautiful, I *am* beautiful, I am *beautiful*'.

Beth slipped back into the room.

"I wrote this in my journal."

"Yes, I know," Beth said, stepping forward, "and then we all read it online." She cringed. "But you are. You are beautiful. Then and now. We just wanted to remind you."

I looked in the mirror, past the gems and the words, and saw my face. It was me; I was still me. I ran my fingers along the red scars, once open and bleeding, now closed and healing.

"How? How is this possible?" I placed the mirror on my lap and ran my hand over the elaborate decoration, then picked it up and looked again. "I look like me, almost."

"Chemistry!" Saafa said smugly. "You can save your miracle for another day."

While I was still studying my face, my mother came rushing into the room.

"Maya!" she called out to me. Ravn and Dalley soon followed, and then, before I knew it, my father and Cristiano.

I felt a surge of irrational panic and had to close my eyes. I could feel them all staring at me. Then I heard his voice, "Breathe, Maya, just breathe. Dalley, can you please take everyone out into the garden and set up lunch?"

The room became still, and I knew Cristiano and I were alone.

"You can open your eyes now."

Then I saw him staring at me, not with pity, but with love. "Let's look together."

He took the mirror from my hands and started reading the words. "*I* am beautiful, I *am* beautiful, I am *beautiful.* Please take over any time," he teased gently, and I did. And as I recited the words, he ran his fingers along my scars and kissed each one.

"You love me."

"Yes."

"All of me."

"Yes. But the most important question is, Maya, do you love yourself?"

I took a deep breath. "Yes, I do."

Epilogue

Maya

"Mama, tell me again," she asked, casting her wide dark eyes up at me as her chubby three-year-old fingers circled over the scar on my arm.

"Tell you what?" I teased. Knowing exactly what story she wanted to hear.

"Argh!" she growled at me, her little forehead wrinkling up like a washboard.

Cristiano laughed, then offered, "I could tell you the story this time, Senda."

"No, you can't. You weren't there, Papa."

"When did you get so smart?"

"That's not being smart, that's good 'membering."

"You mean remembering?" he tried to correct her.

"That's what I said, good 'membering."

Cristiano was about to enter an unwinnable argument with a three-and-a-half-year-old when his eyes met mine and I entreated him to stop.

"You're right. I wasn't there when Mama got the scars on her arm. That is her story to tell."

"You weren't there when Mama was a little girl, but you helped save her from the pirates who did that to her face. Right?"

"Papa saved me, and Auntie Dalley, and Uncle Ravn, and Saafa and—"

"Auntie Beth and Luca, I know, I know. More peach trees and pirates," Senda said, scrunching up her little eye like she was the pirate.

"Yes, more peach trees and pirates."

I started with the faded scar on my arm. "When I was a few years older than you, I was running through the vines at Grandma and Grandpa's vineyard."

"… the one with the peach trees, not like Netuno. Netuno has olives." She added.

"Yes, peach trees, not olives."

"When we get there, I want to climb the peach trees like you used to do when you were a little girl, Mama."

"And you will. We have a few hours before we land. Grandma and Grandpa are so excited to see you. Four months is a long time."

"It's forever, Mama, forever."

"Well, maybe not forever. But I know it feels like it."

I loved the way she called me mama. It made me feel complete, like I had done something right and the decisions I made led me to that moment.

"No, it's forever. That's what Grandma Judith said on the phone before we boarded the plane. And Grandma never lies. Keep going."

"Well, I ran—"

"… smack into the sign and cut your arm open," she took over with great enthusiasm.

"And then?" I asked, encouraging her to tell the story. I loved the way she told it.

"And then there was blood everywhere. Grandpa Phillip came running out and put you on his lap and held your arm until the blood stopped." She paused. "Where was Grandma Judith?"

"Grandma Judith was probably making tea."

"A noisy cup of tea?"

"Oh, I am sure it was a noisy cup." She placed her finger to the side of her face, ready to ask a question, and then changed her mind.

"Scar number two. This is my favorite story," she said, almost jumping out of her seat.

"What story is that?" I laughed.

"The one about the pirates."

She reached up to my face and ran her fingers along the fading scars.

"I hate those pirates, Mama. If I could, I would beat them up."

"No need to hate or beat anyone up, Senda. Hate does not get us anywhere. It's not good for you. It makes you feel icky inside."

"So, you don't hate the pirates who hurt you? Not even the lady pirate?"

I sighed as I looked over at Cristiano.

"Nope, not even the lady pirate. Actually, I kind of feel sad for her."

"Sad?" Senda and Cristiano asked at the same time.

"Yes, sad. Auntie Dalley found out the lady pirate didn't have a mama when she was little, and her papa wasn't always very nice to her."

"Oh." Her little face bunched up again.

"Mama, if she came to the house for a loaf of your magic bread, would you give her one?"

"Magic bread? What do you know about magic bread?"

"Last week, Uncle Puro told me about Great Avo's magic bread and how you make it now."

"He did, did he?"

I looked at Cristiano, and he shrugged his shoulders.

"How about this? If the lady pirate ever came for a loaf of magic bread, I would let you decide if she was ready for one."

"Really?" her eyes opened, and I saw the connection, the excitement that somehow, she had the power to make something important happen, even if she didn't quite understand all it meant.

"Yes, really."

Senda crawled into my lap and held my face with her two perfect hands. "Okay, I promise not to hate her, but do I have to like her?"

"No!" Cristiano said firmly and then smiled at me.

"I love you, Mama."

"I love you more."

"You win!" she exclaimed, throwing her arms around my neck.

Cristiano leaned over and kissed the top of Senda's head while placing his hand on my growing belly. "We all win."

Discover Michelle's latest news and life adventures. Exclusive bonus material available to everyone who joins her reader community.

Slivers of Doubt : The Prequel
Wine, Love, and Friendship

Thank you for reading *Untangled Vines*. Your honest review on your favorite platform will help future readers decide if they want to take a chance on a new-to-them author.

If you have any comments or questions about the story please send me a note at mish@michelleoucharekdeo.com
Follow me on Instagram @moucharekdeoauthor and
Facebook https://www.facebook.com/michelleoucharekdeoauthor

Acknowledgements

I WANT TO THANK MY friends Navi and Sherry whose fast thinking and creative spirits helped me find the title for this book. We jumped for joy when *Untangled Vines* landed on the page, knowing it was perfect. My gratitude runs deep for my alpha readers, Sean and Frances, who worked their way through a very rough first draft but were able to pull the essence of the story out and let me know I was on the right track. I also want to thank my writing groups: Authors in a Pickle and :55 Sprint Writers; two women's writing groups who inspired me daily and kept my head on my shoulders when things started to spin. And what can I say about my beta readers—Kate, Stephen and Jan's feedback allowed the story to grow stronger and pushed me to make it better.

Thank you isn't enough for Jennifer Buchanan whose weekly visits helped me shape the direction of the series and the team at Best Page Forward whose updated covers pulled the series together in the most amazing way. To Ben Kelley, my copyeditor and typesetter extraordinaire, helping me with all the big and little details.

And where would I be without my family, friends, and many readers who cheered me on and poked me with messages of encouragement and anticipation, wanting to know how the story was going to end.

To finish, there would be no book, no series without my husband and son. Their unfailing support and belief in my writing gave me the strength to push through the impossible days and remind me that with love in your life, anything is possible.

Author's Note

UNTANGLED VINES WAS WRITTEN DURING a time when the world was in chaos and we each had to find our own way. I am thankful my path came in the form of knuckling down and finishing the third book in the Wine, Love, and Friendship series.

I want to thank you for walking with me on this writing adventure. During the writing of the series many of my characters faced challenges such as depression, anxiety, grief and loss and abandonment issues but they also embraced finding new ways to face their fears and the pressures that were holding them back from what they wanted in life.

If you ever find yourself in a difficult situation where you can't resolve the problem on your own or with your immediate support network, talk to someone; reach out to a mental health practitioner in your area and ask for help. A positive therapeutic relationship with a competent counselling professional can help you carve a new path or get you back on track after walking through the weeds.

As I say goodbye to my characters in my first fiction series, I feel grateful to have found my way into the writing world. I have learnt so much and met some of the most amazing people around the world and look forward to all the friendships that are still to come.

Many years ago, when I wrote the first book, *The Girl in the Peach Tree* I was nervous about how it would be received. My husband took my hand and said, "Mish, even if one person reads your book and it makes a difference in their life, then it has done its job." This conversation stayed with me throughout the writing of the series and reminded me that once written, it is my job to release it into the world and focus on writing the next great story.

Remember, if you are lucky enough to find something you're passionate about don't let anything stop you from setting and achieving your goals.

If you are trying to find the time to make this happen, keep your eyes open for my next book which will focus on creating time recovery plans for goal achievement.

Walking on the sparkly side of the street,
Michelle